MW01515087

ILLICIT PURSUITS

Marie Harte

Erotic Futuristic Romance

New Concepts   Georgia

Be sure to check out our website for the very best in fiction at fantastic prices!

When you visit our webpage, you can:
* Read excerpts of currently available books
* View cover art of upcoming books and current releases
* Find out more about the talented artists who capture the magic of the writer's imagination on the covers
* Order books from our backlist
* Find out the latest NCP and author news--including any upcoming book signings by your favorite NCP author
* Read author bios and reviews of our books
* Get NCP submission guidelines
* And so much more!

We offer a 20% discount on all new Trade Paperback releases ordered from our website!

Be sure to visit our webpage to find the best deals in e-books and paperbacks! To find out about our new releases as soon as they are available, please be sure to sign up for our newsletter (http://www.newconceptspublishing.com/newsletter.htm) or join our reader group (http://groups.yahoo.com/group/new_concepts_pub/join)!

The newsletter is available by double opt in only and our customer information is *never* shared!

Visit our webpage at:
www.newconceptspublishing.com

Illicit Pursuits is an original publication of NCP. This work has never before appeared in book form. This work is a novel. Any similarity to actual persons or events is purely coincidental.

New Concepts Publishing, Inc.
5202 Humphreys Rd.
Lake Park, GA 31636

ISBN 1-58608-786-x
2005 © Marie Harte
Cover art (c) copyright 2006 Eliza Black

NCP books are available at special quantity discounts for bulk purchases for sales promotions, premiums, fund raising, or educational use. For details, write, email, or phone New Concepts Publishing, Inc., 5202 Humphreys Rd., Lake Park, GA 31636; Ph. 229-257-0367, Fax 229-219-1097; orders@newconceptspublishing.com.

First NCP Trade Paperback Printing: April 2006

TABLE OF CONTENTS

Winner Takes All   Page 5

Seriana Found   Page 163

WINNER TAKES ALL

Chapter One

"No."

"But Gren, you haven't heard--"

"No." Gren shook his head. "Not yes, not maybe, but no." Stretched out on a lounge chair by the side of the pool, the stubborn man sighed and closed his eyes, shutting out the rest of the world.

Sernal of Mardu clenched his jaw. Why had he expected the damned mercenary to hear him out? He glanced around at the tropical paradise surrounding them and grudgingly acknowledged Gren's refusal. What could Sernal offer to compare with a few weeks in paradise?

The resort overlooked Aflera's largest ocean, blushing under the noon sun. Not a cloud marred the sky, creating a scene of almost unreal perfection. Large, green leafed palms surrounded the resort, framing the ocean's beauty. From Sernal's vantage, he overlooked the lavender pool in front of him. Beyond the pool lay white sand so soft the grains felt like silk under one's feet, and the pale rose-colored ocean water teemed with finwhales, mraun fish, and a myriad of delectable marine food available on the resort's high-priced, gourmet menu.

Sernal sighed. This wasn't going to be easy. "Can I at least buy you a drink?"

Gren eyed him suspiciously before nodding. They sat in silence for a moment before an extremely attractive woman joined them. Gren leaned back in the lounger, sighing under the ministrations of his personal *thraia*, one of the resort's legendary massage therapists.

As her many hands crept over Gren's neck, shoulders and arms, Sernal repressed a wave of envy to have those gifted hands over *his* body. Native to the planet, the *thraia* had an innate skill for pleasure. With six hands and eight digits on each hand, they made a simple massage orgasmic. And the sex, he paused and stared at the *thraia's* sensual eyes half-closed in concentration, the sex was rumored to be indescribably erotic.

"I'll take the drink, Sernal, but nothing else." Gren murmured something unintelligible to the *thraia* that had her giggling before she left. "Talk about *wainu*," he said with a groan as he rolled his shoulders. "I've found utter peace without sex. I wouldn't have believed it possible before now."

Sernal waved down a server and ordered them two Aflera Ambrosias. As he watched the server leave, he wondered how best to reintroduce his needs to the wary mercenary.

If he hadn't needed Gren's particular skills so badly, he would have left the overtaxed man alone. But with so many women gone missing in so little time, he needed the legendary Thesha's gifts, and the sooner the better.

Staring at Gren's form clad in swimming trousers and nothing else, he subtly approved Gren's musculature, earned from years of harsh discipline and training. Sernal's gaze wandered to Gren's only imperfection, a jagged scar that ran from his left hand up his forearm. Gren had never offered the story behind the scar, and Sernal knew it best not to pry.

Though friends with the Thesha, Sernal instinctively sensed the danger surrounding the larger man. Gren had earned his reputation as a fierce warrior and tenacious adversary, one who had never been beaten.

Gren sighed and rolled his eyes at Sernal's intense gaze. "Sernal, you're steadily becoming a royal pain in my ass. The first time in three years I'm finally able to take a break, and I find you blocking my sun just hours after my arrival. What is it with you Mardu?"

"What can I say? It's in our blood to be persistent."

"I think you mean obnoxious," Gren muttered and accepted the drink the server handed him. He took a long swallow and smiled, the action drawing the stares of several nearby women.

Sernal noticed and shook his head. "Can't you turn it off?"

"You're persistent, I'm desirable." Somehow Gren uttered the words without sounding conceited. "What can I say? It's hereditary." He guzzled his Ambrosia and set the empty glass by his side.

Sernal stared at the glass, amazed Gren had imbibed the strong liquor so quickly. "I'd say your metabolism is nothing short of amazing too."

"I'm surprised you didn't know that." Gren lowered his voice. "Alcohol doesn't affect my kind the way it does others. We have a natural tolerance for fermented fruits. Certain drugs, however," he paused, his expression darkening, "can be lethal."

Sernal saw a golden opportunity and charged forward. "You know how it feels to be powerless all too well, don't you?" It might not have been smart, but reminding Gren of his imprisonment years ago would have more of an impact than a simple entreaty for help. "Imagine helpless young women undergoing what you suffered. Except they don't escape. No one rides in to their rescue."

"I wasn't rescued," Gren said between clenched teeth. "I was two seconds from killing that bitch Cari when you entered the scene, running late as usual." Then he cursed under his breath. "I'm just not going to be rid of you until you tell me what's on your mind, am I?"

Sernal drained the rest of his glass, feeling overly warm as he did so. Unlike the Thesha, the Mardu *were* susceptible to alcohol. "Nope. So you might as well hear me out."

Gren stared at him for a moment before he stood abruptly, flexing his massive arms as he whipped a towel around his neck. "Fine then. Follow me."

Sernal trailed Gren to the most expensive section of the resort. Whistling as he followed Gren into a suite, Sernal stared in appreciation. "Being a mercenary must pay pretty well."

A small water fountain greeted them when they entered, and the room's soothing hues of amber and pale green blended with the tropical environment directly outside.

Through two open doors leading to an outside balcony, Sernal could clearly see a finwhale leaping in the air before it disappeared beneath the water. The wind blew, rustling the silken drapes framing the balcony doors, and the sweet smell of *florantes* teased his sensitive nose.

He almost felt bad for what he was about to do to Gren.

"Spill it," Gren ordered and wandered outside on the balcony.

"We have a total of fifteen missing women, all grabbed within the past month. All are from affluent families, and all from different provinces in Mardu."

Gren shrugged. "So tap system law. What do you need me for?"

"There's something about these crimes that smacks of peacemaker corruption."

Gren turned to stare at Sernal. "How so?"

Finally, a spark of interest. Sernal prayed to Flor his luck would continue. "The culprits have kidnapped five of the women from their own security. Eyewitness accounts paint our kidnappers as organized, controlled and possibly military.

"They cover all their bases a little too well. Neither Rafe nor myself has detected a trace of evidence at any of the crime scenes."

The picture Sernal drew intrigued Gren on several levels. The idea of women being misused made him itch uncomfortably to rectify the problem. And the idea that peacemakers were involved, lawmen who--with the exception of Sernal and Rafe--went out of their way to make his life miserable, made Gren's mouth water.

Yet he desperately needed a break. While he stared longingly toward the ocean, his conscience warred with his fatigue. "You say only women are being kidnapped?"

Sernal nodded. "All unusually beautiful and within child-bearing age."

Gren's eyes widened. "You don't think it's another Ebrellion Ring?"

"We don't think so. System Observation Posts report normal Ebrellion activity, all from outside system boundaries. No, these crimes point to an internal threat."

"Any evidence to support that?"

Sernal frowned. "Yes and no. Let's just say it's not enough to prove without a doubt, not yet. I've got my suspicions and a clear direction to begin the hunt, one lead peacemaker in particular. I can tell you these criminals have connections above my pay grade."

Gren stared at him. "So you come to me asking for help."

"You've got the perfect reputation for the job I need done. Your abilities with women will make getting information a cinch. And with your resources you can easily plant one of my people undercover. Don't worry. Rafe will be on hand to assist."

Gren grimaced and saw Sernal's patience thinning.

The lawman narrowed his eyes. "Gren, we're talking about saving the lives of at least fifteen women."

Gren shook his head as the wind whispered, *stay.* "No." His principles tugged at him while the ocean beckoned a second glance. He stared at the rippling water, imagining himself floating without a care, rebuilding his strength and peace of mind. He would never admit it aloud, but his imprisonment two years ago had taken a toll on him from which he had yet to recover. His nonstop assignments hadn't helped matters either.

"Look, Sernal," he tried. "You have resources far beyond mine. You have an entire planet of lawmen at your disposal, not to mention you're the damned head of Peacemaker Central. Order your most trusted contacts to help you."

Sernal swore. "I'm not the head of 'Peacemaker Central,' as you like to call it. And weren't you listening when I told you we've got rogue peacemakers? They could be anyone, men and women I trust," Sernal muttered with disgust and ran a hand through his hair. "You call me a pain in the ass? Hell," he growled, "it's taking what little control I have not to *order* you to assist us."

Gren crossed his arms over his chest and locked gazes with Sernal. All the peace he'd felt under the *thraia's* hands disappeared as the tension that had been building since Sernal stepped into the suite came to a head.

Sernal must have sensed the strain for he straightened, no longer at ease but now on edge, ready to spring into action if necessary. Gren had to hand it to the Mardu. He was a pain in the ass, but a dangerous pain in the ass.

Even so, Gren didn't bow to anyone, not even the Elders. "I dare you to order me to do anything," he said quietly, hoping Sernal would lose his cool so he could legitimately toss him out of the room.

Suddenly, the door to the room flew open and a woman

entered in a huff, followed closely by Sernal's brother, Rafe.

"What the hell?" Gren's anger grew as more unwanted guests intruded on his vacation.

"For Narok's sake, Lead Sernal, you should just order him to assist us and be done with it," the woman said, disdain in her voice as she eyed Gren. "It's not as if we don't have enough to worry about without begging for this *drun's* help."

Gren had to blink at the vision standing before him. He gathered his focus, immediately wary at the strong effect she had on him. He subtly looked to Sernal, wondering if the beauty was part of some plot to snag him into helping. But Sernal didn't look pleased at the interruption. Instead he glared at his brother.

Rafe shrugged. "She distracted me and before I knew it, she was busting in."

The woman glared at Rafe over her shoulder. "If you let a little thing like breasts distract you from your mission, you need remedial training."

Rafe glared back at the icy beauty, but before he could say anything, Gren began to laugh. For the first time since he could remember, a woman responded to the Mardu brothers with scorn rather than passion.

All eyes swung to him as he continued to chuckle. Rafe swore. Sernal closed his eyes, seeming to pray for patience. The woman, however, seethed with resentment. He could almost feel her animosity as she glowered at him.

"She does have a point, Rafe." Gren grinned and fell into a plush, oversized chair. Though the woman's attitude amused him, he decided to needle her for her earlier insult. *Drun,* indeed. "But, honey, those breasts you're carrying are enough to drive a man crazy, even a *drun* like me."

The woman stiffened her spine and narrowed her eyes like an angry she-wolf prepared to attack. The combination of long, silken blonde hair and unique purple-gray eyes drew his gaze like a magnet. And her tempting body, long, lean and full of womanly curves, made him contemplate *luring* her for sex, something he hadn't done in a long time. Women came to Gren of their own free will. He hadn't needed to coerce a woman to his bed since, well, since Mara two years ago. And that had been for the sake of the mission.

Sernal spoke before the prickly woman could reply. "Gren, I'd like you to meet Temis Freya. She's one of my top peacemakers. Rafe you already know."

"A peacemaker?" Gren ignored Rafe to study Temis. "She looks more like a pleasurer. Though her attitude needs work."

The first words out of Temis' mouth were obscene, yet impressive in their creativity.

Sernal shot her a sharp look that immediately stilled her clever if barbed tongue. "We've been working on her attitude. It seems we've still a long road ahead of us." Her glare subsided at Sernal's rebuke.

Interesting.

"I'm sorry Temis interrupted us," Sernal continued, "but she has a point. We're running out of time and we need your help. According to my sources, the women will be sold at a secret slave auction in little more than a week's time."

Slave auction. He inwardly flinched.

Gren glanced over his shoulder to the balcony. A raptor flew over the sea, snagging a mraun fish from the water. That reminded him he had yet to eat.

Then he wondered if the missing women were being fed. Were their captors abusing them while he lounged in his overpriced suite? And did Sernal really expect him to refuse to help when images of tortured women began appearing in his mind? The damned peacemaker knew a Thesha couldn't abide harm done to an innocent woman. Damn him.

"You're going to owe me big for this," he growled at Sernal.

The lawman visibly relaxed. "Thank Flor you've come to your senses," he praised. "I'll find us transportation to the ship while Rafe fills you in on the basic scheme of things. For the most part it's like every other undercover mission you've worked."

"For the most part?" Gren's left brow rose, in both curiosity and command.

"This mission you're not flying solo. Temis will be with you every step of the way."

Chapter Two

One day. One lousy day was all he could recoup from a fully paid month-long vacation.

Jahnja, his personal *thraia*, walked through the door clad in nothing more than what her creator had given her. *Damn, but Afleran geneticists had real talent.* Despite his fascination with her unbridled sensuality, hostility lingered over the lawmakers' interruption.

"Do you want me to come back later?"

Gren grinned, forcing his anger at those idiot peacemakers from his mind. "I don't have more than tonight, *seb*," he murmured the *thraian* endearment. "So why don't you join me on the bed?"

She smiled and licked her lips, her tongue glazing the ripe fruit of her mouth, accentuating the promise of fulfillment.

He watched with interest as she fondled her breasts with two hands, while her other hands skimmed her body and fondled the dark nest between her thighs. He'd never before lain with a *thraia*, and had been looking forward to learning if their reputation was as well-earned as had been told.

Now however, as the woman neared, thoughts of that viper-tongued peacemaker stole through Jahnja's image. White-blonde hair and flashing, violet eyes seared his loins, and to Gren's dismay his cock buoyed under the peacemaker's imagined ferocity.

"Ah, such a large gift," Jahnja said with a smile as she crawled up the bed.

Gren mentally cursed Temis Freya from his thoughts and focused on the woman before him. He waited curiously to see how she'd use her hands then sighed with pleasure when she wrapped two heated palms around his cock. With her other hands she stroked his body, teasing his nipples with pinching pleasure and reaching low to knead his buttocks with a finesse that bespoke practice.

He throbbed, needing release, wanting to spill himself inside a warm, willing woman. It had been too long since he'd enjoyed himself sexually, way too long, if his reaction to Temis was any indication.

Jahnja continued to exclaim over his size, and he knew she felt as aroused as he. He could see her aura pulsing in vibrant waves of passion. He inhaled deeply, gratifying his need for untainted energy, for pure, erotic satisfaction.

He watched through heavy-lidded eyes as she licked her lips greedily. She waited until he looked into her eyes before lowering her mouth to replace her hands on his shaft.

Warm, wet pressure engulfed his cock until he thought he might burst from the sensation. Coupled with her skilled hands, Jahnja's mouth easily set her apart from the few pleasurers Gren had frequented in the system. Clearly her reputation had been earned.

"Take the pleasure, Gren, all for you this first time," she ordered as she continued to suck him deep into her throat.

Her sex smelled like honeyed cream and Gren inhaled deeply, taking not only her scent but her essence into his body. The overflow of energy and desire hit him hard.

Unable to stop himself, he envisioned Temis Freya on her knees, sucking his cock with desire bright in her eyes, and he came in a rush. Jahnja swallowed him greedily, stimulating him to another orgasm as intense as the first.

When he could catch his breath, he closed his eyes and prayed tonight's rapacious sexual encounter would cure him of his insane fixation on a certain sharp-tongued woman.

He heard Jahnja sigh and rose up on his elbows. "What a clever little tongue you have," he said, his voice lower than usual. "Now why don't I show you how clever I can be?"

She smiled and rolled onto her back, spreading her legs wide in waiting. He gratefully acceded to her wishes, losing himself between her thighs, thoughts of the future fading as sweet, womanly want finally consumed him.

* * * *

Temis sat before Sernal, forcing herself to be still. She felt mortified at having lost control in front of her mentor, and all because of that bastard Gren.

"We need his help, Temis. I wish it weren't so, but it is. Your attitude and insults earlier were directly counter to gaining the man's cooperation." He frowned and she could almost hear her father's sigh of disappointment.

How hard had he taught her to shield her emotions when in battle? When working, Temis had to assume a warrior's mindset. That ideology had made it possible for her to attain her current position. In the direction she headed, however, she could see her future going up in flames.

She swallowed her pride, a lump that lodged deep in her throat, and said quietly, "I apologize, Lead Sernal. I had no thought but to salvage your standing. It was prideful and unnecessary, I realize now. It won't happen again."

Sernal stared at her for a moment before nodding. "If you're set on working this case--"

"I am," she quickly interrupted.

"--then you have to learn when to speak and when to stay silent." He shook his head and she felt her cheeks redden. "Temis, you continually score higher on tests than your peers, you can take down a man twice your size in the blink of an eye, and your weapon rating nearly matches Rafe's."

She could feel Rafe's gaze burning into her back. Sernal's brother couldn't have made it plainer how he felt about being partnered with a woman.

"But for all your accomplishments, you continually push your limits with your attitude. Quite frankly, were it not for my brother's assessment of your strengths, I wouldn't have agreed to assign you this mission."

She glanced at Rafe in surprise. He said nothing, merely stared back at her. Apparently she'd been wrong in assuming Rafe had a bias against her.

"You seem to think everyone is against you, Temis," Sernal said in a quieter voice. "That may have been true in your last duty station, but on my watch everyone is treated fairly."

She nodded, something within her easing at his words.

He turned to Rafe and murmured a few parting orders, then left them both in the small conference room. Silence settled over them before Temis cleared her throat and turned to directly face Rafe.

He and Sernal shared the same exotic golden-glimmering eyes. And he looked at her with a similar disappointment. "I didn't ask to partner with anyone, Temis, let alone a newly promoted peacemaker from another district. But I'm trying to make things work. If you won't at least meet me halfway, I suggest we request reassignment before our lack of trust results in field injury."

Temis bit her lip. She really had misjudged Rafe. "I'm sorry." The rusty words fell from her lips in a hoarse growl. "I'm sorry," she said more firmly. "The precinct I left had an aversion to female peacemakers, and I'm afraid I took out my resentment on you."

Rafe nodded. "Apology accepted. I have no problem working with women. I like women." He grinned and his face lit up with a sensuality she'd seen only once before. It still made her uncomfortable. "I'm not suggesting anything between us save a working relationship. But hell, Temis, I'm a man. If you shove your breasts in my face, I'm going to get distracted. Especially since I'm not on my guard with you. Now if a female suspect pulled something like that...." He shrugged.

His genuine humor took some of the sting out of his words, but she flushed nonetheless. "I'm sorry I did that." She still couldn't believe she'd nearly flashed Rafe of Mardu to steal into Gren's room. "My eagerness to tell Gren to go to hell overcame my good sense."

"Not that I didn't enjoy it," Rafe said with a wink. "The view or your insults to Gren, but rushing to Sernal's defense wasn't necessary. He and Gren have known each other a long time. There's more to Gren than the rumors would have you believe. You'll see once we start working with him. He's a hard man, a dangerous mercenary, but his heart's in the right place." His stomach grumbled and he rubbed his abdomen. "Now what do you say we get something to eat on this ship? I hear Sernal runs a tight little galley."

Temis laughed and grabbed the hand Rafe held to help her to her feet. "I can work with you, Rafe, but don't ask me to trust a man like Gren. With the bodies he's left in his wake, it's a wonder he can sleep at night."

Rafe smirked as he walked with her to the galley. "I highly doubt Gren has problems sleeping."

* * * *

"Ah, ah, more," Jahnja panted as Gren thrust deep inside her. He gritted his teeth at the sheer pleasure the *thraia* afforded. On her hands and knees before him, her breasts swaying to his pummeling thrusts, she cried and clenched at his welcome intrusion.

She moaned his name as she came, her body flooding him with waves of tremendous energy.

The utter power of the moment shattered his control and he shot inside her, showering her with pleasure upon pleasure.

His body thrummed with sensuality and he gently withdrew from his bedmate. Jahnja closed her eyes and curled into a contented ball on the bed, her steady breathing indicating the slumber she would need to gather her expelled energy. He still couldn't believe she'd lasted a whole night with him.

Gren rose beside the bed, glowing with vigor and unbridled power. He could feel her gift inside him, a new light kindling the flame that had begun to fade under old hurts.

Knowing her gift wouldn't last but grateful to have received it, Gren kissed her gently on the cheek, dressed, and left her a hefty tip for services rendered.

Humming under his breath, he collected his belongings and took an aerotransport to the shuttle that would ferry him to Sernal's legal vessel. Jahnja's coupling had brought him the respite he'd need to deal with the annoying peacemakers waiting on *Lady Justice*. At least now thoughts of Temis didn't make his dick rise every three seconds.

He found the shuttle standing by, waiting for his arrival. The copilot grabbed his bags and pointed Gren to a seat. Fond memories occupied Gren until he was almost smiling. Damn, but he would definitely have to visit Jahnja once he finished this mission. Who knew the *thraia* had the staying power to withstand Theshan lovemaking throughout the night?

Few women could sustain one of his kind for that long. Oh, women had done so for much longer. But those women were special, and could only sustain certain men. Take his fellow Thesha Lurin and his wife, Mara. Made for each other, perfect complements to one another's souls.

His grin faded as he thought about his own life. Gren had lived far longer than his peers, and only slightly less than the elders of his race. He had long since given up hope that he would one day find a lifelong mate. He genuinely believed in true love, but knew such a fate would not fall on him, not in this life.

He swore under his breath as the shuttle landed. No, Gren had committed far too many sins to believe such a tremendous blessing might one day be his. Despite his work to protect the Theshan way of life, despite his resolve to protect the innocent and punish the guilty, he knew he fell far short of deserving when it came to true happiness.

Dark memories intruded and he ruthlessly suppressed them as he stepped out of the shuttle. To his surprise, Sernal stood surrounded by at least a dozen armed and angry-looking peacemakers. The shuttle behind him rumbled to life and left, leaving him at the mercy of Sernal's hospitality, which at this point looked less than inviting.

"You're late." Sernal aimed his phaser at Gren's heart.

"Do you shoot all your late guests?" Gren crossed his arms and leaned casually against a support beam. He read the tension in Sernal's frame and knew this was no game he played. Something had gone very wrong. Eyeing the dozen peacemakers focused on him, he expected to see Rafe or Temis. Instead, twelve strangers glared at him, waiting for him to make a wrong move.

"Gren, you're under Mardu arrest for the illegal weapons trade you conducted with Melan rebels three months past in the southern province. Don't bother denying it," Sernal forestalled with a warning, "because I have at least four witnesses that saw the whole thing."

Gren stared at Sernal, trying to piece the puzzle together. Since he'd never sold illegal arms to Melan rebels on Mardu, he and Sernal both knew the statement to be false. So what did Sernal have to gain by this little drama?

"However did you come to expect welcome aboard a peacekeeper vessel?" one of the peacemakers nearest Sernal asked.

His head tilted at an arrogant angle, complementing the superior glint in his light blue eyes. Long black hair flowed to his shoulders, gleaming under the ship's Eyran crystals. Gren noted the man's obvious vanity, as well as his experienced, combative stance. The peacekeeper eyed Gren and then Sernal, a contemptuous sneer on his face and in that moment Gren understood.

Though Sernal hadn't liked admitting it, the internal strife among the peacemakers was not a huge secret. Apparently those not worthy of Sernal's trust had somehow interfered in his plans. And now, for the sake of the mission, Gren would have to play along and see where things led.

"Well, Gren? Have you nothing to say?" The dark-haired man shook his head in disgust.

"I thought I was here to discuss payment for information I might have on the Melan rebels." He glared at Sernal for effect and saw the peacemaker's tension slightly ease. "I should have known you peacemakers are all scum and liars."

"Quite the ruse, Lead Sernal. Well done." The dark-haired man twisted his lips in the parody of a smile.

Sernal nodded. "Thank you, Lead Rorn. I knew there was no other way to garner Gren's attention, unless of course I had a few naked whores lying about."

The other peacemakers laughed, an ugly sound that chafed Gren's ears.

"Well said." Rorn slapped Sernal on the back and sheathed his phaser. "My men will provide assistance in securing the prisoner, Lead Sernal." He turned to his men. "Make sure he doesn't escape."

Gren eyed the men cautiously approaching. His reputation preceded him, obviously, since they thought they needed a dozen men to put him in a cell. Damned if he'd disappoint them.

In a burst of lightning speed he dove for the ground and rolled into the men in front of him. He knocked down several and continued to barrel ahead. Those flanking him wanted to fire but now chanced hitting their comrades.

Sernal had of course leapt to the side, his Xema reflexes holding him in good stead. Rorn, however, fell hard, and found himself tangled in Gren's attack.

Hands yanked at him and feet kicked at him, but Gren refused to give in too easily. Besides, his aggravation at the whole mess Sernal had involved him in grew to new heights and he needed to vent his anger.

He lashed out, using all of his strength to break free of the bodies atop him. He steadily rose to his feet only to meet Sernal face to face.

"Go ahead, peacemaker." Gren seethed and knocked the phaser easily from Sernal's hands. "Take your best shot."

Sernal frowned at his antagonistic tone but honestly, did he really expect Gren to take a beating just to go along with this stupid mission? In hindsight, Gren would have been better off finding the women and rescuing them without Sernal's interference. But it was too late now.

* * * *

Temis and Rafe entered the loading dock expecting to find Gren waiting impatiently to begin mission indoctrination. Instead he was surrounded by peacekeepers from another district, a few of Sernal's handpicked peacemakers, Lead Sernal and Lead Rorn.

Temis scowled at Rorn Fenhal, a man she despised like no other. He had been responsible for her rude and unprofessional treatment at her last duty station. Thank Narok she'd evaded his advances and transferred before he'd been promoted to lead.

Now she watched with confusion as he and his men held Gren at bay with their weapons drawn.

"What the hell?" She took a step forward when Rafe latched onto her arm.

"Stay here. Don't get involved."

"What's going on?" she asked in a low voice. The tense group by the shuttle bay still had not noticed them.

"Sernal has reason to believe some of Mardu's peacemakers have turned rogue. Well, his number one suspect boarded us by surprise." Rafe cursed under his breath as he glared at Rorn. "This puts the whole mission at risk." He turned to Temis. "Whatever you do, don't let on you know Gren."

Just as she was about to ask another question, a round of explosive action burst. Gren rolled into the mass of armed peacekeepers, knocking several to the ground. Rorn, she noted with satisfaction, was one of the men laid flat.

Gren rose fighting, his arms and legs flowing like the wind through the great Canfer willows of Zephyr. She watched in awe as he moved gracefully but with purpose. Each strike, every movement hit its target. That he exercised economy of energy, assaulting and defending himself in a mixture of techniques she found hard to identify only increased her admiration.

After decimating half the peacemakers around him, Gren turned to confront Sernal. Before the situation could grow any uglier, a pulse from Rafe's phaser brought Gren to his knees.

Dazedly slumping on the ground, Gren gave little protest to the many kicks and curses thrown his way. Temis noted the lack of discipline in Rorn's men, as did Sernal. Scowling at the peacemakers kicking the disabled mercenary, Sernal barked at his men to see Gren to one of the holding cells.

"I'll see him secured," Rafe volunteered.

Sernal glanced over at his brother and nodded, then blinked, noticing Temis for the first time. Rorn had risen to his feet and was glaring at his men when he chanced to look up and see Temis. His entire demeanor changed, from cruel and demanding to arrogant and hungry.

The heated gaze he shot her as his eyes swept her from her head to toe burned uncomfortably. Nothing showed on her face, however, and she approached Sernal at his nod. She barely glanced at Gren when the others led him away, though it took an effort to pretend indifference.

"Peacekeeper Freya." Rorn's voice oozed with practiced charm. "How good to see you again."

Sernal stared from her to Rorn with a polite expression, but she could almost see the kernel of suspicion growing.

"Lead Sernal." She bowed in greeting. "Lead Rorn was one of my peers when last I worked in the northern district."

Sernal's face cleared. "Of course. And congratulations again on your promotion, Lead Rorn. Quite impressive for one so young."

Rorn pursed his lips in displeasure. "And yet I'm a mere year younger than you. Not young or inexperienced, obviously."

Yes, but Sernal had no relatives to see him advanced. Your father bought your promotion, you woman-hating drun, Temis wanted say. She held her tongue instead and waited for Sernal.

He laughed, easily brushing aside Rorn's arrogance. "We are only a year apart, aren't we? Where does the time go?" Rorn's ego restored at Sernal's humor, the two laughed together over Gren's easy capture.

She watched the leads leave the shuttle area, uncomfortably aware of Rorn's private guards ogling her openly before trailing out the door behind their lead officer. No doubt his men later planned on carousing in the common quarters, she thought with a scowl.

She'd hoped for some time there to confer with Rafe, but now they would have to rethink their entire strategy.

She followed after Sernal silently, wondering just how this new development would unfold. As she trailed behind, she couldn't help dwelling on Gren's impressive skills.

His battle moves had been more than that of a man defending himself. With his techniques, he must have experienced some training on Zephyr, a planet that prided itself on training only the best and brightest fighters in the system.

A native of Zephyr, Temis was no stranger to combative training and fighting skills. Nor, apparently, was Gren.

She glanced at the timepiece on her wrist. Since Sernal was engaged with Rorn and Rafe was busy securing Gren, she had time for some invaluable fight sequencing. Lately the mission had occupied much of her spare time. Now that she had the opportunity for physical training, she would be a fool not to use it.

As she approached the conditioning room, she couldn't help but wonder what it would be like to fight against someone with Gren's skills. Oddly enough, the challenge appealed to her, on *several* levels.

Scowling at her wayward thoughts, she focused her mind on the physical disciplines that had thus far served her well in life. As she struggled to attain fighting perfection, she ignored the inner battle not to think of Gren, of his battered body, of what he must be feeling in the narrow holding cell directly below her room.

Chapter Three

Temis felt refreshed after her workout, so much so that she joined Rafe for dinner and a drink before returning to her quarters for some much-needed rest.

Because of the visitors on board, talk of the mission remained unsaid. Rafe had whispered to meet him first thing in the morning in his room, where Sernal would be waiting with new plans. Until that time, however, Temis planned to rest both her mind and body.

She undressed and slid beneath the sheets of her narrow bed, and just as easily slid into sleep.

Comforted by her earlier physical training, her mind readily grasped the familiar dream of her home world.

Zephyr's lavender skies faded into dark black, stars shining like beacons around the planet's brightly glowing moon. The sound of grunts and thuds mingled with the scents of clean sweat and tangy blood, and she smiled at the memories of her upbringing.

Chula, Zephyr's most famous training ground, had given birth to the warrior within her. In sleep, Chula continued to reward her, giving her the peace she needed to combat the fatigue of her day.

Controlling the dream, Temis nodded to her father and master trainer who suddenly appeared, then accepted the hack-staff that materialized at her feet. A faceless opponent shimmered into existence, and for the next few hours she managed her dream, fighting with passion and the determination to succeed.

Reliving her training refreshed her, as it always did. The sweat slid down her body, washing away the mental grime and exhaustion from the day.

Garbed in a slim loincloth and protective breastplate made of rak-hide, Chula's heat comforted rather than oppressed as she fought man after man.

Only one other woman had ever been trained on Zephyr, and she had no desire to fight her daughter. Temis' mother gladly left her daughter's training to her husband, content to raise her children and manage the family estate.

So Temis fought man after man, eventually relinquishing her hold on the dream as true slumber began to overtake her.

She was dimly aware of the dark settling over Chula. Her father and the others disappeared and her world shimmered until only a thin light illuminated a new, foreign area.

Temis blinked sleepily at an unfamiliar world. Three moons sat suspended in an indigo sky, lighting a perfectly round dirt ring surrounded by tropical forests and to her immediate left, an inviting pool of water.

Interest in her new surroundings revived her, and her awareness returned as she found herself holding her hack-staff again, her training clothes fresh but much too thin for the cool temperatures of this strange world.

"Where am I?" she asked aloud.

"You've come to fight, have you not?" a familiar voice called from the darkness in the forest.

She waited curiously, knowing yet not aware how she knew that Gren approached.

He appeared uninjured, as if his fight earlier with the peacemakers had not occurred. Wearing only the swimming trousers she'd first seen him in, he walked lazily toward her, like a cat stalking its prey.

He stopped in front of her, smiling, his eyes lingering over her breasts and thighs before returning to meet her confused gaze.

"You like to fight."

She nodded. "But where am I?"

"In a dream."

"But I command my dreams, and this is not Zephyr."

Gren's left eyebrow rose, an arrogant gesture that irritated her. "We stand in a fighting ring." He crossed his arms, his biceps bulging. "What now, *sura*?"

She wasn't sure what *sura* meant, but on Gren's lips it sounded suspiciously like an endearment. Did he dare dismiss her as some piece of fluff on fighting grounds?

"Now we fight."

He grinned, and the curl of his lips caused her heart to flutter. A curious heat pooled in her loins and to her horror she found herself fixated on the fullness of his mouth.

"If it's a fight you want, *sura*, I'll be happy to oblige," he murmured sensuously. "Hand to hand?"

Imagining Gren's hands all over her made her flush, and she shook her head. "Blunt weaponry."

She didn't understand why Gren had appeared in her dream at all, but decided to accept his presence. Since meeting him she'd been unable to strike the imposing man from her thoughts and unruly imagination. Perhaps her subconscious sensed this and chose to confront the source of her recent confusion head-on.

He flexed his arms and she stared at his muscular perfection. "I like risks, but if it's practice you want, I accept. The winner chooses the prize."

She frowned. "But you could demand anything."

"And I will when I win," he said with a wink.

In his wink she saw condescension and her irritation stirred to anger. Anticipating the heady blow to his ego, she clearly imagined him drawn and defeated by her hand. She taunted him with a superior sneer and was rewarded by a fire in his eyes.

A long, gnarled staff suddenly appeared in his hands. He bowed, then waited for her to attack.

Her blood pumping with excitement, a feeling that owed as much to anticipation of the fight as it did to Gren's presence, she feigned a thrust and struck at his left knee.

Gren nimbly dodged her attack and stepped back. Waiting.

She lunged again and again, each time narrowly missing her aim. Gren continued to dodge and wait, as if toying with her.

"Engage, damn it." She glared at him, wanting him to do more than parry and evade.

"As you wish, *sura*," he answered with a throaty chuckle. "But do not be too angry when you lay flat beneath the victor."

His arrogance chafed and had the effect he'd intended. Caught in frustrated anger, Temis nearly missed the signs preceding his attack. Like a whirlwind of fury, he lashed at her, catching her knee. Off balance, she rolled quickly to her left and managed to avoid a paralyzing blow to the shoulder.

Returning the attack, she swept at his feet. Her staff took his ankle out from under him. While he recovered from her blow, she regained her footing and regarded him warily.

He gave every appearance of a defensive opponent, but he'd clearly just shown his true nature, a deadly predator with unusually sharp reflexes.

She crouched low with her staff held perpendicular to her body, shielding her chest. He faced her, his staff in one hand, a large grin on his face.

"*Sura*, I like the way you fight. But my patience is wearing. Come, let's end this."

Before Temis could blink, she found herself flat on her back, breathless from the speed of his attack. He straddled her, his staff positioned just under her chin. Had he wished, he could easily have snapped her neck.

What in blazes had just happened? She stared in astonishment at Gren. He wasn't even breathing hard. His chest rose and fell evenly, and his powerful thighs held her tightly within his grasp.

"My victory, *sura*," he purred and tossed his staff to the side. "Now my prize."

"Get off me, you oaf." She pounded legs as hard as steel, mortified at having been beaten so easily. Never before had Temis lost so quickly.

His legs tightened around her body in warning and he stared down at her with an unreadable gaze. Much as she wanted to deny it, his victory secretly thrilled her. Temis had never been drawn to the weak. And a man like Gren, handsome, aloof and powerful, made her heart hammer despite her mind's protests. That he had beaten her with ease only added to his appeal.

The sheer strength he possessed stoked the embers of her desire. She could feel the force in his thighs, could see the restrained power in the corded muscles of his arms and chest. Her gaze traveled again to his thighs, to the juncture between them. His erection strained at his trousers, the heat of his arousal burning against her waist.

She glanced up at his face wondering at his thoughts. His eyes darkened to a deep lake green, swirls of energy empowering his gaze so that she felt she looked into the eyes of a sorcerer. He licked his lips and she stared hungrily, any regret at losing gone under a wave of lust so powerful she felt helpless to resist.

Just as suddenly, the voracious need faded. Gren's eyes

still looked impossibly dark, but not as intense.

"This is much better," he murmured, and placed a large, callused palm over her naked breast.

Temis gasped. "Where--" Her breath left her when his fingers rolled her nipple. Helpless to look away from his face, she saw her desire mirrored in his gaze. "Where are my clothes?"

He grinned and leaned forward, grinding his erection between them as his mouth touched her ear. "In my dreams you wear nothing." His tongue flicked along the shell of her ear before plunging deep.

She tensed, her loins tingling with need. She could feel moisture pooling between her thighs and chafed at his legs that kept her still. By Narok's breast, she needed to move, to ease the ache building within her sex.

"Soon, love. I'm going to give you what you've been begging for since I first saw you."

His arrogance knew no bounds, and despite her desire, Temis rebelled. "When I get free you're going to pay for this." She struggled against his hold and soon found her wrists pinned by an unseen force.

Gren rose to his feet, giving her the perfect opportunity for a well-placed kick. But her legs too were bound by something she could not see.

"Wider," Gren said, and that unseen force spread her legs wide before securing them to the ground. "Beautiful," Gren whispered as he knelt between her legs.

He gave her no warning before he buried his face in the nest of curls between her thighs.

She cried out at the sudden onslaught of feeling that burst within her. Never before had she been touched so intimately, and his lips, so gentle in their exploration, created a fire that soon had her trembling.

"Like honeyed wine," he murmured and opened his mouth. He licked at the desire between her folds, his tongue sliding along her walls as if enjoying a great feast.

Temis couldn't help her moans of ecstasy. An unfamiliar need built until she was consumed by it. "Gren," she cried as she shook her head from side to side. "Release me!"

"Not yet, *sura*," he whispered and lifted his head to stare into her eyes. His lips shone with her need, his eyes glittering brightly, two gems of light in the darkness covering them both. "Not until I've had my fill."

He resumed his place between her legs, but this time he added his able hands to her torment. While his mouth worked her sex, stroking her clitoris, nipping with stinging bites that enhanced her pleasure immeasurably, his hands roamed along her thighs.

Squeezing and caressing, he stroked her muscled thighs as if committing the feel to memory. Again and again his hands would venture near her loins, only to shift away, driving her crazy.

Desire spiraled inside her, making the emptiness in her womb all the more apparent, despite his mouth. Though not ignorant of lovemaking, Temis had never before had so much experience. A few stolen kisses, some groping hands. But never such intimacies with another.

Yet she knew what she needed. She needed Gren, to feel him fully within her. She wanted desperately to feel his heavy arousal deep within her womb.

"Please," she begged, uncaring of anything but the feel of his naked body inside of her.

"Now you're ready for release," he said in a thick voice.

He bit lightly at her clitoris and inserted a finger inside her. She arched at the contact, her virgin flesh quivering on the brink of something new, something unforgettable.

"Yes, *sura*, take your pleasure. Ride my mouth, my hand," he rumbled against her mound.

He began thrusting his finger in and out of her, increasing the pressure on her clit, and suddenly the sensation became too much to bear.

"No," she moaned and gasped when a wave of energy flooded her entire body. Pleasure burst like flame, igniting every nerve ending she possessed. She arched, frozen in ecstasy, conscious of Gren's mouth and hands bringing her such bliss.

Energy flowed all around her, and she heard Gren's groan from a distance. On and on her climax continued, the pleasure building and building until finally she crested and quivered helplessly on the ground.

After some time she became aware of Gren's gaze on her, of the sound of their mingled heavy breathing.

She glanced up to see him crouched between her thighs, his eyes bright, his body glowing with vitality.

"What did you do to me?" she croaked, her throat reedy and her body surprisingly weak.

"I think the question is, what did *you* do to *me?*" Gren sounded strange, his voice echoing in the dark void surrounding them. "We'll study this again later. Now you need to rest, and I need to recover."

His eyes flared, unnatural and inhuman. Before she could comment, blackness enveloped her, pushing her into a dreamless sleep until morning.

* * * *

As soon as he withdrew from her mind, he knew he'd made a large mistake. Gren felt on fire, consumed with the taste of her, the need to bury his flesh and plant his seed in the untried warrior woman.

The sight of her naked body alone should have been worth the effort. As he'd imagined, she had full rounded breasts, marble-white and untouched. Her slim waist and taut belly led to the perfection of womanhood, to the blonde curls guarding her woman's treasure.

He closed his eyes, savoring the memory of her taste. Musky yet sweet, an addicting blend of innocence and experience, of femininity and pure rebellion, a goad to his own unruly nature.

Though all contact between them had occurred in the astral state, the energy had been real. Gren had wanted so badly to take her, to thrust into her warm and willing frame. His energy might have joined hers, but his flesh, still stuck in the cell, experienced every jolt of desire. While he'd been fingering her, licking her cream, his cock had been hard, full and ready to come as his body lay still in his prison cell.

Yet he hadn't allowed himself to climax while in the dream state, not wanting a possible tie to the woman before he allowed himself to fully heal. He sensed with a woman like Temis he'd need his full faculties to deal with her. Besides, he figured once he left the dream he'd regain control over his desire. But the lust, the all-consuming need that should have disappeared once he left her refused to fade.

Like Jahnja, Temis' incredible energy had the power of a dozen women. Yet unlike the *thraia*, Temis had somehow bonded with him. Even now, thoughts of her warmed him, made him ache to have her.

The experience left him dazed and more than a little concerned. But more so, it left him achingly hard and needy. He'd wanted to salve his wounds, and, he admitted, to prod Temis, to see what made her different from other women.

Now instead of answers, he had more questions and a hard-on growing to painful proportions. Cursing the woman's pure desirability, he reached into his trousers and unwillingly thought of her.

Squeezing his cock, he rubbed and stroked, imagining Temis' soft lips around his member. He envisioned her swallowing his seed, her mouth milking him of his essence. His hand moved faster as the fantasy built, images of Temis under him, on top of him, being taken from behind ... until finally he groaned and spent himself.

When his breathing evened, he used the small napkin he'd been given with his meal to clean himself as best he could.

Though his body felt relief and the beginnings of true healing, his spirit felt bereft of her presence. Hating such weakness, Gren forced their tie from his mind, worried at how hard he fought to free himself from her grasp.

He would need every faculty come the morning to deal with his imprisonment, with a cagey enemy so close to his allies and with a woman who irritated and aroused him like no other.

According to Sernal, he had to work with Temis on this mission. The lives of more than a dozen women depended upon him. He frowned. There would be time enough to deal with Temis. An idea formed and his mouth relaxed into a small grin.

The idea had merit. It was anti-peacemaker in nature, held a touch of bold thievery, and involved the forced submission of a Zephyr-trained warrior-woman bent on denying him.

Chapter Four

Temis sat across from Rafe and Sernal in Rafe's room, dimly aware of their heated conversation concerning the mission.

She couldn't shake the vague sensation that something odd had happened last night. She recalled dining with Rafe, then leaving him for a solid night's rest. Frowning, she tried to remember what she'd dreamt about, but could only envision a fighting circle and a luminous pool of water.

"Temis, your thoughts?" Sernal asked.

"I'm sorry?"

Rafe sighed. "Pay attention here, Temis. We've got to figure out how to free Gren without appearing to help in the slightest. If Rorn senses anything amiss, he'll cover his tracks before we can trace them."

Her eyes narrowed. "So we definitely know Rorn is involved?"

Sernal hesitated. "He's involved. But I need more proof."

"More?" Rafe's lips quirked. "How about some, any, a hint of proof?"

Temis glanced from brother to brother. "So you *don't* know for a fact he's involved?" she asked Sernal.

His golden eyes blazed as he stared at Rafe. "I know he's involved. He as good as told me so last night. But he's a crafty bastard, and if we want to find those women before they're sold into uncharted sectors, we need to move quickly."

Rafe shrugged. "Then do what I already suggested. Slip Gren a phaser and have one of Rorn's guards check up on him. Gren won't hesitate to escape."

"No." Sernal stood and began to pace. "Gren's working with me on this so far, but he needs answers and a direction to follow. Hell, he hasn't even seen our case file for this mission."

Temis thought about it. "I can get it to him."

Sernal and Rafe stared at her. "How do you intend to sneak him the case file when Rorn's eyes are all over his cell?"

She smiled and winked at Rafe. "I stole into Gren's room on Aflera, didn't I? A little harmless distraction in front of Rorn's men and Rafe should be able to take him anything he needs."

Rafe chuckled but Sernal looked confused.

"Exactly how did you sneak past Rafe?"

"Trust me, Sernal, you had to be there." Rafe grinned. "Let's not waste too much time. If I know Gren, he's already mending from his beating yesterday and frothing at the mouth to return a few lumps to our peacemakers."

Sernal nodded. "I stopped by Gren's cell before I came here and saw at least two of Rorn's men posted by Gren's door. I'll call off our guard and post him elsewhere, and I'll occupy Rorn for the next hour or so. Make sure Gren gets the file and at least a partial explanation for what happened yesterday. Oh, and Rafe?"

"Yeah?"

"Be certain the video of Gren's imprisonment holds under Rorn's scrutiny." Sernal nodded to them both and left to find Rorn.

Rafe turned to her and explained. "We didn't want Rorn able to watch Gren in his cell, so I doctored the vid tape to show Gren sleeping with some generalized movements come the morning. With any luck Rorn won't suspect the vid's been tampered with."

She frowned. "But why did you hide Gren last night? Surely an injured mercenary has nothing to hide while recuperating."

Rafe gave her a strange look. "It's better for all of us if Gren remains a mystery. Especially if he and you have to mingle with peacemakers who know your faces." He tapped the thick file next to him on the bed. "Now let's coordinate our strategy, and fast. Sernal won't have Rorn's attention for too much longer before that *drun* demands access to Gren."

She nodded, feeling slightly sick. "I'm familiar with Rorn's methods. He won't be happy until he beats Gren to within an inch of his life, regardless of any knowledge Gren may or may not have."

"Obviously you know him well," Rafe muttered. "Now here's what I think we should do...."

* * * *

Temis walked in front of Rafe, her hair long and unbound, waving around her hips. She wore a low-cut blouse and tight training pants, and had spritzed a small amount of Mardu pheromone on before leaving her room. Rafe had nodded in approval and followed her with a tray of food concealing the thick mission file he held underneath.

She found Rorn's guards arguing about the best Mardu brawlers sport team. She mentally shook her head at their lack of attention to detail. Neither man had his weapon within easy reach, nor did they stand ready by Gren's cell door. Instead they leaned lazily against the corridor bulkhead, their backs to hers and Rafe's approach.

Temis was almost upon them when they finally glanced over to see her. Their eyes widened as they took in her appearance, and she wanted to smack them for their lustful gazes.

"So, Peacemaker Temis," one of them said as he licked his lips. "What brings you here?"

She squared her shoulders and subtly thrust her chest out, catching both men's attention. "I haven't seen any of you for months. I just thought we could catch up on the precinct news while my partner serves the prisoner his morning meal."

They glanced at Rafe, saw the steaming food tray and nodded.

"If you wanted to take a short break, you three could use the small conference room right next door," Rafe offered. "That way if there's any trouble, I can yell and you'll hear me."

The men looked doubtful, probably dreading the idea of Rorn finding them gone from their post. Temis took both guards by the arm and led them gently toward the room.

"Isn't Rafe the greatest?" she fairly purred. "He knows just when a woman needs to catch up with old friends."

She endured at least twenty minutes of their ogling and clumsy attempts at pawing before giving them a bright smile as she stood.

"Jehn, Marn, I'm so glad we had this time to talk. I'd love to stay," she said and licked at her lips. She hadn't missed their reaction to her appeal, no doubt aided by the pheromone. And much as it disgusted her, their attraction helped the cause. "I just remembered I'm supposed to report to Lead Sernal for the morning's duty roster and I'm already late. Maybe later we can talk more, hmm?"

They readily agreed and escorted her from the room just in time to see Rafe leaving with an empty food tray.

He shook his head, his eyes burning with anger. "The idiot won't say a word about the Melan rebellion. It's going to take more of yesterday's efforts to persuade him."

Temis shrugged, her breasts thrusting against her thin shirt. "I told you he wouldn't respond to a hot meal."

Rafe eyed her speculatively. "Now maybe if you talked to him...."

She stared at him in surprise, wondering why the plan had changed, as the men behind her agreed.

"Yeah," Marn said. "I bet he'd tell you anything you asked." His eyes were glued to her chest. "We'll wait out here while you interrogate him. Then when you have your answers, we'll take them to Lead Rorn."

"And Sernal," Rafe reminded them.

"Sure, sure," Jehn agreed.

"He's bound and confined to the bed," Rafe told her. "We've got him on vid in the control room, so if you have any problems at all, they'll see it right away. And we'll be right here if you need us."

Temis wondered how he planned to add both hers and his images to the false vid, especially since the timing of their visits wouldn't mesh with reality. But he was encouraging her to meet with Gren, so obviously he wasn't too concerned with the cell room monitor.

"Okay, Rafe. Whatever you say." She took a deep breath and entered the cell, aware of the men eagerly awaiting her return. The solid door slid shut behind her and her gaze immediately sought Gren.

"Well, well, well," Gren murmured in a husky voice. "Temis Freya." His eyes roamed over her with an intensity that flustered her, and she had to work to remain still. "I like the outfit."

She frowned. As Rafe had said, Gren sat on his bed, his wrists chained to the floor by long, steel bonds. A small 'x' on the floor dictated the reach of said chains, and she positioned a nearby chair just beyond the mark.

Gren smiled but said nothing.

She noted his vitality, in sharp contrast with the heavy beating he'd sustained the day before, and blurted her concern. "Are you alright?"

"I look the picture of health, don't I?" he asked in a flat voice as he held his arms up for her inspection. She saw no bruising on his face or the part of his chest exposed by his gaping shirt.

"Yes, you do." She stared at him, curious to feel her heartbeat speed at his nearness. She cleared her throat, annoyed that she needed to before she spoke. "I trust Rafe explained everything?"

"He did."

She lowered her voice. "And you have the file."

"I do."

"Then why am I in here?"

"Because my plan is much more solid than the one you peacemakers concocted." He stood and effortlessly broke through both chains holding his wrists, the manacles sliding along his thick forearms.

"Gren?" she asked in amazement. Had he really broken through Mardu steel? Rafe must have done something to his bonds, she told herself, steadying her racing heart. He neared, towering over her, and she glanced up to see amusement lighting his eyes.

"*Sura*, it's time to go."

* * * *

Her eyes widened when he called her that, and Gren wondered if the endearment beckoned forth memories of last night.

"*Sura*?" She looked confused. "What do you mean it's time to go?"

He crossed his arms, aware of the surge of energy spiking his frame. The longer he stared at her, the more he recalled the feel of her silken skin, her taste, the experience of her spirit entwined with his. He could feel his erection growing and growled low in his throat.

Sexual attraction he understood. But his desire for the woman went beyond lust. His energy felt in tune with hers, a connection that was most unexpected and extremely unwelcome.

"Get up and follow my lead."

Her eyes frosted over and he found her coolness as

enticing as her sensuality. "I asked you a question, *prisoner* Gren. And kindly remember who's in charge of this operation."

He smiled, showing a lot of teeth that made her tense with resolve. He watched her body assume a position of readiness, and wondered if she thought to fight with him in his cell. The thought stirred him more than it should. "You really are lovely under that arrogant cloak of warrior."

She glared and clenched her fists.

"Relax, *sura*, and don't fight me. I don't have time to explain." He grabbed her by the shirt collar and yanked her to his chest. One hand wrapped around her slim waist while the other tangled in her golden tresses.

"Nice," he murmured, knowing he had little time for this. She sputtered and squirmed to be free, her eyes now more gray than violet, filled with rage, and he couldn't help himself.

He ravaged her mouth, taking her scream of protest away with a breath of desire. Her lips parted in a soft moan, of surprise or desire it didn't matter. He explored her soft mouth, unable to resist plunging into the moist cavern, teasing her tongue with stroking motions.

After a short pause she melted against him, reacting to each sweep of his tongue with drugging passion. She moved closer to him of her own accord, her full breasts heavy with desire as she strained against his chest. He could feel her nipples surging against his naked flesh where his shirt parted.

Losing himself in her, it took all the strength he possessed to break from her mouth. Panting, he stared down at her eyes closed in surrender, at her mouth glistening with his taste.

"Come, we have to go," he said thickly, his voice echoing oddly in the small room. He blinked as he realized he'd assumed control over her mind and body without trying, his Thesha skills taking charge of his rampant hormones. For some reason he'd lost control of his abilities, and the occurrence startled him out of his passion-induced haze.

Temis, however, remained his to manipulate. Even free of the powerful lust riding him, something within Gren refused to let go of her. With time running short, he decided the easiest course of action would be to take her with him in such a state--helpless to refuse and possibly hinder his movements.

"Open the door, as if nothing is wrong. I'll be right behind you, *sura*," he ordered and waited.

The door slid open under her nimble fingers and he followed her into the corridor, startling Rafe and two guards out of a conversation. Rafe's eyes widened seeing Gren behind Temis.

"What--" one of the men began before Gren silenced him with a chop to the throat. In a blur of speed, he quickly set upon the other guard, paralyzing his vocal cords and movements with an exact strike to the neck.

"Sorry, Rafe, but it's best this way," Gren gruffly apologized before he attacked.

Stunned but too quick to take down easily, Rafe spun out of reach.

"What the hell are you doing?" he asked in a low voice. "You're going to get killed."

"No," Gren said with a smile and lunged at Rafe again, this time bringing the man to his knees with a blow across his chest. "I'm escaping with a hostage in tow." He turned to Temis. "*Sura*? Take care of him."

Rafe's eyes narrowed as he absorbed Temis' blank gaze, at her ready willingness to follow Gren. He turned his attention to Gren, his hands clenched into tight fists. "When Sernal hears about this," he growled before his eyes rolled into the back of his head.

Temis released the pressure point on his arm and watched dispassionately as Rafe crumpled to the ground.

"Very nice, my fierce warrior," Gren murmured. Knowing he had little time before they were found, he prepared for exposure to more peacemakers. He tucked the case file into the small of Temis' back and covered it with her shirt. Then he tore a few pieces of fabric from her blouse and bound her hands behind her, all the while she remained docile under his touch.

He grabbed a phaser from one of the downed guards and set it to high stun, then placed Temis gently over his shoulder and made his way toward freedom. He encountered a half dozen peacemakers that he quickly stunned, not surprised when the alarm sounded just as he reached the shuttle bay.

Thankfully two shuttles sat unused at dock. Using the codes pried from deep within Temis' mind, he unlocked the closest shuttle and belted Temis into a passenger seat. Adrenaline flowed through his system, the challenge, the near victory over the peacemakers like a drug stirring him into overdrive.

Activating the controls and opening *Lady Justice's* outer doors, he maneuvered around the shuttle in front of him and had just reached the ship's outer hull when Sernal's voice leeched through the voice communicator.

"Halt before I'm forced to shoot," Sernal ordered. The peacemaker sounded angry, and Gren couldn't tell if it was for the benefit of the men around him or if he truly was furious over Gren's escape.

Knowing he'd be better off without further peacemaker interference, Gren ignored the command. "Shoot if you must, but know you'll be killing Peacemaker Temis Freya in the process." He heard muttered cursing and grinned, knowing he'd put a major obstacle in his pursuers' path. Without further word he sped toward the hull, narrowly escaping as the hull doors closed behind him.

He set course for Nebe6, knowing he'd never reach the planet but certain once he neared the system's central asteroid cluster he could lose the peacemakers sure to dog his trail.

True enough, not one third of the way toward the cluster he noted four fighters speeding after him. Should Sernal's men be in those planes, he would have no need to worry. He wasn't certain, however, whether Rorn's men would have as much concern over Temis' welfare.

For the next few hours he dodged and wove past several cargo ships and Ragga's smallest moon before he made it to the most dangerous part of his plan, the system's central asteroid band. Having used such an escape route before, Gren managed to lose his pursuers halfway through the static maze. He hoped for Sernal's sake that any decent peacemakers weren't harmed trying to escape the lethal labyrinth of asteroids that were home to many of the system's most dangerous criminals.

Nonetheless, he allowed himself a breath of relief once he lost those following him, and landed in a cavern on one of the smaller asteroids, an excellent hiding spot he'd used before.

Once the shuttle was stable on the surface and in no pending danger, he left the controls to check on Temis.

"You *fregnali* bastard," Temis cursed through clenched teeth, her hands still bound behind her back as she struggled for freedom. "When I get out of these bonds you're going straight back to *Lady Justice!*"

Gren stared at her in bemusement. She should still have been under his influence, but apparently the warrior within her refused to be quelled for too long. Little did she know her contrary nature and inner strength made her that much more enticing.

Her shirt, ripped in places and tattered, bared more of her breasts than it covered, and his cock hardened at the sight of her nipples. Oblivious, she continued to curse him as she fought her confinement.

"Temis," Gren said and cleared his throat, frowning at his lack of control. "Have you not thought how opportune this is to the mission?"

Her struggles slowed and she glared at him.

"Think about it." He sat across from her, unable to look away from her heaving breasts, flushed pink from her exertions. He tried to ignore how 'opportune' their isolation could be. "We are away from the peacemakers, finally. Now I can track the guilty party with you as a believable hostage."

"Hostage?" Her eyes widened, a lovely shade of cool lavender streaked with silver.

He nodded. "I let Sernal know I'd taken you hostage. So Rorn, if in fact he is guilty, won't bat an eye when I eventually show with you at the selling of those abducted women."

She ceased struggling against the ties at her wrists, much to Gren's disappointment.

"I know Sernal had some idiotic notion of using you as my partner," he continued, "but the truth is you'll be much more believable as a potential slave than a peacemaker turned bad."

She simmered with outrage. "Why? Because I'm a woman and therefore not believable as a peacemaker? Or is it because you view my sex as weak, beneath you?"

"I'd like you better beneath me," he muttered and held up

his hand to forestall more acerbic rebuttal. "No, Temis, my suggestion has nothing at all to do with the fact you're a woman. It's more about who you are in particular."

"Well?" she asked after he hesitated.

He stared at her, opening his senses to absorb that essence, that particular aura only Temis possessed. "You're too good. Too honorable," he said bluntly, startling her mouth into a small 'o'. "No one who knows you would ever believe you capable of turning on your ideals. And the plain truth is that your beauty can only aid us in this mission."

"I can't imagine any man turning away the opportunity to bed a woman who looks like you."

He smiled at the return of her hostility and reaching down, removed the bonds from her wrists. She stood up quickly, probably hoping to put them on more equal footing.

"If you men would think with your head and not your--"

"But we don't, so get used to it. I don't know why being told you're beautiful angers you, but you can't hide from the truth." He tucked a wavering strand of hair behind her ear, unable to keep from touching her.

She startled and pulled back. "What was that for?"

"To remind you you're a woman more than a warrior, *sura*." She scowled, but beneath the annoyance lurked the hint of nerves. Curious, Gren stepped closer. "But maybe you need a more thorough reminder, hmm?"

He drew her protesting form into his arms and sighed at her perfect curves. Keeping a tight reign on his powers, he focused on the texture of her mouth, the sweetness of her kiss as he lowered his mouth to sample another taste of *wainu*.

Temis shuddered, not understanding how Gren had done it to her *again*. She'd never before fallen pray to the lusts affecting her peers, and now she found herself a victim of her own needs. That Gren, a man suspected of dozens of system violations and heinous crimes should be the one to spark her desire made her simultaneously disgusted with herself and strangely excited.

As his lips touched hers with surprising gentleness, she felt her will to resist melt under his confusing presence.

Her fingers curled against his shoulders to push him

away, but instead pulled him closer.

He tasted of raw strength, of passion, and of a disturbing wildness that teased her with the promise of unending ecstasy.

Images of Gren kissing her under a foreign sky flashed through her mind and her loins throbbed, releasing a flood of moist desire between her legs. She clearly felt a remembrance of Gren's mouth on her sex, his tongue expertly bringing her to orgasm with ease.

Though the kiss he gave her now was gentle, it held the same heat, the same promise of more to come.

She trembled in his arms and heard him murmur her name as his large arms caged her protectively. Her breasts tingled where they touched the heat of his body, and she could feel his erection through his trousers pressed like steel against her stomach.

Wanting to break free and yet not willing to end this sweet torment just yet, she shifted against his chest, brushing her hardened nipples against his bare flesh.

He cursed against her lips and pulled back, his breathing as harsh as hers.

Staring down at her with an intensely powerful expression on his face, he traced her lips with a callused finger, the roughness of his hand at odds with the gentleness of the action.

"You see, *sura*? You can be both warrior and woman, and the stronger because of it."

His voice, both husky and deep, shook her. She could almost feel his need pounding at her body, and the imagined foreign sensation of male desire made her back up a step.

"I don't need you to analyze me," she answered in a shaky voice. Angered at her loss of control, she sharpened her tone. "And regardless of what you think of your role in this, you and I *will* be partners. I won't let you get distracted by the legion of criminal acts you're no doubt currently involved in. For whatever reason," she scorned, "Lead Sernal wanted your help to find those missing women. And it's up to me to see that you do."

She ended on a forceful, controlled note, secure in her role as peacemaker and disciplined Zephyr-trained warrior.

Gren stared at her as if he wanted to throttle her. "You,

lady, are one piece of work," he growled, his eyes dangerously dark. "Fine, have it your way. I've tried to be nice. Hell, I've even tried to show you the parts of yourself you don't want to see. But you want to call the shots? Go for it, sweetheart," he mocked, and the endearment sounded bitter on his tongue. "I'll find those women, and when I do, you're going to owe me one hell of an apology. One I mean to collect," he threatened and strode toward the control panel.

Temis watched him huff angrily away. Despite knowing him for less than a few days, what she'd seen of him had hinted at a cool criminal, one with a sense of humor at least. But this side of Gren, the angry, cutthroat mercenary, was more of what she'd initially expected.

Bemused, she dwelled on the differing sides of his personality, wondering what the hell Lead Sernal had been thinking to ask for Gren's help, when the ship fired to life.

She jolted into a bench of nearby seats when the shuttle tilted at an odd angle, then rushed to the front.

"Where are you taking us?"

"We need answers we're not going to get sitting on our asses in the middle of nowhere. Hang on." He piloted the ship due east toward Mornio, a planet known for its rich mine deposits.

"Now shut up and don't talk to me until we set down in Mornio, or so help me I won't be responsible for what happens next," he said with an ominous glare that pierced through the retort she thought to make.

They spent the next few hours in silence, and all the while Temis wondered just what might have "happened next," and why the thought of his worst made her want to kiss the scowl off his darkly handsome face.

Chapter Five

Temis and Gren successfully ignored one another for the duration of the trip to Mornio. Once they landed, however, Temis couldn't help asking the questions that had been building.

"Why Mornio? And why did you land here, of all places, when we're trying to keep a low profile?"

She looked through a portal at the seedy little town of Reykhold, Mornio's infamous port town. It was popular reading material for Mardu's peacemakers, a sterling example of what they worked so hard to prevent happening on their own planet.

Mornio's rich mine deposits attracted huge numbers of criminals bent on plunder and power. She shouldn't have been surprised by Gren's familiarity with Reykhold, yet he seemed a step-up from the scum that normally frequented the town.

"Right now you need me a hell of a lot more than I need you. This is my world, Temis," Gren said in a low, no-nonsense voice. He spoke without heat, the ice in his expression alerting her to be extremely wary. "Do what I tell you when I tell you and you'll get out of here unharmed. Play with me and you'll wish you hadn't."

He opened the shuttle doors and strode out without a backward glance.

Steamed, Temis followed intending to set him straight when he stopped suddenly, causing her to ram into his back.

"What--" she began when a large shirt hit her face.

"Put that on."

She noted the small clothing stand they'd stopped in front of, the older Mornian giving her a wide-eyed stare.

"Excuse me?"

"I said put it on." Gren turned to face her after saying something to the man in his native tongue. "Unless you'd rather showcase your breasts to the rest of Reykhold?"

She stared down at her torn shirt and flushed with

embarrassment. Furious, she threw the shirt on. Gren's face, she noted, didn't soften at all, and she began to see just how he'd earned his dark reputation. He seemed wholly untouchable, his emotions locked under the cold, cruel demeanor that now encased him from head to toe.

"You'd like that, wouldn't you? Molesting me in public. You tore it in the first place," she murmured, earning a dark frown. Secretly pleased she'd managed to rile him, she waited for him to explain just where they were headed.

Instead, he nodded to the old man, then continued down the road toward the more crowded center of town.

The reality of Reykhold was far worse than the vids she'd studied. Finished red Mornian steel filled the town, making the village a bloody scene of gluttony and filth. The roads were dusty, a pale yellow reminder of what the raw steel of Mornio looked like before it had been melted.

Peopled with races from every planet, Reykhold served as a conglomeration of the desperate and greedy. Slavers and merchants commingled, no one reviled in a town filled with the underbelly of the system's richest planet.

As they passed vendor after vendor, coming closer to the actual storefronts in the shopping center, she noticed the growing number of stares and murmurs thrown their way.

"Gren," she said in a low voice, but he ignored her. "Gren," she said louder and grabbed his arm to stop him.

He turned around to stare at her, his lips flat. "What?"

"People are staring," she said bluntly.

"I know."

"You know?" When he turned to continue, she latched onto his forearm again, uncomfortably aware of the tingle that spread down her arm at the contact. "That's it. You're going to explain a few things to me now. Right now."

Gren's eyes seemed to glow from within, a startling flare of emerald annoyance as he took a step closer to her, pinning his chest to her breasts. "A slave has no say against her master, and direct disobedience is handled promptly, without question."

She opened her mouth to ask what the hell he meant when he hoisted her over his shoulder and swatted her behind with a whack loud enough to be heard down the street.

She heard several snickers and outright laughter and lashed out at Gren's back. Unfortunately, he held her with arms of iron, and pounding his back was like pounding a steel slab. When she tried kicking at him, he smacked her again, then followed with an uncomfortably warm caress that sucked the breath out of her.

"That's right, *sura*," he purred as he continued to walk down the street. "Relax and ask no questions. The less you know the better. And if you think to keep fighting me, know I'll strip these trousers off you and give the people on the streets a real show." His fingers traced the cleft between her cheeks and moisture pooled between her thighs.

She froze, completely stunned at her body's response to his touch. That Gren could so manhandle her in public, and that her body apparently *liked* it, made her question her sanity. An image, a flash of Gren's mouth between her legs, popped into her mind again and she wondered what, by Norak's breast, was happening to her.

Her mind sifted through the facts and strange memories she'd had since meeting Gren, working in a frenzy to make some sense of his seeming manipulation of her mind and body. Something wasn't right, and the tense coiled sensation in her loins proved it. Her reaction to Gren was anything but normal.

* * * *

Finally, the damned woman had stopped fighting. Gren swallowed a sigh of relief and wound around Nikos, a popular tavern, to a back staircase. Finding Jora guarding the entrance, he nodded a greeting and waited for the large man, a native of planet Ragga, to give him entry. Coming from a planet that gave birth to inhumanly strong inhabitants, Raggas were the best in security, and worth their weight in currency.

After a careful study, Jora grinned and punched in the appropriate codes on the security panel. He motioned a crudity at Temis then stepped aside to allow Gren entry.

"You're all secure," Jora rumbled before stepping back to guard the stairwell.

Gren took the steps quickly, glad the beks he'd spent to safeguard this hideaway had finally come in handy. He punched in the key code and waited for the door to open to his room.

He stared into the darkened room warily, entering only when his senses told him the room was indeed secure. That

Temis lay serenely over his shoulder gave him pause, but at least now he'd have only her to worry about in the relative safety of this room.

He flipped on a nearby light and set her on her feet. She glanced around her in bemusement, still silent, though he could feel her seething, no doubt about his less-than-gentlemanly treatment.

A large bed, locked chest, scarred table and scattered chairs were all that occupied the room, with the exception of the built-in wall storage common in Mornian buildings. A small lav sat off to the corner behind the room's only other door, and Gren made a mental note to have Jora turn the facilities on for his brief stay.

Temis' gaze eventually returned to him. Instead of the fiery glare he'd expected, her stare fixed on his hands.

Not sure what that meant, Gren waited for her to speak. He wondered just how far she would try to push him this time, and if he could control himself enough not to throw her down on the bed and take her until she begged for mercy.

It had taken all his control on the shuttle not to show her how *criminal* he could actually be. The little peacemaker pushed his buttons like no one else ever had. After all he'd been through to help the peacemakers on this disaster of a mission, and she had the gall to accuse him of wanting to engage in criminal activity?

He'd lost his first vacation in years, been beaten unjustly, and thrown away his first taste of *Thraian* passion. And the knowledge that Temis reacted to him, that she could be his for the taking while she ranted and raved at him made him burn with the desire to fuck her until neither of them could speak.

His Theshan senses constantly reared whenever near her, teasing him with the idea of *enthralling* her, of chaining her to his side until he tired of her delectable body. He felt the temperature rise, could feel his cock hardening at thoughts of Temis at his command.

Shaking his head, he glared at her, almost wishing he'd never met her. Almost.

"What is this place?" she asked in a soft voice, her violet gaze finally rising to meet the heat in his face.

"A safe place, for now."

She blinked and stepped back, away from him, as if sensing the precariousness of her position for the first time. Then, realizing what she'd done, a hardness settled over her face and she straightened.

"I want you to tell me what's going on, Gren. No more excuses. I want to know what you're planning. Now."

Her hands settled on her hips in an authoritarian stance, and against his better judgment, Gren found himself admiring her courage. Her determination to control the situation and him finally penetrated his irritation, and his lips curled into a grin before he could think better of it.

"You do realize I can do anything to you in here, and no one will come running?" he asked in low voice, the threat he'd intended buried under his amusement.

She rolled her eyes. "I'm shaking with fear," she said wryly.

His eyes narrowed. "You're not afraid at all, are you?"

"I can handle anything you throw at me," she said coolly, her hands clenched over her hips. "And if you don't start answering my questions," she said and closed the space between them, "you'll take what *I* throw back."

He groaned with frustrated laughter and left her to sink down into the bed. "I can't believe fate would be so cruel to stick me with a woman like you instead of the vacation I deserve."

She smiled through clenched teeth and stared down at him. "Like it or not, fate definitely has a sense of humor. Trust me, I'd much rather be working with my peers on this than a man I don't trust, and don't like."

"You like me well enough when my lips are on you though, don't you?" he asked slyly, pleased at the pretty blush that stole over her cheeks.

She cursed under her breath and made fists at her sides.

His earlier good mood restored, he relented enough to tell her, "You want explanations? Fine. Pull up a chair and listen *without interruption*." He waited until she sat, her brows set in that stubborn line he was coming to know all too well.

"After you peacemakers beat the hell out of me, for no justifiable reason I might add, I did some thinking in that cell. I didn't think Sernal had turned on me, but that Rorn had somehow interfered with the mission. Sernal mentioned bad peacemakers, and obviously Rorn is one of his main suspects."

"Yes, but--"

"So I decided to escape without Sernal's or Rafe's help," he continued with a glare. "The less interaction I have with them, the better my cover. You, on the other hand, made a perfect hostage. A beautiful woman, a peacemaker no less, under my control would ensure a safe escape from *Lady Justice*, at least until I could find security.

"Then something Rafe said made perfect sense to me. He mentioned something Sernal had said, about how obsessed Rorn seemed with you. And I had my answer. I'd take you and turn you into my 'slave,' to barter for easier entry into the slaver's market.

"Once there, I have no doubt we'll find those women. I just need to find out exactly when and where. In the meantime, I have to make sure we're seen together, and you're appropriately subservient."

He couldn't contain a smile at the thought. She bristled but said nothing, absorbing what he'd just told her. He waited for the questions, the objections sure to follow and wasn't disappointed.

"Okay, I agree with most of what you've said. But me, a slave?" She snorted. "No one will believe that."

"They will. You have no idea what the slave markets are like, do you?"

She frowned and shook her head.

"Almost without exception potential slaves are drugged to ensure cooperation. They are led to the auction after blatant displays of what pleasure they're capable of bestowing," he said with disgust, memories of the two auctions he'd attended burned indelibly on his mind. He stood and began to pace. "Then they're positioned for sale. But the special ones, the most beautiful and treasured slaves, are sold at private parties. And you don't want me to tell you the things they make the slaves do there."

"How do you know all this?" Temis asked quietly. Her eyes narrowed. "Have you bought and sold slaves of your own?"

He immediately shook his head, regretting he'd been so open about the market in the first place. "No. Never. I'd rather die than be a party to--" She stared at his vehement denial with burning curiosity, and he quickly changed the direction of conversation. "The reason I mentioned this, Temis, is to let you know why you have to appear under my control."

"The barbaric display in the street," she murmured with disapproval.

"Exactly." Thoughts of what she might have to do to get them into the auction disturbed him, so much so that he began to reinvent his plan of attack.

"What are you thinking?" she asked and stood, coming to his side.

"Maybe you should return to *Lady Justice* and your peers," he said distractedly. He paced away from her, away from the bed, and imagined his next course of action. "I hadn't thought this plan all the way through. No, it won't work. Go back to *Lady Justice*. You'll be safer there."

"Oh no, you don't." She strode to his side and wrenched him to face her. "I'm in this until the end. This is my mission, and it's my duty to help those women. Lead Sernal trusted me with this and I won't let him down."

Irritated, he scowled at her. "Sernal? What the hell does he matter in this?"

"He's my superior, a man I deeply respect." He heard nothing but professional attachment in her tone and relaxed. "Besides, rescuing those women will be a lot easier with a woman, namely me, involved. Trust me, you'll be just as scary to them as their kidnappers. Maybe more," she added, aggravating him all over again, as she eyed him with a discouraging frown.

Being Thesha, he could easily command the missing women to obey his orders. He held more power over the female mind than any other creature in the system. But he couldn't tell her that. The Thesha lived in secrecy, and for good reason. Too many slavers had made them ready victims. At the thought his anger grew and he focused it on Temis, trying to combat his desire.

"So you find me intimidating, do you?" he asked softly, glaring at her nose to nose. "Good. But that's nothing compared to the fear of what you might have to do to prove your compliance once we reach the enemy."

Her shoulders straightened and she pursed her full, luscious lips. "I'm not afraid of you, Gren. And I'll do whatever I need to for the mission."

He felt an answering heat well within him at her carelessly thrown gauntlet. "Anything, hmm?"

Her eyes mirrored his need, and he sensed her desire easily, her sweet scent of wild spice beckoning him onward.

"I'm not an innocent young woman to be protected, Gren. I can hold my own, and I can definitely take you on." Her chest heaved and her eyes glittered with unfulfilled desire. He could see how excited she became at thoughts of tangling with him, of possibly besting him.

His cock swelled, almost hurting with the need to be inside of her, and he threw caution to the winds. He took a small step back. "Then, *sura*, I know you'll be able to dominate this challenge with ease."

His fingers teased the front clasp of his trousers and he watched her eyes grow wide, with anticipation and a hint of alarm she tried to hide. "Not scared, are you?" he taunted.

She shook her head, her gaze fixed on his hand. "I can handle you, Gren."

"Good," he murmured and reached for his straining cock. He withdrew it from his trousers and held it before her, completely hard, aching at the need to feel her mouth around him. "Then take me in your mouth."

Temis stared at him and he grew larger, feeling her gaze like a caress. "Is this what you mean about proving my submission?" Her voice was throaty, thick with want. He could smell her cream, and remembrances of the dream state when he'd tasted her forced him to control a shiver.

"I told you you're going to have to be convincing at the auction, *sura*. The drugs you'll supposedly be under lessen inhibitions and enhance the user's sensuality. You're going to have to be at ease with your sexuality or it won't work."

Temis heard his voice lower and thicken. His eyes remained glued to hers and he began stroking his cock. Her mouth watered at the juicy offering. A small bead of dew poised at the tip of his shaft and she licked her lips, drawn to his sex like a magnet.

Much as she knew Gren was testing her, she couldn't help wanting to meet his challenge. The thought of licking him, of tasting his seed made her wet, and she knew the time of discovery was at hand. Her woman's core demanded she let free.

"Do it, Temis," he said, his eyes a brilliant emerald against his hardened face.

She glared at him defiantly even as she knelt before him. He saw her look and his eyes narrowed, but still he leaned forward, his cock almost brushing her mouth, and Temis heard him try to stifle a gasp.

She licked her lips and heard him mutter under his breath. His eyes were twin slits of lust and need. She breathed in the musky scent of his desire and rubbed her legs together, feeling an answering pulse in her clitoris.

Gren pressed forward, bringing his cock in contact with her mouth and Temis swallowed hard, no longer able to pretend this was all an act. She wanted him, as a woman wants a man, and the warrior within her would allow no half-measures.

She touched her tongue to his shaft tentatively, curious, and felt him tremble. She glanced up to see his face tight, his lips compressed, his eyes closed as he maintained careful control.

On her knees she should have felt subservient. But his expression returned all the power to her. She licked him again, this time harder, and saw his face a mask of agony as he held still.

Smiling, she opened her mouth wider and pressed forward, engulfing him. He swore and surged deeper, unable to keep from moving. Heady with her newfound power, she began stroking him with her tongue, applying pressure when he jerked or moaned.

To hear Gren moaning her name, to feel his hands in her hair, teased something within her to break free.

"Temis," he groaned and rocked against her after she sucked on the head of his shaft before taking most of the rest of him in. He was huge, silky soft and rock hard, the perfect vision of manly desire.

"Yes, *sura*, more," he demanded.

Lost in her sexuality, Temis did more than take all of him. She reveled in his taste. More fluid leaked from his arousal, a hint of the desire he couldn't hide. He began pumping slowly, aided by her hands around his tight, lean buttocks.

She smiled around his cock and stared up at him.

"Now who's in charge?" she murmured and licked the

underside of his shaft.

He caught his breath and stared down at her with such hunger she felt helpless to stop. Watching him, she slowly eased her mouth back over his cock, taking him deep to the back of her throat.

He swore softly and began thrusting into her mouth, all the while he stared at her, watching her suck him to oblivion.

On and on Temis licked and sucked and teased, utterly enthralled at how good he tasted, at how addictive his scent was. She wanted, no needed, to swallow him whole, to feel his seed trickle down her throat.

As if Gren sensed her thoughts, his cock hardened like a rock and he pressed deeper into her mouth, his strokes shorter but more forceful.

"Oh, yes, yes," he groaned and pumped, his hands clenched in her hair. Yet all the while he remained careful not to bruise her, not to choke her with his massive shaft.

Temis felt a gush of warm wetness seep from her body. The more she sucked him, the greater his pleasure, until she could almost feel what she did to him.

"Now, *sura*, now," Gren uttered in a hoarse voice and came hard, shooting deep inside her mouth.

She swallowed his cum, the thick, sweet mass of seed that coated her throat like honeyed cream. And in the doing so felt a coil of heat spiral in her core, enveloping her in a desire so intense, a bliss so profound, she saw stars as Gren continued to come.

Sometime later she heard him call her as if from a distance. She blinked sleepily and felt a large hand on her waist, stroking her side. She focused on the blurred form in front of her and saw Gren looking at her with concern.

"Hmm?" she asked lazily, feeling satisfied in a way she'd never felt before. She lay on her side facing Gren on the bed, and she imagined he'd placed her there. Yet her mind, her spirit, soared on another plane altogether.

She watched Gren's eyes darken to black. "You're in *wainu*," he said with amazement. He stopped stroking her hip and pushed her flat onto her back. "How is this possible?"

She smiled dreamily and caressed his hard face with tingling fingers. Everywhere she touched him she felt heat, and she wanted to feel that marvelous pleasure with him all over again. Even as she thought it, she saw his eyes shine with understanding.

"Are you reading my mind?" she asked curiously. "You're some kind of telepath, aren't you? Or did you drug me like you said you would?"

He shook his head and smiled, a mysterious grin that made her loins quicken.

"*Sura*, you have no idea what pleasure you've been missing. And before we're done, you're going to beg me for more."

Chapter Six

Gren stared at Temis, caught in a wave of lust and tenderness so intense it shook him. Her white-gold hair lay in waves around her, framing her heavy-lidded eyes and passion-kissed lips.

He quickly disrobed her, eager to see all of her again, this time in reality. His breath caught at the sight of her pale white breasts heaving with desire, and he bent to taste their perfection, unable to help himself.

She arched into his mouth and groaned his name, and his cock hardened as if he hadn't just come inside her delicious mouth. Energy swirled around them, a drugging haze that threatened his promise to himself.

Coming inside Temis' mouth had been akin to dying and being reborn in *wainu*. The warmth of her lips and giving spirit that brought him such ecstasy called forth his need to truly join with her, to bond them together.

Certain if he did indeed make love to her he'd be forever changed, he determined to give her every pleasure without entering her womb. Yet seeing her thus, naked and bare to his gaze, knowing of her virginity, threatened his will to stay strong.

Her nipple hardened and quivered in his mouth and he sighed, his cock stroking her thigh even as his trousers slid along her legs. He reached down to hide himself behind the cloth, refastening his trousers, and knew the effort to be a pitiful one.

Nevertheless, he felt a fraction more secure in his resolve not to surge deep within her with more than his mouth and hands.

"Take them off," she urged in a throaty growl, tugging at his waistband. She slithered around him, her curves tantalizingly sweet. Despite being a virgin, Temis' warrior instincts made her decidedly aggressive.

He could smell her need, could feel her climax surging closer and fought to slow down her pleasure, to draw it out.

"No, *sura*, lie back and enjoy," he ordered.

She withdrew her hands with protest but did as he asked.

He leaned over her, his body tense and straining as he pressed against her. Her eyes were slanted, a bright violet ringed by silver.

"I want you," she said boldly, letting her gaze settle on his lips. "And I don't care about anything else right now but having you."

Her words stirred his blood and without a second more he sealed his mouth to hers. They both moaned at the contact, the heat between them blazing with raw desire and energy. Power flickered around them, shooting blue sparks in the dimly lit room.

Gren thrust his tongue into her mouth, needing to taste all of her. She followed quickly, learning through imitation what he liked and pleasuring herself in the bargain.

Her nipples scored his chest with burning marks of desire, until he had to fight not to rip free of his trousers and sink deep inside her.

He withdrew from her mouth, needing the respite, and focused on Temis' pleasure. Running his tongue along her neck, biting her pulse point with a savage desire to possess her, he felt her climax building as she coaxed him further.

He nipped at her collarbone and continued down to her breasts. Licking her nipples until she cried out for ease, he then suckled and drew on the tips, pressing his cock into her clit and riding her until she cried out in climax.

Her orgasm went on and on as he continued to lave her breasts with a skilled mouth and tongue, her energy washing over him like pounding rain.

His hands, meanwhile, wandered all over her body, feeling her strength underneath soft, womanly skin. The contrast excited him, and he brought her to orgasm again with the touch of his mouth and hands in Theshan bliss.

She cried out his name and came in a gush that had him aching to taste her sex, to take her essence into his body.

Her energy wound around him tightly, making him doubt his ability to resist joining her. Already he felt near to bursting, his trousers wet with both his and her arousal.

"I'm going to lick you, to eat you up, Temis," he whispered in a raw voice. She tilted her head to stare down at him, the passion clouding her eyes a heady aphrodisiac he could no longer resist.

"Do it," she breathed and spread her legs, her sweet scent drifting on the air like a drug.

He needed no further urging, and buried his face between her thighs. He opened his mouth wide and began lapping her cream, licking and teasing her clit with a tongue as needy as his cock.

His shaft swelled as he devoured her body. He couldn't get enough, and he licked and nibbled until he felt her climbing yet another orgasm, this one more intense than the last two.

Unable to withstand the pressure on his erection, he reached down with one hand and freed his member, sighing at the feel of silken sheets against his skin.

"Love me," Temis moaned as he thrust a finger inside her sheath while his tongue stroked her clit. "I need you inside me," she begged.

He shook his head, shaking at the conflict within him. Everything in him urged him to do as she asked, yet a part of him knew it would change his very existence.

Hurting, so hard he could barely think, he stripped his trousers off and swiftly juxtaposed his body so that his mouth remained between her thighs while his lower body straddled her head.

"Even better," she whispered and closed her mouth around his cock.

He groaned and resumed pleasuring her sex, thrusting two fingers inside her as he imagined fucking her, shooting deep within her womb.

He nipped at her clitoris, excited anew when in response she sucked hard on his shaft.

Energy swirled and shimmered in the air. He could feel the end coming, so close, so near.

Yes, yes, she mentally screamed as she came, arching into his mouth. Her lips clamped around him and he could no longer hold back.

The taste of her as she shuddered pushed him over the edge, and he came hard in her mouth, surging deep as she swallowed his every drop.

Stunned at the ferocity of their lovemaking, Gren could only close his eyes as *wainu* overtook him. Great waves of energy flowed through his body, a healing peace that lingered in his blood.

Gradually the drugging ecstasy of the moment faded and he gently withdrew from Temis' grasp, turning to gather her in his arms.

He had no explanation for what he felt. Nothing had ever felt as right as this moment, and yet he still felt a niggling emptiness, a part of Temis he had yet to reach that beckoned him closer.

"Gren," she murmured and kissed him gently on his chest. The tenderness of her action, so at odds with the warrior woman he normally interacted with, stunned him, and he hugged her closer, not wanting to let her go.

She hummed her contentment and soon fell into an exhausted slumber, her hands pressed trustingly over the steady beating of his heart.

Gren reluctantly donned his trousers, not trusting himself to lie naked with her in his arms. He soon followed her into sleep, needing to relax and accept the large amounts of healing power now surging through his body. His last thoughts were of how he planned to resist the tempting fate lying in his arms, and if he should even try.

* * * *

"I can't believe you let him get away," Sernal growled in a low voice and glared at his brother. "Do you realize how precarious our position is?"

Rafe rolled his eyes. "I told you, it wasn't like I had a choice. Gren always was a hothead, and he didn't exactly appreciate sitting in a cell after being beaten by Rorn's bastards."

Sernal let out a heavy breath and began pacing his room, running his fingers through his hair. "You told him what I told you to tell him?"

Rafe nodded.

"And gave him the file?"

Another nod.

"Then why the hell did he take Temis hostage when he could have left the ship in one piece undetected?"

Rafe wondered just how much to tell his brother. Sernal normally had an even temper and open mind. But when the safety of his people was involved, he had been known to explode in a fierce temper.

"Well?" Sernal's eyes blazed, definitely not a good sign. And yet, Rafe wasn't too pleased with the position he'd been placed in either.

"It was your idea to use Gren, remember, not mine. I was happy playing an anonymous information broker on Mardu." He grimaced, wishing again he'd refused to become part of Sernal's team. He loved his brother, but honestly the man thought too much of rules and regulations.

"My patience is wearing."

"Fine. You want to know why Gren took her? He wants her, plain and simple. She was the one who knocked me out, per his orders. And she wasn't herself, if you know what I mean." At Sernal's blank look, he sighed. "She was *enthralled*."

"You mean to tell me Gren's using his powers to control my peacemaker?" Sernal glowered and seemed to grow twice as large in his rage. "That son of a--"

"But to his credit, I think Gren is onto something." He ignored his brother's cursing, waiting for Sernal to regain his temper. "You said it yesterday. Rorn has quite an appetite when it comes to women, and it's obvious he's hungry for Temis. Imagine how intense his search will be looking for Gren, giving us more time to build a case against him."

Sernal remained silent, listening.

"I'm not Gren's biggest fan by any stretch," he said with a small scowl, remembering the large man's attack. "But he's unable to harm Temis and you know it."

"Not without severe repercussions."

"I thought he couldn't harm a woman, ever. Theshan skills don't work that way."

Sernal shook his head. "They're not supposed to work that way, but occasionally a Thesha strays. Of course, for Gren to harm Temis he'd do at least twice as much damage to himself."

Sernal sighed. "Dammit. I'm just aggravated that Gren never does anything the easy way. No, he won't hurt Temis. With her looks, he'll no doubt want to take her to bed." He grimaced. "That's all we need. Another complication."

"I don't know. Temis seemed like she could use a little relaxation, and it's unheard of for a woman to complain after being visited by one of his kind." Rafe grinned at his brother's exasperation.

"I'm so glad you're amused. I'm not," Sernal huffed. "But I'm beginning to think Gren's plan might have some merit. By taking Temis hostage and escaping unaided, he's taken the suspicion off of us. And with Temis at his side, an irresistible lure Rorn will no doubt follow, he should have no trouble locating the missing women."

Rafe nodded, seeing additional benefits. "He'll especially do well if he uses Temis as a 'slave' rather than a partner. Come on, brother, open your eyes. You may be her superior, but you can't deny she's one of the most beautiful women you've ever seen."

Sernal frowned but didn't disagree. "Right now we're in a good position to do more digging. Gren should try to contact us within a day or two. He won't want to, but he knows it's better to keep us in the loop and out of his way." He rubbed his jaw and gave Rafe a small grin. "Gren always manages to annoy the hell out of me when we work together. I can only imagine what Temis must be feeling."

* * * *

Temis woke with a stretch and yawn, feeling more rested than she had in months. Her body felt as if it had been exercised hard, sore in places yet limber enough to engage in anything at the moment.

Turning her head, she gazed at Gren's profile and her heartbeat accelerated.

He slept peacefully, his lashes dark and thick against his weathered face. Even in sleep he looked hard, a warrior one second from waking into full readiness. His strength awed her, his control impressed her, and his lovemaking overpowered her.

She blushed furiously, recalling the pleasure he'd given her. That he'd touched her so intimately, been so gracious fulfilling her desire didn't quite fit with the savage mercenary of legend.

He'd been truly angry when she'd accused him, perhaps unfairly, she admitted now, of criminal activity on the shuttle. But he'd scared her, somehow seeing beneath the defensive shield she'd worked so hard to build. A tough warrior mindset had earned her way into the peacemaker corps, not her womanly softness.

Only Gren had come this close to her woman's heart.

Gren, a mercenary, supposed criminal, a man she didn't dare trust, and a man she was beginning to care for.

Her previous limited sexual experiences had left her ill prepared for a man like him. She still couldn't believe how bold she'd been. She stared at his chiseled lips, at his straight nose and uncompromising jaw line. She, Temis Freya, a woman of little sexual experience, a virgin, had brought Gren to climax with her mouth, not once but twice.

The memory made her loins quicken and she strove to contain her breathing. Sharing such intimacies with a man had never before occurred to her. Oh, she knew eventually she would marry and raise children, like her mother. But Temis had yet to meet a man that she respected and made her heart race, her blood pulse with desire.

Until Gren.

He stirred and she placed her hand on his chest to calm him. At her touch he resumed his slumber, mumbling low under his breath in a language she'd never before heard spoken.

She petted him gently, stroking the impressive muscles beneath her palm with warmth, wondering about him.

Gren truly was a mystery. No one knew of his origins, and most of what she'd read or been told about him came from rumor and pirate gossip. For a man who had supposedly killed hundreds without blinking an eye, he had treated her with an affection and care surprising for one so "hard-hearted."

As she recalled all they had done, she puzzled over his refusal to mate with her fully. Perhaps he worried about getting her with child. He shouldn't have. She was only fertile in the summer months of Zephyr, and then only with the right mate. But he would have no way of knowing that.

Thoughts of a child with Gren caused her womb to flutter and she hurriedly turned from that line of thinking. Her touch stilled on Gren's chest and he frowned in his sleep.

She resumed petting him while she chastised herself. Just because Gren had given her pleasure she'd never before experienced did not mean emotion need be attached. So he'd been an extraordinary lover, so he'd brought her to peak time and time again unselfishly. That meant nothing.

She had given him ecstasy as well. In fact, she'd started it. Temis nodded to herself and began stroking Gren's nipples, curious when the little buds hardened under her touch.

She glanced down his body and noted the bulge growing beneath his trousers. Then she noticed she wore nothing at all and flushed.

Never before had any man seen her naked, though she'd seen her share of nude bodies during her early days of training on Zephyr. She glanced again at Gren, studying his powerful muscles when something wrong hit her.

No scars or bruises marred his flesh save the scar on his left hand that led up his forearm. He'd recently suffered severe trauma at the hands of Rorn's men, yet he wore no mark to record the event. She frowned. He'd looked perfectly fine to her in his cell as well. Then he'd done something to her, something that made her head swim trying to recall the exact memory.

She leaned up on an elbow to better study Gren's body, his face, trying to understand him. Temis knew her own mind, and still had no explanation for Gren's impact on her senses. It had been like this since she'd first laid eyes on him.

He held some odd sway over her, and she began to look deeper into his unfathomable control. She had left *Lady Justice* and knocked Rafe unconscious, and all because Gren had ordered her to do so. She paused as the obvious hit her.

Of course. He was a telepath.

Somehow he had wormed his way beneath the mental guards she'd been taught in her peacemaker training. *A telepath.* She finally made sense of her odd behavior. Only using such rare and powerful abilities could he have caused her to leave her ship without Lead Sernal's permission. She couldn't fault Gren's sexual magnetism though, and acknowledged his physical attraction readily, despite not wanting to feel so drawn to him.

His apparent lack of injuries, however, deserved some explanation, one she determined to receive once he woke. She surprised herself at her willingness to let him rest when her mind demanded answers. Gren's lovemaking had definitely softened her, and though she loved what he'd done to her body, she didn't like the softening of her will.

After such a tumult of events from *Lady Justice* to Mornio, after leaving behind her world of order and discipline only to discover the erotic side of herself, she should have been more on edge. The warrior within her should have been clamoring to know the why's and how's of her adventure.

But her body refused to rise. The calm lethargy that relaxed her stole through her very pores, leaving her mind free to roam while her body rested.

And though thoughts of Gren confused and at times aggravated her, the emotional connection she felt with him soothed when it should have worried her.

His large palm suddenly covered her hand on his chest, startling her. But still he slept, a small grin tugging his lips.

Temis shook her head. She could only imagine what dreams pleasured Gren's sleep. Treasure? Battle? Or more likely naked women, a lot of them, doing whatever he commanded.

Why thoughts of Gren with other women bothered her, she refused to consider. Tired of such puzzling thoughts, she laid her head on his shoulder and curled into his warmth, dreamlessly accepting the comfort he unknowingly provided.

Chapter Seven

Heat centered in the core of her body, then spiraled outward, until her blood pulsed with need. She felt rough palms caressing her breasts, a warm mouth trailing their touch.

Temis squirmed, seeking the source of such pleasure.

"Yes, *sura*," Gren murmured in a rough voice, alternating his mouth with stroking fingers. He paused at her navel and moved back to blanket her body with his, finding her lips with the practice of a skilled lover.

Thrusting his tongue deep inside her mouth, he mimicked the action with his fingers, sliding between her thighs into slick heat.

She arched into him, demanding his passion, reaching for any and every place to hold him, to cement them together. He groaned as she aggressively sought his tongue, and answered by thrusting a second finger inside her.

Temis wanted to devour him. He tasted of ambrosia, the sweetest spice in the system, and she wanted more. She could feel something within her reaching out to him, an inner self she had no control over.

Gren shuddered and deepened the kiss, his fingers quickening over her sensitive bud, thrusting faster and deeper toward her womb.

Temis was lost.

The waves of desire suddenly became too much and as she crested, the overpowering feelings she had crashed hard in an explosive orgasm.

On and on the pleasure pulsed. Intermingled with her desire, she imagined Gren's bliss as well, a strange sense of masculine satisfaction that beat with energy. It felt so real, so pure, and it fed her own rapture.

When her heart finally calmed, she lazily opened her eyes. Gren stared down at her with an intensity that roused her to real wakefulness. His eyes looked darker than she'd ever seen them, and her pleasure began to fade under the sense something was wrong.

"Gren?" she asked hesitantly.

He leaned into her, his body heat like a blanket. Running a finger down her cheek with surprising tenderness, he murmured in a foreign language, so beautiful and exotic she stared in wide-eyed fascination.

"What does that mean?" she whispered.

He shook his head and like that, his eyes resumed a normal green hue. Amazed, Temis stared at him, all of him, suddenly riveted by the odd glow that hugged his body.

Aware of her study, the look in his eyes shuttered and like that, he *dimmed*, if such a thing were possible.

He leaned up off of her and rolled to his side, sighing heavily.

"What just happened?" she couldn't help but ask.

"We experienced morning's bliss." His gravelly voice was tinged with humor. "And my clothes are definitely in need of some washing."

Temis blushed at his frank teasing. Apparently she hadn't imagined his groan of release. Yet she clung to her need for an explanation. "I know what we did. I want to know how your eyes turned from green to black. And your skin...." She narrowed her study, seeing him in the faint light that filtered through the room. "You look better than alright, Gren. Are you sure you aren't suffering any injuries from yesterday?"

He sat up and looked at her casually, too casually. She read his body language, surprised that she *knew* he was hiding something. His uncanny ability to mask his expressions seemed to have disappeared.

"I'm fine." He gave her a masculine smirk. "In fact, I'd say I'm more than fine, wouldn't you?"

She rolled her eyes but didn't have the heart to refute the truth.

"Come on, *sura*," he teased and leaned down for a brief kiss. "Isn't that the best way to waken, in the arms of a master pleasurer?"

She chuckled and tugged at his trousers, amazed the familiar heat began to build after such intense lovemaking-- after such intense *sex*, she corrected herself.

"I must admit I've never before had the pleasure." She felt his elation and blinked in surprise. It must have been her imagination, for Temis was not an empath. Yet all the same, she swore she could *feel* the immense satisfaction flooding his system.

He left the bed and punched a few codes into the wall monitor near his door. "The lav should be activated in a moment. Ladies first?"

Temis shrugged, determined to get her answers sooner or later. Curiosity burned at her to discover his dark secrets. With that in mind, she strode confidently toward the lav, all the while aware of his burning gaze on her back.

* * * *

The minute she closed herself behind the lav door, Gren uttered a low groan and allowed himself the release of energy his body demanded. Like a star, the brilliance of his and Temis' shared energy poured into the room, illuminating the dingy area better left in the dark.

Scarred wooden flooring, dented Mornian steel and the few mismatched pieces of furniture now visible in the morning light streaming through one shuttered window made the room seem seedy, not fitting for his first sexual encounter with Temis.

At the thought, his mouth drew tight and he rubbed at his eyes in frustration. These feelings he had concerning the stubborn woman were strange and more than a little disturbing.

Sharing Temis' body, absorbing her essence, her woman's power, had shaken him to the core. He'd resolved to keep his distance after last night's incredible intimacy, but woke to a burning desire that no other but Temis could satisfy. He absently rubbed at his well-used cock, now covered in spent passion.

Where the hell had his discipline gone? Growling in embarrassment, that he'd come not once but twice while pleasuring her this morning, he whipped off his trousers and paced the room unencumbered by clothes. As he paced, he consciously burned off lovemaking's residual glow and strove for some inner peace.

Temis Freya was trouble with a capital 'T'. He'd known it from the first time he'd seen her, and the impression had only grown stronger. She attracted him unnaturally, especially so for one of his kind. Her energy lured him all too close, like a siren's call, and now he felt truly hooked on her scent, her taste.

He stared down at his growing erection with distaste, aware the control he'd mastered and lived with for years seemed to have vanished at just the thought of the warm woman bathing in the lav.

With conscious effort he focused to ignore his desire and instead tried to formulate a plan for the sake of the mission. Yet even there he stumbled, for he knew what he and Temis must do.

In his mind's eye Temis wore slave's clothing, skimpy rags designed to showcase her body to anyone with interest. Just the thought of her breasts straining the thin silk made him want to sink deep inside her and never let go.

He knew it had been a good idea to refrain from a true joining, but damn it all, his body wouldn't quit the idea. Even now he wanted her more than before, as if he hadn't sampled her delights a few moments ago.

Scowling down at his troublesome cock, he cursed under his breath and decided to make the call he'd been avoiding.

He found the telecom unit he'd stowed on a previous trip and dialed the private number.

After several buzzing tones a husky male voice greeted him, reminding him the hour was most likely too early for anything but emergency communications.

"*Mara's Light*. And this had better be good."

Gren grinned at his friend's surliness. Lurin Vez, a fellow Thesha, had taken to bounty hunting as if he'd been doing it all his life. Of course, he had the best teacher. His wife Mara had the skills and determination to whip the Thesha into shape.

"This is Gren." He could feel Lurin's surprise. All Thesha shared the ability to communicate telepathically, and in some cases empathically.

"Well," Lurin's voice cleared, sounding less tired and more welcoming. "Not that it's not great to hear from you, but why call so early?" *You are alright?*

"I'm fine," Gren answered. "What's the matter, Lurin, Mara keeping you up late at night? Can't rise the way you used to?"

He heard a female chuckle in the background and knew he'd caught Lurin in bed.

"I have no problem getting up," Lurin mocked. "Thanks for asking. If anything, Mara's made me into a tougher, *harder* man thanks to all her training." *You have no idea how hard*, Lurin added under a burst of pleasure.

Gren felt a wave of heat from his friend and knew he'd best get to the point before Lurin and Mara forgot about him.

"I'll get right to the point. I can't contact a friend of mine and I need you to get an untraced message to him."

Lurin's attention refocused. "Tell me.'"

Gren refused to mention Sernal out loud, just in case his message was intercepted en route. Thanks to the energy he'd recently received from Temis, he had the resources to span the large distance between him and Lurin.

Over a dozen women have been abducted from Mardu thanks to some rogue peacemakers, so Sernal called on me for help.

Rogue peacemakers? Damn.

Yeah. I had the misfortune of stepping right into the middle of Sernal's problem, screwing this undercover mission. I snatched one of his people and escaped peacemaker involvement. I just need you to tell him all is well, and to use you to contact him later with more information.

He felt Lurin's surprise.

No problem, Lurin answered without hesitation. *You want me to put some feelers out for the abducted women?*

Gren thought about it. *No. I'm trying to keep my cover as untainted as possible, and having you look into things might tip off the men I'm trying to find.* One of the crewmembers on *Mara's Light* was Sernal's brother, Catam.

Okay. I'll have Catam get with Sernal and pass your message, discreetly. You need anything else, let me know.

Gren thanked him and would have disconnected the call when he felt Lurin's tentative probe.

What was that? Gren asked without heat. Never before had his friend mentally trespassed.

I'm not sure, but I distinctly feel a woman's presence in your mind.

That's impossible. She's not a telepath. Gren immediately envisioned Temis naked in the lav and heard Lurin's laughter.

Ah, so the mighty have finally fallen.

What does that mean? Gren asked, irritated. Why the hell couldn't he keep thoughts of Temis at bay? And just how much had Lurin seen from Gren's brief vision?

You'll figure it out, Lurin added smoothly. *And after all the help you gave me and Mara, maybe I can return the favor?*

He ended their conversation with more laughter and it took Gren a moment to remember to disconnect the electronic transmission.

Anger burned when he realized what Lurin had meant about "returning the favor."

"As if Mara would let him," he mumbled, still scowling at the telecom.

"Gren?" Temis asked cautiously. She stood in the doorway to the lav, a thin towel wrapped around her.

He stared at her gorgeous body but his thoughts were on Lurin's words. Years ago Gren had enthralled Mara, Lurin's wife, into making love with him in an effort to regain energy needed to save Lurin's life. His intentions had been pure even if he had derived a great deal of satisfaction from the coupling.

At the time he'd been surprised at Lurin's possessiveness of Mara, not used to Theshan jealousy. The Thesha shared women pleasurably, not tied to any one female. Yet even then he'd clearly felt Lurin's bond to Mara.

He stared at Temis waiting on him expectantly and suddenly understood what had bothered Lurin about sharing Mara. Just the thought of Lurin touching Temis in any way made his blood boil.

"I was just contacting a friend of mine to let Sernal know we're fine," he said and mentally cleared his thoughts.

A ripple of unease passed over her face and he neared her with concern. "Temis? Are you okay?"

She smiled and shook her head. "Just hungry." She glanced around the room with a wry expression on her face. "I don't suppose you have anything clean I can wear?"

He studied her curves clearly outlined by the towel and his libido leapt in answer. "I would say you can wear me, but I'm not clean either."

She flushed and it took all of his control not to lay her back down on the bed and fuck her senseless. "Let me clean up and I'll get us food and clothing." He walked toward her, willing her to step away from the lav doorway before he did something extremely undisciplined and took her against the wall, mindless of his vow to let her be.

She blinked and quickly moved toward the bed, well out of his reach. Uncomfortably aware of his erection, he grumbled under his breath and shut the lav door behind him, needing the brief respite from Temis' potency.

* * * *

Temis stared at the closed lav door in shock, now free to give way to the emotions rocketing through her. During her much-needed cleansing, she'd been conscious of a buzzing in her mind.

Focusing to discover the source of her worry, she'd been shocked to hear Gren's voice communicating with another. *But not out loud.* The sounds she'd heard had been directly within her mind.

She'd stood staring at nothing, the warm water sluicing over her as pieces of their conversation drifted to her. Understanding gradually dawned. She could hear Gren's thoughts, could feel what he felt. Her previous imaginings of his satisfaction, of what he felt when making love with her, had been *real*.

Puzzled, she'd finished her shower. She was no telepath, but apparently Gren and his friend Lurin were? No, telepathy didn't seem to fit, not when she could also sense Gren's feelings. He must have empathic abilities as well that he unknowingly passed to her, somehow.

But envisioning his flawless skin, healthy, with the earlier preternatural glow hanging over him, not to mention his incredible sexuality and stamina, she dismissed his abilities as merely empathic.

His gifts didn't bother her, however, instead they intrigued her to know more. When she'd felt his friend's subtle probe, she'd quickly pulled her mind away, shutting everyone out. Like the dreams she crafted, she used her mind to create a mental wall, a talent she'd found useful when dealing with known telepaths.

Had she known about Gren's gifts earlier.... She blushed as embarrassing thoughts hit her. Had he read the desire she'd felt upon first meeting him? Had he somehow used the knowledge to make her want him enough to succumb to his advances yesterday?

She thought about it and relaxed. No, Temis had been in control of her actions if not her sensual nature. For once in her life she'd allowed the woman within her to take charge, and she couldn't for the life of her regret it.

The door to the lav opened and Gren walked through, his body a study of male perfection. She watched admiringly while he dressed in standard trousers and a tan shirt he grabbed from a nearby storage bin.

"Much as I like you in that," he said in a husky voice, "I need to pick up some clothes that lend to the mission. And before you think to protest," he paused and held up a hand to stall her. "Remember we've got some women to save."

Not thinking of protesting, she shrugged and nodded. "I know, Gren. I remember why we're here."

"Good. I'll be back as soon as I can. And don't answer to anyone but me."

Her brows rose. "You're expecting company?"

He shook his head. "I always like being prepared. And people know better than to bother me. But there are those wanting to make a name for themselves--" He stopped and frowned at her. "Never mind. Just don't open the door."

He strode to the door and jerked it open, slamming it behind him and making her wonder what he'd been about to say before he stopped. Shaking her head at the mysteries of the male mind, she stared around her, wondering where to start.

She wouldn't have long before he returned, and she planned to make good use of the time. She knew Gren would never willingly reveal details about himself, not to her, a peacemaker. So she began snooping through the room, hoping for a hint of the real man behind the sword.

As she looked, she couldn't help recalling how thoroughly they'd made love, and secretly wondered when and how they would again. She flushed and threw herself into her search, reluctantly admitting to herself being captured by Gren wasn't torture at all. That to this point, it had been more an exercise in the erotic arts.

But she'd be shot before she'd admit it. Her newfound sexual imagination burned at thoughts of Gren doing things to her she'd heard of but never had the nerve or interest to pursue. Silk scarves came to mind and she felt her heart race.

"This isn't good," she muttered to herself as she studied the contents of a dusty drawer. The warrior within her now bowed to the sensual woman within her, growing in power, and she had a hard time finding the will to battle her back. Just imagining Gren deep inside her made her want to lay down and accept everything on his terms.

She slammed the drawer shut and muttered a curse. This was why she'd been smart to avoid sex before. A little bit of pleasure and she was almost willing to forego a lifetime of learned caution.

Her jaw clenched tight, and she resolved to stay strong. "Great sex or no, I won't be anyone's puppet." She yanked another drawer open, this time not so careful to conceal her foraging. "If Gren thinks pleasure will make me more pliable, he's got another thing coming."

Chapter Eight

Gren strode down the street, his thoughts in turmoil when he should have been focused on the mission. Fifteen women's lives were on the line, and he couldn't stop thinking about making love to Temis.

Get a grip, he mentally admonished himself, harnessing his Theshan abilities for a clearer focus. It took him the length of the dusty street before he managed to take hold of his senses and banish Temis from his thoughts.

He entered Margo's, his favorite eating establishment, and left carrying a heavy sack filled with fruits, nuts, and a juicy cooked rak flank for Temis. He didn't eat meat, an extremely uncommon trait among the system's inhabitants, but his Theshan abilities worked better on a diet devoid of animal flesh.

The sweet smell of ripe fuave and maneo root made his mouth water, and he realized he hadn't eaten in two days. The meal Rafe had brought him in his cell had gone uneaten while the lawman had briefed him.

He left Margo's and headed east, toward an unsavory establishment that catered to Reykhold's true underbelly. A diverse group of cutthroats, thieves and slavers filled the bar under the lingering smell of vomit and body odor mixed with sour ale.

Keeping a straight face when he wanted to exit the crude dwelling, he nodded to Maruk, the pub's monstrously large security guard, and made his way to the back, where the infamous informer Ceril undoubtedly sat.

Sure enough, Ceril sat looking bored, listening to a scruffy looking miner drone on about hidden Mornian mines and treasure maps.

Gren had to grin. Ceril's fleshy lips drew into a thin line and the paunch around his middle shook as he drew in a deep breath. "Get out!" he shouted, having apparently lost patience with the fool seeking a backer. "I cannot believe you wasted my time with treasure-hunting drivel!"

For a large man, Ceril was surprisingly quick. He kicked

the miner with an overly large boot, stunning the man with the ferocity of his strike.

Scurrying away, the miner gave Gren a wide berth. Gren shook his head and settled himself across from Ceril with a knowing grin. "Bored, are we?"

Ceril grinned, his teeth surprisingly straight and white, the only clean things on his person. Like most occupants on Reykhold, Ceril sat covered in the pale gold dust that covered everything from the streets to the buildings in town. Known for his ability to appropriate anything for the right price and as a font of information, Ceril's particular odor and common grunge did little to dispel his popularity with the dregs of the underworld.

"Gren! I'd heard you were in town. Took you long enough to come and see me." Ceril's crafty eyes narrowed. "Though from what I heard, you've your hands full of voluptuous peacemaker."

Gren lifted an eyebrow. "Ceril. You know better than to listen to gossip."

The large man chuckled. "Word has it she's ripe for the Sale, if you were so inclined."

"The Sale?"

"Come on, Gren. Don't play innocent with me. You've no doubt heard about the major slave trade happening a week from tomorrow."

Gren's mind raced. He hadn't expected Ceril to have so much information on the missing women. Interesting that the big man knew so much and wanted to share it freely. "What's so major about this trade?"

"You've heard about the massive abductions on Mardu?"

Gren nodded. A man of his reputation had to keep his ears open to all major criminal activity in the system. So he would have had the knowledge regardless of his dealings with Sernal.

"Those Mardu women are the ones to be auctioned." Ceril belched and motioned for another glass of ale.

"And you think I might be interested because...." He dangled the bait.

"Word is already circulating through space that your little peacemaker is worth at least fifty thousand beks, unmarked and properly subdued."

Gren allowed his disbelief to show. "I captured her

yesterday. How the hell did word of her disappearance spread so fast?"

Ceril shrugged. "Most likely one of her shipmates leaked it for some currency. You know those peacemakers." He sneered, his attitude like so many others. "They arrest those of us trying to make a clean living, but have no problem using us to their own advantage, legal or otherwise."

Gren nodded with understanding. Rorn Fenhal topped his list of detestable lawmen. "So you're telling me Temis Freya is worth fifty thousand beks at auction?"

"At least," Ceril concurred. "But I heard you can get a lot more if you find your way into the auction's private party."

Gren pursed his lips as if in thought. Someone wanted Temis very badly. The question was, did that someone want her unharmed and returned to Sernal's folks, or for his own malicious play? He was betting on the latter.

"Where and when?"

Ceril grinned, and Gren figured the hefty criminal would be cut a large finder's fee when Temis was sold. A likeable fellow and impressive drinker, Ceril nevertheless was not one to be trusted. "Like I said, a week from tomorrow, midday. The where is still being debated. Most likely an uncharted sector beyond Jaron."

"I'll be in touch." Gren stood to leave. "I take it Drorna is still in the slave trade?"

"Yes, but I told you you'll get much more for the woman if you attend the auction." Ceril looked worried.

Gren smothered a grin. "I need some clothes for my little slave. Can't have her wearing her peacemaker's finest at the auction, can I?" he added sarcastically.

Ceril beamed and gave him directions to Drorna's newest location, several doors down.

"One other thing." Gren paused and looked around him, glad of the privacy surrounding Ceril's table. He lowered his voice. "I need a small cruiser with fighting capabilities and a sennight's worth of provisions."

Ceril nodded. "Your standard provisions?"

"Yeah. But throw in some rak meat as well. Oh, and I've a peacemaker shuttle to use in trade."

Ceril grinned. "Perfect. That will cut your payment in half."

"By two-thirds."

Ceril paused, his eyes narrowed as he calculated his profit. "Fine. Two-thirds it is. You know where to wire the beks."

Gren left by a back door, conscious he'd picked up some followers. He paused by the reflective window of a nearby storefront and noted two large men trying to blend unsuccessfully with their surroundings.

"Should have shed the peacemaker boots," he muttered as he eyed their top-quality rak-hide leggings. He continued to Drorna's, his senses alert for trouble.

To his relief, Drorna stood alone on the bottom floor of the slave house. Frail in appearance yet strong in mind, Drorna's sweet smile and innocent blue eyes gave the impression of a grandfatherly type. In reality, the older man could shred a tome to ribbons with his trader's tongue.

"Gren." The old man's eyes widened, then narrowed as if he smelled potential business. "I thought you avoided the slave trade as a matter of principle." He looked beyond Gren and his eyes showed a hint of disappointment.

Apparently Gren's 'barbaric' display of ownership with Temis on the city street yesterday had done its job. "No, Drorna, I'm not going to sell her to you." The man sighed with regret. "I need some clothes appropriate to her new station."

Drorna's eyes lit and he motioned Gren to wait. He returned shortly with an armful of clothing. "I happened to notice her with you yesterday," Drorna said softly as he carefully displayed the clothing on a nearby table. "Such beauty wasted on a peacemaker." He shook his head. "But on a trained pleasurer ... take a look at the blue set."

Gren contained a grimace. Every article of clothing on the table was short and sheer, just what he'd been afraid of. But what else would a slave wear? Especially when her owner planned on selling her?

Staring at his choices, Gren selected several pair of matching tops and bottoms, to include the dark blue set that would barely cover her breasts and ass. He paid Drorna with the beks he'd kept for emergency currency and left the house just as the slaves began to rouse.

One young woman traipsed down the stairwell wearing nothing and looking worn and tired until she spied Gren. Then the glow of avarice appeared in her eyes and her downtrodden expression turned to one of allure, of suggestion.

Both disgusted and spiritually pained by the display, Gren left the house quickly, damning Drorna and his kind to everlasting hell. What once had been an attractive young woman was now an addicted, hopeless prostitute with little remorse and even less self-worth. He knew their kind all too well, knew the hurt of watching the life drain out of them.

He clenched his jaw tight and returned to Nikos to find Jora still guarding the back. "Don't you ever sleep?" he grumbled.

"Two hours a day," Jora answered with a chuckle. "We Raggas don't coddle our young like so many other races." He sneered at Gren good-naturedly. "What's wrong, Gren? Not enough sex to keep you happy last night?"

Gren forced a grin, pushing thoughts of the slave trade away. "There's never enough sex to keep me happy."

Jora chuckled and motioned him to pass.

"Jora," Gren warned on his way up the stairs. "I've got two peacemakers watching for a way in. Don't disappoint me."

Jora nodded, a militant gleam in his inky black gaze. "The only way they'll pass by me is if I'm dead. And believe me, I won't go to my grave silently."

Satisfied the Ragga would maintain protection over his hideaway, Gren returned to his room, pausing outside the doorway.

He'd been so distracted by Drorna's he hadn't thought about Temis since entering the slave house. Would she be as receptive and friendly as she'd been earlier? He hoped not. He didn't think he could handle any more temptation. Then again, knowing Temis, he thought perhaps she regretted their intimacies as much as he did. If that were the case, the warrior would be back, a hard-hearted peacemaker vying for order over a situation she couldn't control.

He entered cautiously to find his room in complete disarray. Much as the disorder aggravated him, he couldn't contain a small grin. So, the warrior had returned. Thank fate. With her resistance added to his, he might just make it through the mission without fucking her senseless.

"Took you long enough," she growled from the corner of

the room. "I'm starving."

With another silent thank you to whoever watched over him, he tossed the bag containing food onto the room's only table. "Enjoy."

She quickly perused the contents of the bag before settling into the rak meat, and he gave himself credit for anticipating her needs. Temis hailed from Zephyr, a fierce planet that produced some of the best fighters in the system. And they were well-known for their fierce appetites.

He emptied the contents of the clothing bag onto the bed, sorting through the different outfits and praying they fit larger than they looked.

"What is all that?" she asked around a mouthful of food.

Gren straightened and stared down at his handiwork with a frown. "These are your clothes for the remainder of this mission."

She approached, her hands full of food and drink, and stared blankly down at the bed. "You're kidding, right?"

He sighed. "I told you before, Temis. Slaves have few rights and even less to wear. For my cover to hold, I have to try to sell you. In order to do so I have to showcase your wares." He gave her scantily clad form a heated perusal. "Trust me, our scheme is already working. Parading you around in any of that," he paused and motioned to the rags on the bed, "is sure to keep us in the auction loop."

He explained his visit with Ceril.

She finished her food and set the drink back on the table. "Are you going to fill Sernal and Rafe in on what you've learned?"

"Later." He mentally calculated their timetable. "We need to show you off downtown and then get off this planet before Rorn sends any more peacemakers to keep an eye on you."

"More peacemakers?" Her lavender eyes darkened with concern.

"We've got two outside keeping watch. They're too sloppy to be Sernal's men. Besides which, I've got a feeling once we're in the open they'll make a play to snatch you back."

"No, we can't have that." Temis approached the bed and held up the blue silken top and bottom. After a moment she sighed. "You need to dangle me out there so Rorn keeps his attention away from Sernal. I'll change and be right back."

Gren felt a bit disappointed she hadn't argued overly about the clothing. But apparently even she realized the necessity of playing out this role.

He sat down at the table and filled his body with nutrients while he tried to master the control he would need dealing with Temis in such skimpy attire. The sexual drive he'd been master of since his sixteenth year flared out of control again at thoughts of Temis in next to nothing, and he swore silently at his pubescent excitement.

Should have soothed my cock earlier in town.

To his shock a vehement *No!* filled his mind and he started out of his seat, his hands reaching for his absent sword still on Sernal's ship.

He glanced around, his mind and body poised for attack. Expanding his senses only proved he and Temis shared the hideaway alone, confusing him all the more.

"Well?" Temis' voice floated through the air like a physical caress, her husky voice a prelude to the vision that soon followed.

Gren stood motionless as he watched her sashay forward. The thin silk stretched taut to encase her generous breasts, the material barely enough to hold the round globes tight, plumping them for inspection.

The pale skin of her corded abdomen invited touching, looking soft as velvet and just as luscious.

His eyes lowered further to the thin triangle of silk protecting her golden curls, framing the muscular expanse of long leg that seemed to go on forever.

Swallowing to bring moisture to his suddenly dry throat, he glanced up to see Temis watching him warily. Her pink cheeks told him she found the outfit highly uncomfortable, but her stubborn refusal to protest showed him she understood why he'd brought it.

"It's typical slave garb," he said, aware his voice sounded overly deep. He cleared his throat and strove to keep his eyes on her face. Damn but he was as hard as a pike. "I figure one or two turns around town to gather a few supplies should do the trick."

He frowned down at her bare feet. "There are thin sandals in the bottom of the bag."

Still flushed, she nodded and bent over to remove them from the bag. Gren clenched his teeth at the sight of her taut ass. The backing of her bottoms was a small square that when she stood, would cover most of her cheeks. But bent over like that, the material sliding over her skin like warm water, she was an invitation few would be able to resist.

He lunged forward and grabbed the bag out of her hand, careful to minimize physical contact with her. "Here," he growled and stalked back to the food on the table.

She gave him a quizzical glance before sitting on the bed to don the footwear. Flat soles strapped to her feet by long cords wrapped around her calves. When she finally stood, she stared at him in the eye, almost daring him to say something crude.

Not wanting to disappoint her, he leered and winked. "Damn, Temis, but half the town will be a walking hard-on this morning."

She blushed bright red. "You are so crude." He noticed she carefully avoided looking at his crotch.

"But honest. If we had more time...." He let his words dwindle and looked down at himself.

He felt her answering heat, a wave of feminine craving that hit him hard. "There'll be no more of that," she spat, though her body and mind protested her words.

Good. The more she protested, the better his chance of steering clear of her treacherous attraction. All too easily he imagined her wrapped around his body while he rode her to climax. Just the thought of doing so jarred something deep within his mind, a union of spirit too encompassing for a loner like him.

"Temis?" he asked in a low voice, determined to avoid the uncomfortable feeling of togetherness at all costs. "Did you hear someone say 'no' in here earlier?"

She refused to meet his eyes. "What do you mean?"

His study sharpened. She knew something, and to his surprise, he couldn't read her mind. His attempt to pry into her thoughts, to make her tell the truth, fell flat.

"No. You said 'no.'"

"I did not." She tossed back her hair and started stuffing the remaining slave clothes into a sack. "I don't know what's wrong with you, but we have to get moving if we're going to help those women."

Gren closed his eyes as she bent over again.

"Although," she paused and straightened. "Now would be an ideal time for *you* to come clean."

"Excuse me?"

"I know you're either telepathic or empathic, and maybe something else."

He stared at her, wondering where the hell this was coming from. *I distinctly feel a woman's presence in your mind.* Lurin's words echoed in his thoughts. Then he recalled entering her dream, feeling the strong hold she had on her dreamworld reality. It appeared Temis had mental powers of her own.

"You 'know' I'm telepathic? Seems like I should be accusing you of the same."

She shook her head. "I have no such gifts. But I know you do. Don't try to deny it, Gren. There's no way you could have gotten me off *Lady Justice* the way you did unless you drugged me, and I know you didn't. Then there's the fact that you look in perfect physical shape despite the savage beating you took only two days past."

She waited and he knew he'd have to tell her something. She was too intelligent not to notice his differences.

Damn Sernal. Why had the peacemaker demanded Temis work with him? The situation was growing annoyingly difficult. That a Thesha had to go so far to hide his powers....

"You want to know my secrets?" Gren glared at her, pressing her mentally to accept his explanation. "I'm a telepath with strong empathic traits. I don't know why, but I've always been a fast healer. And I don't like my gifts advertised because it makes people less inclined to share information. And information is power in my line of work, but more than that, it's a lifeline."

He focused hard, harder than he should have had to, and saw her frown and reach for her temples. Sensing her pain he immediately withdrew his mindtouch, taking with it the hurt he'd caused.

Because of his nature, the pain he received tripled, and it took all of his concentration not to appear injured.

"Okay," she said slowly, staring warily at him. "I believe you." She tossed the bag of clothing at him. "Now what?"

"Now you wait while I finish my food." He cursed all peacemakers to such torture and replenished his energy with several succulent fauve fruits. Aware of her stare the entire time, he kept his attention on the food.

Once he finished, he swept the remaining fare into the bag and tossed it and her clothing bag over his shoulder. He then opened a hidden storage cabinet in the wall and pressing the necessary security keys, withdrew a long, sharp saber and scabbard.

He turned and noted the angry expression on her face.

"Missed that, did you?" he asked blandly. He shoved the blade into the scabbard and affixed it to his waist. Then he withdrew the silken leash and collar he'd hidden earlier in his pocket.

"What is that?" she asked suspiciously.

"This is your handler's way of holding onto his property." He stared at the items with disgust. "It's a common slave practice and one I've adopted because it's necessary, not out of any desire to degrade you," he added softly.

She eyed him warily, but must have sensed his aversion to the practice for she slipped the collar on without a murmur. She attached the leash and walked to him, placing the end of the strap in his hand.

"Well, *handler*, what are we waiting for?" Temis gave him a cocky grin before she schooled her expression into one of vague adoration. She stroked his bicep, curling her fingers over his muscle. "Let's show Reykhold your captive peacemaker."

Gren stared at her, aware at this moment that though he held the leash, she somehow held the reins.

Chapter Nine

The walk through town made Temis want to cringe every time she thought about it. Men appeared out of nowhere on the sparsely populated street, all begging to touch, to sample her delights.

Gren managed an arrogant yet frighteningly intimidating demeanor, stating boldly that he had other plans for his tasty little slave anytime asked.

Tasty little slave.

She eyed him through narrowed lashes in the private smoke-filled room, waiting on her knees docilely by his side, while his friend Ceril tried to see through her clothing.

"By Feru's balls, Gren. That is the finest set of tits I've ever seen," Ceril said, managing to conceal the drool no doubt pooling between his fat jowls. The large man made her want to cringe in embarrassment. Not only did he smell awful, but he spread his legs wide, making no effort to hide the puny erection beneath his barrel of a belly.

Gren grinned and stroked her shoulder, petting his *slave* before his friend. She wanted to bite his hand off. As if he sensed her turmoil, he eased his hand lower toward her breast in warning.

She immediately calmed herself and focused on Gren. She knew meeting his 'friend' Ceril hadn't been necessary, but a test to see if she could pull off her ruse. The only thing making her feel slightly better was that she could feel the open hostility lingering around Gren like full body armor.

He disliked parading her around as much as she hated it. And though he hadn't joked any more about it, she knew he wanted her with every breath he took.

She leaned closer to his touch and he moved his hand to her shoulder, letting her know he'd received the message that she was in control of herself.

Temis sat on her knees waiting for him to finish small talk with Ceril. She still didn't believe Gren's tale of being a "telepath with empathic traits." She'd never heard of a telepath being able to cause telepathy in another. And she knew for a fact she had no psychic abilities of her own. Controlling dreams was one thing. Hearing another's thoughts, feeling another's feelings, was a distinct impossibility for a woman with her background.

The fact that she still felt Gren's desire so strongly, that every now and then she heard a glimpse of his powerfully projected thoughts, captivated her imagination and she knew she would do whatever it took to learn his secrets.

When earlier he'd thought about relieving his aching arousal in town, she been enraged enough to protest. That he'd mentally heard her answer had shocked her into instant retreat. That and the fact she was jealous in the first place.

Ever since she'd shared intimacies with Gren, she'd been acting like a stranger to herself. And hearing voices, sensing his sexual desire, was more than a foreign concept. It was downright scary.

Though a strong woman, Temis had never thought she might have to face such challenges in her lifetime. Being tortured or taken hostage, forced to kill in order to preserve life, those instances she had easily imagined and come to terms with. But sharing another's thoughts?

She still couldn't be sure Gren wasn't *hearing* her. Yet the solid barrier she'd erected earlier in the day held fast. She'd felt his tentative probe several times along their walk but refused to yield.

A tugging pulled her attention back to Gren and she stared up at him with a hazy expression.

"She sure is beautiful," Ceril said.

"I know. But you should have seen her before I dosed her food with *mernal*. A peacemaker with attitude who couldn't see herself as anything but the law." Gren's full lips curved into a grin that made her catch her breath. "Of course, after a night with me she toned down quite a bit." Ceril chuckled and she wanted to bite Gren wherever she could reach him. As if a night with him had tamed her. Ha. "And with the drug, well, my friend, let's just say there's a core of fire running through her blood."

He trailed a hand over her nipple and a burst of heat exploded in her core. Stunned, she couldn't contain a moan of pleasure, and saw Ceril fairly leap out of his chair.

"You're sure you have to leave now? Just an hour with her, Gren. Okay, a half hour. Ten minutes?"

The man pleaded but to no avail.

"Sorry, Ceril. Those peacemakers are breathing down my neck. I guarantee the minute I leave here they'll be on me. No. Better I get her safely aboard the shuttle and gone before they come after you for helping me."

Ceril nodded dejectedly. "Good point. But damn me, she's got me so ready.... Carrna, come here, girl!" he called to a pleasurer lingering outside the small room. "Good luck, Gren. And let me know how things turn out."

Gren waved and stood, careful to wait until Temis stood with him. The leash between them wasn't very long, and could easily hurt her as tight as the collar felt. Once she'd attached the leash to it, the collar had tightened to automatically cinch her neck. Made of Nebe silk, it didn't pinch, but it left little room to escape.

"Come, love," Gren cajoled as he pulled her toward him. She stared straight at him, conscious of Ceril's moans behind her. She couldn't help a blush, nor the niggle of irritation at hearing Gren chuckle.

He took her with him out a side exit and immediately guided her into the darkened portion of the alley away from the main street. Pressing her into the steel wall of the building, he ground his iron hard arousal against her belly.

"What--" she whispered before his lips closed over hers. Immediately a wave of desire hit her with such intensity it knocked her knees from under her. Only Gren's firm grasp kept her upright against the wall.

"Don't move," he growled against her mouth. "The peacemakers are at the end of the alley waiting to take you from me. Just go along with me to distract them."

"Are you sure this is all for their sake?" she asked in a soft, breathy voice, angry that he so easily stoked her passion. "I don't think--"

"Yes, *sura*," he said softly and thrust against her, giving her the full feel of his growing cock. "But I admit it pleasures me as well." He nuzzled her neck and the need to come burst through her as heat welled in her center.

She began moaning and pressing closer to him as he pumped against her belly. Odd sensations filled her mind, visions of intimacies with Gren so shocking they could only have come from him.

Definitely more than a telepath, she thought as she exploded into orgasm, right there in a public alleyway still wearing what little clothing she'd been given. Before she could say anything Gren left her sagging against the wall.

She dazedly stared at the scene before her, not sure any of it was real. Gren fought two peacemakers, whom she recognized as Rorn's men, taking both men down with ease. He used his bare hands to disable both peacemakers before leaving them in a heap on the ground.

He turned to her and she saw a ferocious glow in his eyes, a blazing green light that called to someplace deep within her.

Then he blinked and returned to her side.

"Are you alright?" he asked in a husky voice.

"Just fine," she answered before yanking his head to hers and sealing their mouths with an aggression that surprised her.

He tasted so sweet, so full of life and energy. She thrust her tongue inside his mouth and heard him groan. She needed to feel him, to touch the very center of his being.

Reaching between them she burrowed her hands into his trousers, sighing when her palms closed around his turgid length.

"No, Temis," he gasped and pressed helplessly into her. "No time," he whispered as she began pumping his cock.

"Yes, Gren," she said as she stroked him, sending back the images she'd recently viewed. She felt him harden further, his warmth burning through her palms and making her wish for closer contact. "Now's the perfect time," she purred and fastened her mouth to his.

She couldn't explain her desperate need to touch him, to bring him to the edge of desire and further. But touching him was like a drug, addicting as it pushed her higher and higher. She was conscious of nothing besides his pleasure.

His large hands grasped her shoulders as if to push her away, but instead he held her tight as she primed him, readying his climax.

"Oh, *sura,* I can't take any more," he groaned and spilled into her hands. He tensed as warm cream filled her palms and she smoothed it over his aching shaft. She fondled his sack, sucking on his tongue and felt him shoot a second time over her hands.

Then a burst of energy filled her, a joyous flare of power that made her feel stronger and more alive than she'd ever felt before in her life.

She opened her eyes and stared at Gren's harsh face thrown back in bliss. He seemed to glow, his body bathed in a preternatural light that lit the alleyway.

His breathing was unsteady when he finally opened his eyes, and his fathomless black gaze pulled her until their souls seemed to touch.

She must have blacked out, for the next thing she knew, she laid in a small cabin aboard a foreign vessel. As she sat up, she wavered, lightheaded yet in no way pained.

Gren's voice floated to her from another part of the ship, and as soon as she regained her footing she joined him in the small cockpit of what looked like a shuttle-fighter hybrid, a Mornian craft judging from the steel construction around her.

"Hello," Gren greeted her with a husky voice, his eyes lingering on her breasts before lighting on her face. "Feeling better?"

"I feel amazing," she admitted and sat next to him in the only other seat available in the narrow room. She stared at him hungrily, confused and yet wanting him again. "Did you drug me?" she asked bluntly, needing an answer for her odd desire.

He gave her a sharp glance. "No. Why? Do you feel ill?" He set the autopilot and turned to her.

"Not ill, exactly," she hedged. How the hell was she supposed to tell him she still lusted after him without feeling extremely foolish? This made no sense.

"Tell me, *sura*." His voice sounded strange, an odd echoing of slightly different pitches, and she found herself nodding, content that her answer would soothe the ache inside.

"I can't stop wanting you." Saying it out loud lifted a giant burden off her chest. "What I did in that alleyway." She paused. "I've never done before. In public! I can't believe I did that." She stared into his eyes, the deep green of his gaze darkening with desire, and she felt herself grow wet. "Gren, what's happening to me?"

She licked her lips and saw his eyes narrow on the

movement. "I feel hot everywhere, but at the same time I feel powerful, full of energy."

He frowned and closed his eyes.

At once the greedy want within her faded, replaced by a soothing need to sleep. Her concern left her and she blinked up at Gren tiredly.

"Sorry, *sura*. I should have realized you needed rest."

He gently drew her to her feet and led her to the bed at the rear of the ship. His gaze was shuttered as he lowered her to the blankets and tenderly tucked her inside.

With a soft kiss to her forehead, he whispered, "Pleasant dreams."

* * * *

He stared at her in concern and bafflement, not able to understand what Temis experienced. In all his years, he'd never seen a woman so affected by Theshan bliss. Nor had he ever been so absorbed in a female. It was as if she were Thesha and he her hapless prey.

Shaking his head, he sat beside her on the bed, trying to piece together the puzzle.

All day he'd been trying to read her thoughts and been rejected each time. Only with Ceril distracting her had he glimpsed a hint of her troubled feelings, and of her disturbing ability to read him.

Wanting to exert control over her, he'd sent her a wave of sensual energy, more than pleased when she'd responded.

Then outside in the alleyway, he'd initially thought to use her to distract the peacemakers after them. Knowing Temis, he decided to avoid an argument and used his gift to bring her to a quick and satisfying orgasm. He hadn't counted on the effect her pleasure would have on him.

Once the peacemakers had been dealt with, she'd sucked him into her bliss with an aggressiveness that shook him. That a virgin's hands could still his common sense, could bring him such ease unnerved him.

And then to watch her *absorb* his energy! He'd stared in astonishment as Temis bathed in *wainu*, then glowed with his energy. Thankfully she'd passed out and didn't seem to understand what had occurred.

More and more around her, his Theshan abilities were being brought into the open. How foolish he'd been to take pleasure with her in an open alleyway where anyone could have witnessed the energy transference. Yet he'd been helpless to refuse her. Once in her grasp, he'd been her willing puppet.

Grimacing at the remembrance, he tried to recall any history of similar occurrences between Theshas and their partners. The few mated Theshas he'd met experienced a mental and spiritual joining, but he didn't think the women had ever absorbed their lovers' energy.

Gren swept a lock of golden hair from Temis' face, fascinated by the silken texture. Sitting so near her wasn't smart, but at least unconscious she presented much less a threat to his sanity.

Though aroused, he felt a distinct tenderness for the spirited woman lying under his protection. And that fast, he realized he was beginning to feel deeper emotions for her. Admiration mixed with frustration, sexual attraction with a genuine caring. He stood abruptly, eyes wide, as he realized the danger she presented.

Once again he saw his future spiraling out of control. A master Thesha, a skilled warrior felled by an erotic, young woman at odds with herself. He strode from her side in dismay at how out of sorts he felt.

Swearing aloud, he moved as far from Temis as possible and signaled *Mara's Light* from the ship's controls. Catam answered and Gren waited while he fetched Lurin, in no mood for the smart-mouthed Xema.

"Lurin here."

"It's Gren." *Pass this information to Catam and have him send it to Sernal right away.*

He shared the information he'd gathered with Lurin and gave his friend his ship's identifiers, should Lurin need to get in touch with him.

Gren? You don't sound right.

He shook his head. *It's nothing. Just a woman I can't understand.*

He heard Lurin's whistle of delight. *Now that's something new. Rumor has it she's gorgeous. Go figure. You and a peacemaker. Must be fate.*

Laughter was the last thing Gren needed right now. *Just make sure Sernal knows I'll get him the where when I know more.*

Now don't go away mad, Lurin teased. *Sernal passed*

along he has proof of Rorn's involvement. But he doesn't have enough yet to put the bastard away for good. Rorn needs to be caught in the act at the sale. That's the only way to get around Fenhal's lofty contacts in the peacemaker realm.

It would have been too easy for Sernal to pin the crimes on Rorn before the auction, dissolving Gren's association with Temis.

Gren sighed. *Right.* He paused. *Lurin? Has Mara ever absorbed your energy during an exchange?*

He felt Lurin's puzzlement. *No. I've shared* wainu *with her, but only after an intense joining. You already know she can read my thoughts when we're together. The sharing is strongest after we make love, of course. But even now she could listen if I hadn't asked her not to.*

Gren didn't know what to make of Temis' abilities.

Gren? What's going on? Is there something you need me to pass to the elders? Lurin sounded worried, another complication Gren didn't need.

Nothing some raw sex won't cure. He made his tone light and was relieved when Lurin laughed.

Go for it. But be warned. Once with Mara was all it took. Next thing you know I'm married and she's reading my mind.

I'll be careful, Gren answered with wry amusement. He disconnected and stared thoughtfully out the front viewport.

Intimacy with Temis went beyond special. Despite his wish to remain apart from the woman, they had somehow bonded. The connection remained susceptible to breakage, however, since he had yet to truly join with her. Perhaps he should just throw caution to the wind and explore all of her.

In doing so he would become vulnerable, he knew, for sexual intimacy with Temis already stripped his control. Yet in order to understand her abilities, to protect the Theshan way of life, he would sacrifice whatever necessary.

He flushed as honesty compelled him to admit making love to Temis would hardly be a sacrifice. Sex with Temis would ease the ache deep inside him and give him the respite needed to focus on his mission. Never mind the possessive nature that consumed him concerning one blonde peacemaker. He needed to forget the contrary feelings she stirred in him, feelings he had no business experiencing considering his true purpose in life.

As he sat gazing out the viewport, he continued to rationalize his need to bed Temis. But after continued staring into deep space, he felt his eyes getting heavy. And with a reluctant breath, he fell into an unwelcome slumber.

Chapter Ten

Temis stared at Gren lying so peacefully under the Canfer willows of her home world. She often placed herself in this calming forest when dreaming, especially when needing a gentle respite from the rest of the world. But she hadn't counted on Gren sharing her private space.

Closing her eyes, she breathed in the scent of sweet yala blossoms just opened. The steady drone of market bees hard at work and the pleasant chirping of overhead birds reminded her that spring harvest would soon arrive, and soon after, the pre-tournament games at Chula--her favorite time of year on Zephyr.

Her gaze once again found Gren and she frowned. Why had she brought him here, of all places? This private place was hers alone, never shared with anyone. Yet his presence seemed to complete her paradise, as if she'd been waiting for him to finish the scene.

He certainly looked the part of her perfect lover. Approval surged within her as she stared at his golden skin exposed under Zephyr's molten sun. Despite the shade the Canfer trees provided, the growing heat encouraged her to discard the scraps of slave clothing she still wore, a residual from her waking state.

Feeling free in her nudity, she wandered to Gren, wondering when and even if he might wake. If not for the subtle rise and fall of his chest, she might have thought him dead, he slept so soundly.

His muscular body showed no sign of ease during rest. Instead his strength seemed more pronounced now that she could look her fill without interruption. She inspected every inch of him, curious about the scar that creased the knuckles of his left hand and traveled along his arm stopping just before his elbow.

She traced the darkened scar with soft fingers, surprised at the groan and ready awakening of his body. His eyes remained closed while his nipples hardened and his shaft stirred.

Licking her lips, she stared in curiosity as his erection grew, the velvety rod no longer relaxed in that thatch of silky black hair. Her body instantly responded. Moisture gathered between her thighs, her breasts tingled with anticipation, and a need to feel him deep within her called for action.

"Gren," she whispered as she straddled his body, pressing her moist heat directly along his shaft. She closed her eyes at the pleasure such contact afforded, and decided to fully take advantage of this dream where embarrassment and weakness didn't exist for her. "Wake and love me, Gren," she ordered softly.

His eyes fluttered open, a brilliant green that made her think of precious danstone, a coveted gem throughout the system. Multifaceted and deep, danstone was worth more than most could afford, her included.

She rubbed along his arousal and he growled low in his throat, an answering need in his eyes. "What are you doing to me?" he groaned as she rubbed along his length.

Testing for just the right friction, she found the perfect spot as his shaft grazed her ripe clitoris. "Oh," she moaned and continued to stroke herself with his body. "I want to feel you inside me. I want you to pleasure us both until we can't think anymore."

He shook his head, his eyes straying to her hardened nipples. With two large palms, he cupped her breasts, his calluses a wonderful contrast to the soft touch he used. "Why must you break down every barrier I think to make?" He sounded desperate to refuse, but his body said the opposite.

"You need me," Temis said boldly, running her hands over his hardened chest. She squeezed his nipples and watched his head tilt back, felt his hands tighten around her breasts.

He rolled her nipples between his fingers and she gasped in pleasure. Riding his steely arousal, she slipped back to increase her rhythm and felt the tip of him ease into her. She immediately stopped, wanting all of him.

"Blessed fate," Gren groaned, his eyes glowing brighter than they had a right to. "I can't hold back any longer."

He shifted his hands to her hips and levered her over his penis. Then he coated himself in her moisture, his breath quickening as he played with her position. Temis let him settle her over him, eager to feel this newest sensation. She'd been unable to stop thinking about him inside her, a burning curiosity that built into all-consuming want.

Then Gren whispered something soundless and eased her body down slowly, inch by delicious inch, stretching her with a pleasure so intense it was painful.

"Oh, more, oh," she moaned, spreading her legs wider around his torso to allow deeper contact.

He grunted and pushed further into her, until she sat flesh to flesh atop him, the whole of his shaft within her.

He laid still, his eyes closed and his breathing rapid, the utter joy of the moment spreading around them both like a warm pool.

"*Sura*, you don't know how good you feel," he said in a thick voice, opening his eyes to stare into hers. "I want you so much."

Like magic, his words forced her to move, and guided by visions suddenly in her mind, she began to ride him, up and down, slowly, feeling all of his thick length.

He gasped her name and fondled her breasts, pinching and plucking until she would die if he didn't take them in his mouth.

Sensing her unspoken need, he suddenly sat up, thrusting deep inside her, and took one rosy bud in his mouth.

She rocked hard onto him, her clit near to bursting, and grasped his head to hold him to her. Her fingers slid through hair softer than Afleran silk, and she nearly climaxed when he suckled her other breast.

"Please Gren," she begged, needing more, needing the completion she'd only ever felt with him.

Then something powerful passed through her, as if a huge ball of warmth suddenly exploded within her. She screamed her pleasure as he rocked inside her, coming around him so hard she felt mindless with ecstasy. She couldn't stop the rapture from overtaking her, knew he could feel it too as he shuddered and spilled inside her.

Amazingly she felt him pulsing within her, and as he groaned and continued thrusting inside her, she sought his lips.

The kiss stole her very breath, her ability to reason without him. Together they moved in nature's rhythm, climaxing as one, their bodies and souls melting into one another.

It seemed like forever before they finally stopped, when Gren let go of her mouth long enough to take a breath.

"*Sura*," he groaned and pressed deeper inside of her. "What have you done?"

* * * *

Suddenly the world stopped spinning and she blinked up into angry green eyes.

"Gren?" she asked hesitantly, glancing down to find herself garbed in skimpy slave clothing and lying in bed. Gren too wore clothing, and she couldn't help the disappointment that filled her. Tears gathered in her eyes, a horrifying reminder that she was most definitely not herself.

"Temis?" His antagonism faded a bit as he studied her. She prayed he accepted her hesitation as one of confusion, that he hadn't seen her eyes well.

She blinked rapidly, relieved the tears would not fall. "I must have been more tired than I thought," she said, aware a blush fired her cheeks. She couldn't stop thinking about what they'd done in her dream, and the slick heat between her legs was a physical testament to her imagination.

His nostrils flared and he stared deliberately at her groin. He clenched his fists and placed them slowly on his hips. "I thought I heard you call out for me."

Damn. Please let her erotic dream have been silent. She would be all too embarrassed if he'd heard her moaning his name.

"No," she answered in a high pitch. Clearing her throat, she sat up and swung her feet to the floor to feel less vulnerable under his stare. "Must have been a nightmare."

"Funny, because I just had one too," he said in hard voice, his gaze suspicious and not at all like the one from her dream.

"Where are we?" she asked to change the subject.

"Between Jaron and Eyra, on the outlying side of the system." He stepped back and took a deep breath, staring out one of the room's two portholes. "If you're done resting, you might want to fill up on some of the provisions I brought. There's a small galley barely big enough for two people past the lav." He thumbed the direction. "I thought

I'd get some rest while you eat. We still have several days until the auction, so I figure we'll rest in shifts until we get closer to go-time."

He stared at her expectantly, and she slowly rose from the bed. Unfortunately the quarters were narrow, and she had to brush by him to exit the room.

She heard his intake of breath and stifled one of her own, then left the room with a queenly nod.

Puzzled and slightly hurt, she entered the galley and selected a meal. Obviously Gren wanted to spend as little time with her as possible before the mission.

What had happened to stir such a change in his attitude? She pondered his erratic behavior and dug into the meat tray with gusto, a little surprised at her appetite.

"Touchy merc," she mumbled, peeved Gren was acting more like a moody woman than a warrior with something clearly on his mind. She'd thought he would be one to identify and clear a problem, but apparently she'd been wrong. As she dug into her food, she decided distance might just be the thing to better her perspective.

Women's needs were all well and good, but once let loose, played havoc with reason. Her disciplined nature reveled at her new mind-set, and after digesting several spiced meats and fruits, she began to look forward to the mission, despite the moody warrior keeping his distance.

* * * *

"I bet she's miserable," Rorn Fenhal muttered under his breath as he stared at a hologram of Temis Freya's likeness. He'd had his men post wanted notices, anonymously of course, for the capture or purchase of said abducted peacemaker.

He stared at her picture, images of owning her never far from his mind. From the moment he'd seen her again, aboard Sernal's ship, he'd had a raging erection that wouldn't quit. Luckily he'd thought to bring along two of his favorite female peacemakers, women who, unlike Temis, understood their extreme good fortune to pleasure such a powerful man as he.

Sitting inside his quarters, he pondered the eventual success of his latest operation. Selecting the women for the upcoming slave auction had been simple. He'd simply chosen the most beautiful women from Mardu he'd had the pleasure to meet, then studied their security detail with the aid of peacemaker resources, and like that, he had plans in place.

With the aid of Nero, his second in command, and a small handful of greedy peacemakers more concerned with power than right, he'd begun steadily creating his own hedonistic world.

He leaned back in his chair and closed his eyes, thoughts of the future exciting him. Soon his growing estate, Fenhal Lands, would run the outlaw Colony6. In the "civilized" portion of Colony6, his estate was a kingdom. The poor masses of outlaws and castaways owed him their allegiance, for without him, more than half the economy of the small moon would be nonexistent.

The slavers market he'd started years ago had taken off, and deciding he'd had enough of peacemaker politics and righteous fools like Sernal of Mardu, he'd decided to end his tenure as a peacemaker on a grand scale. He had no desire to follow in his father's footsteps. His father could keep his lofty position as Peacemaker Legion Director. Rorn had a better idea of the perfect life.

Abducting Mardu's wealthiest and most gorgeous women to sell as playmates to the system's most powerful underworld leaders would cement his position in the criminal classes. Already whispers abounded of his power and contacts.

He smiled and buzzed for Calia and Zerona.

Temis would regret that she'd ever rebuffed him. He wondered if Gren had raped her yet, then thought by now he must have. The thought of her violated pleased him, and he looked forward to continuing her introduction into the violence of desire.

With Gren's reputation, the chance existed Temis might have fallen prey to his seduction. But since Temis thought herself too good and pure to waste on the best of the peacemakers--namely himself, what were the chances she'd willingly give her pussy to a murdering mercenary?

His cock ached, thoughts of Temis on her hands and knees, begging for rescue, enhancing his desire. He unfastened his trousers and waited impatiently for his peacemakers to attend him.

He wondered in what ways Gren had taken Temis. Had he

spent in her mouth, her ass? Had he creamed her slick pussy with his unrefined seed?

Feeling himself nearing climax, he stared down at his impressive erection, knowing it was only a matter of time before Temis begged him for it.

A short buzzer sounded and he pressed a button, opening the door to allow Calia and Zerona entry. They stopped short at the sight of him in the chair, not sure what to do, he supposed, since he'd never before called them to him together.

"Take off your clothes," he ordered.

Calia began stripping while Zerona stared as if unsure.

"I gave you an order, peacemaker," he said silkily, amused and slightly disappointed she quickly did as he bade. Temis would have fought, at least at first, before succumbing to his orders.

When both women stood naked before him, each stunning in her own way, he motioned them closer. "Calia, tie Zerona to the wall."

"Lead Rorn?" Zerona asked in a nervous voice. He'd only slept with her once, a gentle coupling to get her to trust him. Calia, on the other hand, knew what he liked, and her widening grin told him she knew what he wanted. She'd spent a good amount of time chained to the wall while he used various means of taming her.

She roughly grabbed Zerona and bound her naked to the grips in the wall, Zerona's hands and legs spread apart in an upright position.

"She's all yours, Calia," he said, and Calia smiled with pleasure. Zerona, however, shook her head, not wanting to verbally resist his order but clearly not comfortable at thoughts of having no control over the situation.

Control. How he prized the feeling.

He groaned as Calia bent to her knees and began showing Zerona how to play the game.

After much resistance, Zerona began to respond to Calia's rough if sensuous treatment. As he watched the last of Zerona's innocence being ripped from her, her protests fading under the unwilling moans of pleasure she uttered, he began touching himself.

The corruption of another was always so satisfying. And after Calia had finished, he had a few games of his own to play. He eyed a leather whip sitting on the corner of his nightstand. Oh yes, he had such beautiful things to teach the uninitiated.

Thoughts of Temis mixed with the sexual deviancy before him, and his patience fled. He strode to Calia and shoved her out of the way. Then he ripped Zerona from her bonds and threw her down on her hands and knees.

A swift thrust and the fire in his groin started to ease, the swiftness of his climax fast approaching.

Zerona's protests were half-hearted at best, beginning to bore him. Calia, however, captured his interest. He watched as she maneuvered under Zerona so as not to be left out of the sexual play. She buried her face between Zerona's thighs, and he could hear her sucking and licking, could feel her tongue as it swept over his balls.

He groaned realizing Zerona finally cried out in ecstasy, exultant once again at having broken down yet another woman. From now on Zerona would do whatever he ordered her to do, like all the others.

And as he continued to fuck the replaceable woman in front of him, visions of Temis never left his mind.

* * * *

Gren knew it couldn't last. For the past four days he'd done a remarkable job avoiding Temis. Though he knew they needed to work out their strategy to free the women from the slave auction, they still had plenty of time to rehearse.

He sat in the galley imbibing fermented honey ale, and made no apologies for doing so. Though he'd purposefully left out a few of his shirts for Temis to wear over her ragged clothing, she apparently hadn't understood the message for she continued to flaunt her body in the slave garb he'd given her.

She didn't try to speak with him, just gave him those disconcerting looks that made him want to punch a wall. She'd shake her head, her long white-blonde hair shimmering like the golden waterfalls of Eyra. Then she'd bat those silvery purple eyes at him, as if humoring his "bad mood."

He wanted to wring her neck.

No, he wanted to stroke her lovely neck, pinning her helplessly to the ground while he fucked her without mercy.

He growled low in his throat as his cock *again* stirred to uncomfortable life.

Given his rationalizations four days ago, he might eventually have made love to Temis if she hadn't taken the matter out of his hands.

The dream they'd shared had all but vanquished his will to resist. Since then, he could no longer read her, nor could she read him. A wall of mental silence had been erected, one he had no idea how to scale--an unheard of occurrence for an advanced Thesha like himself. And to make matters worse, his libido was in constant readiness while she strolled around the small, suffocating ship as if she had not a worry in the world.

He took a quaff and finished the ale, then poured another. With Temis asleep in the ship's only berth, he had at least three more hours before they switched watch.

Sitting by the control panel had become an exercise in boredom, and at the rate he was eating and drinking he'd likely gain enough weight to rival a Ragga. He stared morosely down at his flat stomach and sighed. His metabolism refused to let him turn to fat, a Theshan gift and now a curse. He'd thought if his body grew too sluggish it wouldn't want Temis with his every breath.

But no. She'd broken his willpower with a dream he couldn't shake, the sensation of coming within her, of blending their energies and souls mesmerized him until he could think of little else.

Something simply had to give, but he'd be damned if he'd let a virgin bring him to his knees.

He downed the rest of his drink and stared dejectedly into space. He'd do well to remember why he was here in the first place. Guilt rode him as he realized he'd spent little time worrying about the abductees.

But then, what good would worrying prove? He could do nothing about their situation until he knew their precise location. At least Ceril had contacted him yesterday with good news. Apparently those running the slave auction knew he had Temis, and an elite invitation was issued in his name. In a few days, Gren would learn the location of the auction, but Temis had to be prepared for sale.

According to Ceril's source, the other women were hearty

and healthy, if unaware of their circumstance. More *mernal* drugging their systems. The poor women would be lucky to pass their captivity in ignorance.

He clenched his jaw, memories pushing to be let through. *Women running, screaming. Men falling upon them, raping and wounding without distinction. Mindless acts of violence, and all under the auspicious tent of the slaver's ring.*

"Gren?"

Her voice shook him free from the past, but when he saw her, he wasn't sure what was worse, haunting memories or Temis in the flesh. She had finally taken one of his subtle hints to cover herself and now wore his shirt.

The garment came to mid-thigh on her, the buttons gaping above her chest, where a hint of lavender silk peeked through.

As he stared at her, all thoughts of the slave trade left him, the blood rushing below his waist. She looked more erotic wearing his clothing than Drorna's silken scraps, and he had to remind himself to steer clear of her.

"I think I'll turn in," he said with a straight face. He nodded politely and sought quarters. As he lay down in the warm indentation where her body had just laid, he smelled the subtle scent of Temis, a wild yet feminine perfume all her own, and he groaned.

He felt feverish, his need to join her bordering on pain, and thought anything would be better than this hell. Ripping his shirt off, he threw it to the ground, a poor substitute to cooling his overheated body. A traitorous thought occurred, a weakness of the mind, no doubt.

Would bedding her be so very bad?

Yes it would. For once he had her, he feared he'd never let her go.

Chapter Eleven

Temis stared after Gren with a disgruntled frown. Enough was enough. She'd tolerated his sulky mood for several days now, and thought she might explode if they didn't come to some agreement to restore the peace.

She'd been on tough assignments before, even with those less than professional, but she'd always managed to make the best of things. With Gren, her best was one step away from punching him in the jaw.

Fuming, she rechecked the autopilot, the messages and the security measures encoded into the ship. Satisfied all ran as it should, she left the narrow bridge with a purpose.

Standing in the doorway of the berthing quarters, she watched the muscles of Gren's chest ripple as he sought comfort in bed. Helpless to turn away, she could only stare in fascination at the strength he so effortlessly exuded.

Gren, though at the moment more a headache than a welcome diversion, was a warrior through and through. She recalled the way he'd bested two peacemakers on Mornio, the way he'd fought almost a dozen armed men on *Lady Justice* with an instinct that left her stunned in awe.

His arms were corded with power. The dim light of the hallway shone on the bulging muscles and she had to force herself to swallow around the lump in her throat.

He froze at the sound and quickly turned on his side to face her, the golden expanse of his chest a temptation in the extreme. Nevertheless, Temis forced herself to focus on his face, on the stubborn expression that didn't fool her for a minute.

Though she could no longer *feel* Gren the way she had, she knew he still wanted her. She hadn't missed the massive erection he sported whenever she walked by him. She knew she hadn't helped by deliberately teasing him wearing the silken outfits. But honestly, something had to change before she went stark raving mad.

"What are you doing here?" he asked in a gravelly voice, the tone threatening and not at all welcome.

She stared, unbelievably drawn to the danger surrounding him. "It's past time to set things right, Gren. I can't take much more of your surliness."

His eyes glittered, and she could feel a battle about to begin. Her blood churned at the thought, and she deliberately set out to provoke him.

"My surliness?" he murmured, his brows narrowed fiercely as he rose from the bed. "I've been more than polite to you, *princess*. I'm not here for your amusement." He glared at her and closed the distance between them until they stood nose to nose.

She could smell his raw power, could see the control he fought so hard to master, and felt her insides quiver with desire.

"But you aren't amusing, Gren. And I'm tired of watching you sulk when we have a job to do." She took a step back and dropped the shirt from around her shoulders, gratified at his swift breath. "This is what you need to be used to before we get to the auction. If you can't handle being around me, then I doubt we'll be able to pull off a rescue."

She stared at him with scorn, secretly elated when she noted the arousal straining his trousers. His chest heaved and she wanted him more than anything. A fight was just the way to break down his barriers.

"I can handle you, Temis," he said through clenched teeth. "I'm just tired of you throwing yourself at me. Enough already."

Had he said those words without a desperate growl, had his body not stiffened noticeably when she neared, she might have taken offense. But Temis found the challenge of besting him too tempting.

Her decision to keep her distance had given her an objective viewpoint from which to reason the future. She was a peacemaker, a woman warrior in a man's world. And like men, she had needs. It was time to stop ignoring her sensuality, time to exploit every aspect of her nature to the fullest. Only then could she begin to know and understand herself.

Funny that it had taken Gren at odds with himself to show her the way.

She stood facing him with her arms akimbo, the position thrusting her silk-clad breasts toward him, a motion he seemed determined to ignore.

"Enough already?" she repeated. "Enough of what, Gren?" she asked softly and took a step nearer.

His nostrils flared and he clenched his fists. "I don't want you in here, Temis. I'm trying to get some sleep."

"Coward." His eyes widened in shock. "You do want me, Gren. You want in here," she said, cupping her mound, not surprised to find the silk wet between her legs.

He suddenly grabbed her shoulders and spun around, throwing her on the bed. In a blink he was on top of her, his weight familiar, domineering and altogether sexual.

"You're playing with fire." His voice was guttural, and she could feel his erection bruising her hip. "You don't know what you're doing. I'm not one of your civilized lawmakers, Temis. I'm like nothing you've ever seen."

His eyes flared, an inhuman green inferno that promised she would suffer the burn of his desire.

"And I'm like nothing you've ever had," she dared, licking her lips in anticipation of his kiss.

Without another word he ravaged her mouth, his arms tight around her shoulders as he pressed into her. His weight was heavy but manageable, and soon forgettable. The pressure of his mouth took away every thought but mating with him.

His tongue plunged into her mouth, tasting and teasing as he brutally let free his passion. His savage need aroused her own, and she ran her fingers through his hair in an effort to urge him on.

He groaned and allowed her a breath, sighing with pleasure at the feel of her hands touching him, all the while he stared at her through slitted eyes.

"I tried," he rasped and nipped at her neck. "Now it's too late."

She shook her head, not wanting talk when her body desperately needed relief. Warmth unfurled from her core, ecstasy from without, and she moaned while her body wept for more.

"I can make you come with a thought," he whispered in her ear. He plunged his tongue inside, sensitizing her lobe with love bites and the sweet sting of soft lips. "I'm going to fuck you so hard you'll beg me to never stop."

"Never." *Never stop.* She gasped, arching into his

questing hands as he ran them over her taut breasts. He leaned up and with a hard jerk ripped off her miniscule clothing. Then he quickly shed his trousers and slowly lowered his body to hers.

The electric shock that passed through her at the contact felt like an orgasm, and she caught her breath as she realized this had only just begun.

"Yes, *sura*." Gren's voice echoed strangely in the small room, his eyes sparkling. "You're mine now."

His lips scorched a trail from her neck to her breasts, his thick arousal straining, stroking wherever he touched her. She wanted him so badly she shook, while he took his time pleasuring her breasts.

"Please," she gasped as his mouth closed over one turgid peak.

He suckled and pulled, earning moans and pleas she wasn't consciously aware of giving. His hands pleasured her skin, caressing and petting, moving lower down her body.

His mouth closed over her other breast, the contrast of cool air on her wet and exposed globe extreme opposed to the hot tongue stabbing her pleasured nipple.

Then his hand teased her mound, rubbing and pressing, until she thought she'd go crazy. He began thrusting against her thigh, as if unable to stop himself, and she wanted to throw herself around him and take charge.

"I need you now," she ordered and yanked his head from her breast, angered and needy and frustrated all at once.

"Not yet," he said softly, the threat still there in his striated gaze. Black threaded through green, making his eyes a spectral wonder she could little dwell upon. Instead her body clamored for completion, needing him deep inside her.

He stared at her a moment and when she would have protested his stillness, inserted a finger into her wet sheath.

She bucked and groaned, closing her eyes at the intrusion. Another finger quickly followed, stretching her, loving her, as he began thrusting his digits in and out with a rough tenderness.

"You won't come, *sura*," he promised. "Not until I'm deep inside you. It aches, the pain, the need, but I'll make it so much better." He kissed her, taking away her moans and pants while he slid his fingers through her wet passage.

She could feel the steel erection burning her leg, could feel the moisture around his penis and knew him close to climax.

"Please," she moaned when he let go of her mouth to pleasure her breast. "Love me."

"I do. I will," he answered and rose between her thighs, spreading them with muscular legs. "Watch me while I enter you. Watch the joining and *know.*"

She did as he bade, wanting everything and more. She stared down and saw him thick and silky, impossibly large. But still she didn't feel a moment's fear.

He slowly entered her, and her eyes flew to his face. Instead of the slight discomfort she expected, only fullness and pleasure stole through her. The further he pressed, the hotter she felt, until her body seized with flame.

"Yes, *sura,* so perfect," he groaned and sank the rest of the way inside, until he reached her very womb. He gave her no time to think, to reason, and began thrusting, long deep thrusts that shook her with desire.

She moaned and shivered, needing him like she needed breath. Lights danced around them, the ship quavering with the power of their coupling, and she met him thrust for thrust, locking her ankles around his waist to take him deeper.

"Come with me, Temis," he commanded, his voice thick. "Swallow my seed deep in your womb. Give me the power inside you, your woman's voice crying for more."

"Yes, yes," she gasped. Anything he wanted, everything he wanted.

And he thrust harder, powerfully conquering any will to resist becoming one with him.

Sparks showered them as he cried out and came hard inside her, pushing her into an orgasm that changed her very existence.

Lights danced and colors whorled. Her body shook as her walls tightened around his shaft, milking him of his seed. She felt him shooting deep inside her, felt the tingling warmth of their joining and the fire that now burned in her womb.

The orgasm kept on, a continued conflagration of need and want that opened barriers and closed an impenetrable wall around them.

"I'm with you now, *sura*. Forever," Gren rasped as he slowly withdrew only to slide forward again. He was still hard, and suddenly she felt all of it, his thoughts, his desires, his passion.

Overwhelmed, she struggled to free herself from the onslaught of sensation, but could only drown in his feelings.

She dimly heard him groan her name and felt him coming again, this time bringing her with him. His orgasm was fierce, triggering her own, and she felt him steal into her soul, bonding with her, until she could no longer tell where she stopped and he began.

When he finally withdrew, she felt shaken and confused, and too tired to care. Spent, yet sated down to her bones, she reached for him, still needing his touch.

"Shh, go to sleep now, love," he murmured and curled her into his warmth. The loud beat of his heart calmed her and within seconds she slept, replete and protected in his strong embrace.

* * * *

When Gren awoke, he felt refreshed and for the first time in his life, truly whole. Temis stirred slightly in his arms and he soothed her, knowing she needed more rest.

Sleep, sura. I'm here.

She immediately snuggled closer to him and his heart thumped steadily at the contact.

It was too late now to change things, and having experienced utter *wainu*, he wouldn't change his circumstances even if he could. Never had he thought to find a woman like Temis, a woman to join him in all ways possible.

He felt the oneness between them, could feel her breathing, her heartbeat just by searching within himself. Her thoughts he would respect, her feelings as well, but he would have to teach her how to shield them. She already had the knowledge as she had done so previously, but now that they'd joined, she was open and susceptible to him at all times.

Worry reared its ugly head but he ignored his responsibilities for once and took comfort in the woman beside him. Temis had just entered into a sacred bond, whether she knew it or not, and he intended to take advantage of her loving for as long as he could. Reality would be upon them all too soon. For now, he would love his mate and share with her the pleasures few would ever know. Satisfied with his decision, he let drowsiness take him into the dark, his arms locked around his woman.

Hours later he felt the heat of warm breath on his groin, waking him to unbearable pleasure.

He opened his eyes and looked down. Temis lay between his thighs, waiting for him to waken. The minute she saw him blink, she closed her mouth around his engorged cock, licking and sucking while she watched with a swirling lavender gaze.

He thought it the most erotic thing, watching her pleasure him. She knew just how to stroke him, how to lave the sensitive spot beneath the head of his shaft, to fondle his sack while she consumed him.

His breathing quickened until he was panting, and still she continued.

"Wait, *sura*," he breathed, not wanting to come in her mouth when he'd been waiting for what seemed like forever to join her woman's core. "I want to come inside you."

She smiled, like a cat toying with prey, and crawled up his body, pressing her breasts into him, twin trails of fire.

"More," he growled and mentally showed her what he wanted. Her eyes glittered and she straddled his face, teasing him with her wet need.

He grabbed her hips and lowered her clit over his mouth, hungrily licking her nub as she rode his tongue. She tasted like sweet wine, and he nipped at the ripe fruit of her clit, wanting more.

She cried his name and came hard, her moisture flooding his tongue as she convulsed. He felt his cock near to bursting and with a final lick, hurriedly sat her atop his erection.

She slid down his rod with ease, bouncing up and down with his hands guiding her hips. He felt her orgasm building again and *pushed* her further, a burst of Theshan bliss causing her to cry out as she gushed around him.

Her scent fed his excitement and he shot hard, grinding against her as he came, sexual energy flowing between them like ethereal gold.

The power between them lit the room, so that he could see every nuance of her perfect body. Her full breasts heaved in the aftermath; her tight belly quivered with satisfaction.

She stared down at him, her lips full and passion-stung, her eyes cloudy with lust and energy, the irises a glowing combination of silver and lavender that made him want to take her again.

"Yes," she moaned, feeling him stir within her.

"You won't feel sore, after," he promised, knowing he was large enough to hurt her with so much passionate sex, especially as it had been her first time. He sat up, hugging her curves to him and thrusting deeper. "I'll make sure of that."

"And you'll explain why I can't stop wanting you," she ordered, not giving him time to answer as she plastered her mouth to his.

Chapter Twelve

To her amazement, Temis and Gren spent hours upon hours making love, an exhaustive but thoroughly satisfying exchange. She wouldn't have thought it possible, but each time she touched him she wanted him more.

After finally succumbing to their bodies' need for sleep, the two rested.

Waking with a deliciously well-used soreness, Temis stretched and discovered Gren already awake, staring at her with a sleepy smile on his face.

He brushed his lips over hers and the soreness vanished, replaced with a languid peace.

"Not that I'm complaining," Temis said as she traced every facet of his brutally handsome face. "But when are you going to explain how you're able to do things like *that*," she finished, referring to her loss of pain.

He sighed. "Do we have to go into this now?"

She nodded. "I can't help it. My curiosity is killing me." She rose to sit up and saw his eyes darken. Flushing, she pulled the sheet up to cover her breasts. "Focus, Gren."

"I am," he murmured, stroking her leg through the thin sheet covering them.

"How is it I want to smack you and kiss you at the same time?"

He shrugged, his grin stirring confusing feelings within her. Needing some answers, she pressed forward.

"You took me to places I had no idea existed. I saw stars, Gren. Real stars. And though I don't have much experience with this kind of thing, I know that's not normal."

He continued to stroke her thigh, his gaze shifting from her eyes to the blanket covering her.

"And what about the flashing lights? The surge of energy that rocked the ship while we made love?" She took his chin in her hand and brought his mysterious stare back to her. "Tell me, Gren." Her voice softened. "Please. I need to know."

He pressed a kiss to the center of her palm that quickly

turned her insides to mush.

"I told you I'm a telepath."

She stared at him, waiting.

He sighed again. "And I should have guessed you wouldn't believe me. Temis...." He paused and sat up, his stomach flexing and his pectorals tense, an unwelcome distraction. "I'm somewhat of a rarity, quite different from those you normally meet."

"Tell me about it." She grinned, but her smile faded when she saw his lips flatten.

"I can do things most others can't. I--" He stopped. "I don't know how to explain, exactly."

She frowned. "Just tell me the truth. I won't tell anyone else." A sudden thought struck her. "Are you an enhanced psychic?"

"Enhanced?" He looked confused. "Oh, you mean the genetically altered Eyrans? Hell no. My gifts are inbred, a natural part of my heritage." He sounded proud, his tone that of the arrogant mercenary she had first met. "And unfortunately they're worth far more than what the Eyrans are paying for recapture of their *scientific experiments*," he added caustically.

"I've never much cared for biological tampering either," she admitted. "My home planet looks down upon skills acquired through artificial means. We prize true strength and power." She eyed him curiously. "I don't understand why you can't tell me what you're hiding. I've seen you fight. I know your strength is your own and that you've spent at least some training time on my planet."

His brows rose, a hint of humor in his eyes. "So it's my body you're attracted to, and not my mind?"

"Can't you just answer the question?" she asked in a huff.

"It's more complicated than you know." He pulled her into his arms and rested his chin on top of her head, making her feel warm and protected. "I can tell you I'm not telepathic, at least not with everyone. I have an affinity toward women."

She stiffened. She couldn't help it.

He chuckled. "I mean my psychic abilities, as you call them, only work on women."

"But I heard you communicate with Lurin." She tried to squirm out of his hold to look at him, but he tightened his arms around her.

"So you heard that, hmm? And you say you've no mental gifts of your own?"

"Only the ability to structure dreams, and that's not all that uncommon among my mother's people. I only started hearing some of your thoughts and feeling some things you felt after we, uh, well, after we were intimate that first time."

"You mean after I licked your honeyed cream, swallowed the sweet sobs of your body, crying out for mine?"

"Really, Gren." She tensed, knowing he laughed at her discomfort. Temis simply wasn't used to talking about sex, and only recently felt comfortable *doing* it.

"I'm sorry, *sura*. But you're so easy to tease." He exhaled a deep breath. "What we shared, Temis, is something I will never share with another. Nor will you." He squeezed her, hugging her tight. "Our souls connected on a spiritual plane my people call *wainu*."

"Your people?" She finally managed to free herself and glanced up at his somber face.

"I've never heard of a foreigner reaching that state. And I wouldn't have believed it possible had I not seen you there with me." She wanted to take exception to being called a 'foreigner' but his earnest expression stopped her. "We are bonded, Temis. And though I tried to avoid it, it happened regardless."

"Bonded?" she grew nervous. He seemed to be talking about permanence, and she still didn't understand just what he could do, who he really was. "And what do you mean you tried to avoid it?"

"I felt drawn to you from the first, and thought if I could steer clear of your sexuality, I would be safe. It worked at first, but you grew too tempting."

"I don't understand." Her heart stuttered hearing how drawn he had been to her. At least it hadn't been one-sided.

"Making love to you fully, taking your virginity." His voice deepened with lust. "That I tried to avoid."

Her lips formed an 'o,' suddenly understanding why he'd been so reluctant to spill his seed within her.

"So by doing that, we bonded?"

He shook his head. "We bonded before that. When I tasted you, something in me shifted. With you, Temis, I can communicate the way I do with those of my kind, mentally." So Lurin was one of his *kind*. "And only with you does the lovemaking get so out of control."

His eyes burned. "Every time we touch I want you. It's an ache that will never fade. And though it's typical of my kind to share everything, know I won't ever let another touch you," he promised.

She stared at him in surprise. She hadn't thought into the future, at what it might be like to experience sex with another.

Nor will you.

She blinked at his familiar voice in her mind. "You can read my thoughts? Whenever you want to?"

"I can now, but I will teach you to shield yourself." He gave her a tender look and brushed his knuckles over her cheek. "You are so very young, so very beautiful. I'm not really sure how this works, but I'll do everything in my power to please you, *sura*, in all ways."

He closed his eyes and she felt a sweltering burst of energy within her. She gasped as her loins flooded and cried out in ecstasy.

After catching her breath, she stared at him in awe. "You just, you--"

"Brought you to orgasm, with a thought. I wasn't bragging earlier when I said that." He stared at her hungrily. "It's one thing my kind does very well."

She didn't know what to say. Still trying to collect her thoughts, she could only watch him with helpless fascination.

"Quite a talent, I know," he murmured, reading her thoughts. He pressed a kiss to her lips and stroked her hair. "It will be alright, Temis. Since I know you're feeling uncomfortable with me reading your thoughts, I'll show you how to counter that right away. Then we'll focus on our mission, a goal that's been evading me ever since I laid eyes on you," he conceded with a rueful sigh.

She had more questions, but her body hummed with passion. That he had shared as much as he had made her take stock of the importance of their relationship. She couldn't say how, but she knew he had never shared so much with another before, at least not with a *foreigner*.

Like a cat, she crept over his body, brushing subtly

against him. She felt him tense and feminine satisfaction surged within her. "We have time yet," she whispered in his ear, and plunged her tongue in the sensitive cavern. He shuddered and ground her on top of his steel hard erection. "I think part of my mental training should start here." She slid over him, joining them as one. "What do you think?"

"Yes, *sura*," he groaned. "That's the perfect place to start."

* * * *

Two days later Gren received the call he'd been expecting. After disconnecting with Ceril, he felt Temis watching him expectantly. The touch of her warm gaze caressed him, both arousing and comforting, and he knew his life was forever altered.

He thought it interesting that the thought of a bonded future no longer bothered him.

"Well?" she asked, clad in another of his overlarge shirts.

He liked her wearing his clothing, a testament to his new possessive nature. Her eyes sparkled with amusement, and he realized he needed to keep a better shield on his thoughts. Normally he didn't have a problem shutting everyone else out, but with Temis it felt like closing off a part of himself.

She had picked up the shielding skill with ease, mentally keeping him at a distance without fully separating herself. Despite not being fully at ease with him, a part of her wanted the spiritual contact they shared.

"The auction will proceed as planned, tomorrow at midday on Colony6."

"Colony6?" Her eyes widened. "That's outside peacemaker jurisdiction. I'm not sure we can follow them there legally."

"You mean Sernal can't." He smiled with satisfaction. "I can do whatever the hell I want. And with no peacemakers to interfere." She glared at him. "With one exception, of course." He gave her a polite nod.

She grumbled under her breath and left the bridge. He understood nothing outside the word "galley" and decided to leave her to her musings.

As he dialed Lurin's private number to forward the news to Sernal, Gren wondered when and if the time would ever be right to share his heritage with Temis.

It wasn't as if he didn't trust her, but their relationship was so new. And added to that were his responsibilities to his people. He still had no idea how to make his guardianship mesh with his new relationship.

He couldn't imagine any of the elders being pleased he'd taken a mate. Then again, as deeply as he felt for Temis, he still felt guilty he'd found her. At his core he knew he wasn't worthy. And his weakness in taking her anyway, regardless of his duties and stained past, only reinforced the notion he had no business being with a soul so strong and pure.

"Lurin here. What's new?"

Lurin's voice shook him from dark thoughts. They made pleasant conversation while he mentally projected the information Sernal needed to know and Lurin filled him in on Sernal's projected role in the operation.

Got it. Anything else I should pass to Lead Sernal, the biggest legal pain in the ass in the system? Lurin asked in a gruff voice. *By Flor's dagger, the man's been calling us at all hours wanting to know where you are and what you're doing.*

Lurin paused, aware of the humor Gren projected.

Laugh it up, friend. But you're going to have a lot of explaining to do when this is over. I hear you not only captured a peacemaker, but Sernal seems to think you've enthralled *her.*

Sernal's an idiot. I didn't enthrall her. A recollection of her abduction from the ship flashed through his mind. *So I lured her off the ship. That was as far as her subjugation progressed. She's here now, helping me of her own free will.*

A moment of silence passed. *So you finally mated, hmm?*

Gren grimaced. *Is this really any of your business?*

Hell no. But I told you your time would come. I can't wait to tell Mara.

Feminine humor bled through the conversation. *So what's she like, Gren?* Mara joined the silent communication. *I hear she's a peacemaker from Zephyr who's absolutely gorgeous.*

Who told you that? Irritation filled him. Of course she was beautiful, but who had described her as 'absolutely gorgeous'? Sernal or his idiot brother Rafe?

Wow, jealous already. Lurin whistled. *Didn't I tell you--?*

Yeah, yeah. You told me the whole of it, he directed to Lurin. *Now pass my message to Sernal and stop wasting my time. I've got a mission to prepare for.*

And a woman to love, Mara added with amusement. *Best of luck, Gren. And tell Temis we're dying to meet her.*

He disconnected and left to find Temis. She sat in the galley eating a plate of seasoned gnom, a delicacy loved on Zephyr.

"I can't believe you have this on board," she said with enthusiasm, the food having apparently rid her of her earlier hostility. "This is my favorite dish."

He smiled and grabbed a plate of fruit before sitting next to her. "I thought that might be the case. Many years ago when I trained on Zephyr, I learned as much about the inhabitants' customs as I could."

She stared at him with curiosity. "Just when did you train there? Did you know Master Zephu?"

He shook his head. "I trained there a *long* time ago." Smiling, he decided to tease her curiosity. "It was long before you were born, Temis."

Her eyes widened. "Just how old are you?"

He gave her a mysterious grin. "That's my secret." He felt her probe at his mind and shook his head. "Good try, *sura*, but until you've earned the right to know, I'm not telling you my age."

"Earned the right to know?" She looked affronted.

He nodded, pleased with the fire lighting her eyes. She was so easy to rile, and so much fun to watch.

"You leave so many holes in your history and your present. You're a walking mystery. And you stir so many questions!" She looked like she wanted to throttle him, and he wanted her under him again. "Will you at least answer me this?"

He waited.

"What, by Narok's sword, does *sura* mean?"

"*Sura*? Didn't I tell you before?" She shook her head. "It's my people's word for *drun*."

Her face flushed bright red at the insult and he laughed.

"I was just joking, Temis. It means sweetheart or 'one who is cared for.' A pleasant endearment, *sura*, nothing more."

She huffed and crossed her arms. "It had better not mean *drun*."

"Though you will recall that's what you referred to me as when we first met."

She flushed again. "I didn't know you then."

"And now?"

Her eyes narrowed. "Now I still might call you that." Her lips quirked as his expression soured. "But then there are a lot of other names I could think to call you as well."

His eyebrows rose in question.

"But before I get sidetracked, I think it's time we talked specifics about tomorrow. Why don't you tell me a little bit more about what to expect at the slave auction?"

Temis watched as all humor leaked out of Gren's expression.

"You're going to see it soon enough."

"I'd like to be prepared," she said quietly, knowing how much this bothered him. Though she could no longer read his thoughts unless he shared them, at times she still sensed his emotions. Right now she sensed anger, guilt, and surprisingly, shame.

He sighed and pushed aside his food. "The auctions are different and yet always the same. Captured women, normally drugged and therefore obedient, once prepared, trudge through long lines of disreputable men, some desperate, others sickly depraved.

"The women are naked, pawed and prodded as they walk from the entrance of the slave tent to the center cage, where they await the bidding wars." His face didn't change expression but the dark feeling around him deepened. "The women are prepared within the cage to be ogled on center stage. A beautiful woman, called an *ogra*, rubs dyes on their breasts and pubic region, calling attention to the women's femininity. The *ogra* will at times engage in sexual play with certain slaves, to entice them to behave or excite the mongrel onlookers."

Temis listened in horrified awe. She could imagine it, the helplessness, the dirty feeling of dozens of eyes on her in her most vulnerable state. Then to be sexually molested by a woman for the amusement of those watching....

He nodded. "It's extremely unpleasant for the women involved. The *ogra* works for the auctioneer and derives pleasure from her work. The men and few women watching the orgiastic event chant and cheer. But the women in the cage remain oblivious, drugged to remain docile. Every once in a while the auctioneer will allow one or two women to go undrugged."

"Why?"

"To watch them fight and see them subdued before the crowd. It isn't uncommon to watch them raped before the masses."

She sat in troubled silence. "It sounds like hell."

"Believe me, it is. But that's not the worst part of the auction. The private party, normally held after the main auction, is decidedly worse."

"How could it be any worse?" She cringed just thinking about it. Maybe she'd taken on more than she could handle. She didn't think she could participate in the events he'd described, peacemaker or no.

"The private party is smaller and, like its name implies, is extremely private. Only the richest and most powerful are invited to attend."

"Are you?"

He nodded grimly and gave her a burning stare. "Because of you. Rorn Fenhal wants you, Temis, badly."

She swallowed. "Go on."

"Inside the private parties all manner of perversities can occur." His jaw clenched and she had to urge him to continue.

"I'm sorry, Gren. But I need to know. I'm going to be there tomorrow, remember?"

"I know." He cleared his throat. "I really hadn't thought this through before, Temis. I can stomach the auctions for the sake of those women, but I don't think I can handle you there."

"How bad can it be? I'll have you there with me, right?"

He nodded. "And I won't let anyone but me near you, that I promise. Some "owners" get possessive, so it won't seem too odd if I want no one near you but me, at first. I am supposed to be there to sell you." He cursed and ran a hand through his hair. "Owners don't care for their slaves, so using them and sharing them means nothing. Public coupling is a way of advertising.

"It isn't unusual to watch the owner and slave engage in

intercourse, or to watch the slave pleasure her owner in other ways. There's also the option that the slave may pleasure anyone the owner chooses."

"What are you thinking to do?" She wished at that moment she could read his thoughts. His mood shifted from angered to enraged to aroused and back again.

"I won't let you do anything with anyone other than me, and only if it's absolutely necessary. As obsessed as Rorn is with you, he might want a private viewing. I could push for that."

"But with you there, right?" She tried to act professional, but thoughts of having sex in public shocked her. Temis did not consider herself a prude, but lovemaking was new to her and with Gren, utterly meaningful. She couldn't imagine dirtying it for the likes of Rorn Fenhal.

"Don't worry, *sura*," Gren murmured, reading the panicked look on her face. "I won't let anything happen to you."

She couldn't help it. She might be unnerved, hell, even frightened, but Temis fought her own battles. "I won't let anything happen to myself," she corrected, and saw an answering flash of heat in Gren's gaze.

"Then you'll be doubly protected, won't you?" His eyes glowed brightly.

"You still need to explain that," she said with a nod to his eyes. He scowled and immediately the aura around him dimmed. Pleased that she'd taken control of the tense situation, she smiled. "Don't worry, Gren. I'm a peacemaker, remember? We'll enter the auction, save the women, and nail Rorn Fenhal to the wall like the insect he is."

"Sernal didn't say he had to be brought in alive." The look on Gren's face froze her to her seat. She'd only seen him appear that deadly once before, when he took on a dozen peacemakers on *Lady Justice*. And then he hadn't been out for blood.

She felt uneasy about Gren's attitude, and decided it was time she talked to her superior to make sure she knew what he wanted. Until now she'd been content to have Gren exchange encoded messages with Sernal's contact, as he'd explained.

Peacemakers, however, had standards, and "dead or alive"

didn't figure into the law.

"I need to talk to Sernal."

Gren glared at her, and she could almost see his body thrumming with energy. "Why?"

"Because he's my superior. I'd like to know exactly when and where he plans to arrive with back-up, and to hear *him* say it doesn't matter if Fenhal is brought in dead or alive."

Gren scooted closer to Temis, deliberately trying to intimidate her with his large frame. Instead of threat, however, Temis felt arousal.

He must have felt it as well for he cursed and moved back. "Look, once we land on Colony6 we'll have a few hours at most before the auction begins. At best, Sernal and the others will arrive during the auction. But most likely they'll arrive just as it's ending. In the time we're there, we'll have staked out the necessary extraction points for the missing women."

"But how are we going to drag fifteen, and possibly more women who've been drugged and Narok knows what else, amidst a crowd of murderers and slavers? Even you can't take on the dozens that will likely be there."

He smiled and she couldn't help the shiver that raced up her spine. Though she felt completely safe in his presence, she knew those at the auction would not be so lucky.

"I told you I'm different, Temis. Trust me when I say I can move the women to the extraction points. Drugged or not, as long as they're capable of walking, they'll be saved."

"Are you telling me you can control any woman's mind? Whether it be in passion," she paused and the heat rose in her cheeks, "to clear her head, or to simply order her about?"

He nodded slowly, his eyes fixed to hers.

She frowned. "But that can't be." He couldn't possibly be saying what she thought he was. "You can't control men, but women are virtually bound to your every thought, your every desire?"

"Let's save the rest of this discussion for after the mission," he said brusquely, not pleased at her questioning. "And if you absolutely *have* to talk to Sernal, come with me."

Chapter Thirteen

The morning spent on Colony6 made Temis more than glad she lived in the charted sector of the system. This small moon, if it could be called that, was more like an outlying tundra set apart from planet Jaron, and the sun, by mind-numbing cold.

Had Gren not outfitted her with one of his extra exploratory suits she would surely have frozen to death amidst the ice and snow covering the ground.

She hadn't expected such cold, especially considering the skimpy slave garments she'd been "forced" to wear. She could only hope the slave tents had heat.

They do.

She glanced up at Gren leading the way through the heavily packed snow. He had insisted they remove all inner shields to allow communication at all times, especially should something go wrong. She wholeheartedly agreed.

She still had a hard time believing she'd spoken to Sernal via Catam, translated from thought by Lurin. That had been the strangest conversation she'd ever experienced.

Talking with the Mardu brothers is always strange. Gren waited for her to catch up to him.

Temis curbed her grin and strode to the top of the hill. The rocks and fallen needles of the trees pricked at her feet, even clad in tough rak-hide boots. Winded, she couldn't help noting Gren breathed evenly. Envious and a little annoyed at his strength, she hurried to his side.

I'm bigger than you, sura, *it's natural I can handle the cold better.* His words were meant to calm, but the arrogant humor in his tone made her snap her teeth together.

You wait until we get back. I'm taking you to Chula for a proper fighting match. I'll have you flat on the dirt in no time.

Such a short memory, he chided, and a familiar vision of a fight with Gren surfaced, one that had already happened on Chula if in a dream.

"You know about that?" She flushed three shades of red.

"Wait a minute. You were there? But it was my dream."

"Your dream that pulled me in, but my control of the outcome," he said with a husky voice, mentally broadcasting the memory of that first shared intimacy.

She was blushing hotly as she reached him. "I thought that a dream."

"It was," he answered aloud. "One I long to have again." He looked hopeful and she swore under her breath, ignoring the quickening in her womb.

"Just wait until I have you in a challenge ring on Zephyr, in *my* world, with *my* rules."

They continued down the hill into a thatch of trees, pausing when a crude looking village came into view, curls of dark smoke escaping the dismal houses dirtying the clear blue sky.

"I need you to stay here," Gren said in a low voice as he studied the stone dwellings before them. "I'm going to get us some answers." Before she could argue, he turned to her with a stern look in his eyes. "You can't appear until the auction. If Rorn's men see me, no one will think twice. I'm known for being cautious. I can't risk you being seen, *sura*."

She didn't like it, but she agreed. "I'll be with you every step of the way." She tapped her head.

He nodded and left. After what seemed like an hour and was likely no more than half that, she "heard" him talking with a woman, someone named Cherel.

I've an affinity for women, Gren's words rang in her mind, and she forced away the surprising surge of jealousy. When she clearly focused on Gren, she felt his disdain for Cherel. The tight band around her heart eased a fraction, startling her. When had she become so possessive?

"Tell me, Cherel, where does Fenhal plan to hold his party?"

The woman he spoke with was a barkeep who often worked on her back for extra coin. Per Gren's blunt thoughts, she had a pleasant visage and a figure made for sex, but too much greed in her eyes to be truly attractive.

Cherel answered him with breathy phrases, pressing her breasts invitingly against his forearm.

Temis wanted to throw her through a wall. She felt Gren's warm amusement and wanted to throw him through a wall as well.

"Why don't we talk in a more private place?" he murmured in Cherel's ear. Temis heard his vague mental comparison of the woman's hair to her own, startled to find the woman was blond.

Have a thing for blondes, hmm? She couldn't help the heated comment.

Steaming, Temis waited in the cold, tall needle trees and large gray boulders her only companions, while Gren joined the blonde whore in a private room behind the bar. She felt him expel a ball of energy and listened in amazement to the woman moaning her pleasure. Oddly enough, Gren remained unmoved. What the hell was going on down there?

Remember, sura, he whispered to Temis, *I can instill pleasure with a thought.*

Slightly mollified but still not liking Gren's "quest for information," she impatiently awaited his return. When he finally appeared sometime later, he sparkled with vitality and amusement, she felt, at her expense.

"What was that all about?" She tried to hold onto her anger but knew he felt it all the same.

He chuckled and enfolded her in his arms. "*Sura,* don't worry. The woman was nothing more than a means of information. When she experienced bliss, she opened her mind to me. I know where the women are being held, and the layout of Rorn's estate."

Temis relaxed enough to look up at him. "I felt you doing something to her, but didn't recognize what."

"She is a sad example of the inhabitants of Colony6, castoffs from the system with no morals or ideals. She would as soon have slit my throat for a pocket of coins, or spread her legs for the promise of besting her competition across the road."

"Nice friend you made."

"Rorn seems to like her well enough. Apparently he's been building himself an empire for the last few years. When he visits, he brings women, drugs, and other illegal substances to Colony6. He uses the people here for work, binding their loyalty." Gren twisted his lips in disgust. "And the things he's done to that woman would make you cringe."

Temis didn't want to know. "You found the information we needed, but you took something else as well, didn't you?"

He looked uncomfortable with her question, piquing her interest.

"When a woman experiences bliss," he began slowly, "she produces energy. The energy is pure, despite the woman who creates it, and it enhances my abilities."

"What are you talking about?" She'd never before heard of such a thing.

"I absorb her energy. It's like the surge you receive after replenishing your body with food, only much more powerful."

He absorbed the woman's energy? Her eyes widened. She *had* heard about energy transference from the stories of her youth. Men capable of controlling a woman's mind, of making her do whatever they wanted while they stole the very soul from her being.

The legendary Thesha.

"You can't be!"

His eyes shuttered and she felt him erect mental walls. "You have such an imagination. Come on. We have a lot to do in a short time."

As they walked back to the shuttle hybrid they'd arrived in, Temis pondered Gren's heritage. Too many pieces of the puzzle pointed to the impossible.

A Thesha. Temis had met and bonded with an actual creature of legend.

I'm a man, not a creature. The heated reply shot through her system. *And definitely not that nightmare you were thinking of.*

Get out of my head, Gren. She pushed him out, aware he still had a small hold on her thoughts, but not enough to accurately read more than her emotions.

The Thesha were rumors, myths told during adolescence, when hormones ran rampant. She remembered her friends giggling about them in her youth while she'd been focused on learning to fight.

She could never have imagined they were *real*.

Theshas had the ability to control women, but more so, to pleasure a woman until she wanted to die of the rapture. Rumors still abounded throughout the system that the

Thesha existed. And she knew the black market value for a real Thesha could be anywhere from hundreds of thousands to millions in currency.

Just a few years ago she'd heard of a rich woman on Jaron who had supposedly captured two Theshas. The story of not one but two legendary creatures even existing killed any speculations of truth about the rumor instantly. In actuality, the woman and her daughter had killed her daughter's betrothed, then kidnapped and tortured the victim's alleged murderer--the "Thesha"--and the bounty hunter who'd captured him.

Her eyes widened. Hadn't Sernal been on that case? She stared at Gren's broad back as they entered the ship.

Cari Elaran was a crazy witch, Gren growled. *And her daughter was just as bad.*

"It was true? You were there?" Her heartbeat raced.

"I was there helping a friend." He didn't sound pleased at her curiosity.

"Lurin," she said, seeing the face that popped suddenly into his mind. Then the connection snapped. "He's Thesha too?"

She heard Gren mutter something under his breath but he refused to answer her. The ship took off and she sat beside him, stunned. If he was Thesha, did that mean he'd been controlling her thoughts all along? She suddenly felt extremely uncomfortable around him, not the reaction most women would have, she knew. But then Temis' priorities had never been her own pleasure first, her responsibilities second.

"Just forget about it until we complete the mission, okay?" Gren sounded angry and she could feel his dejection like a heavy fog pressing down on her.

She wasn't quite sure what to do or how to make things right. The thought of losing her scared the hell out of him.

Losing *her*? She blinked, realizing she experienced *his* emotions.

Glancing at him in her periphery, she noted the stiffness of his shoulders, the resolute set of his jaw. Confusion pulsed in her but so too did concern and compassion, and the bead of arousal that never faded when in his presence.

Worse, she could feel his hurt and it gnawed at her.

More than bothered, she sighed and reached to cover his

shoulder with a gloved palm. "We'll talk about it *after* the mission."

He relaxed at her touch and nodded. For the next few hours they marked outer extraction points while Gren shared information about Rorn's estate. Using the ship's advanced cloaking device, they were able to get fairly close to the estate, a massive conglomeration of native rock, Mornian steel, and Eyran technology. Obviously Rorn had currency to spend, and he'd clearly spent it here.

When they hovered above the estate, Temis saw the slave tents for the first time. At the rear of the estate sat a large rectangle of red material connected to a smaller square of red, both effectively hiding whatever occurred beneath.

"The tents are heated and lit from within, ensuring total privacy from outsiders. Not to mention they're easy enough to tear down when the auction is finished. They're standard among slavers," Gren explained.

"How do you know so much about the slave trade?" She had to know.

Silence fell heavily over the cabin until he sighed. "I lived with a slaver when I was young. My parents died unexpectedly." She saw his face tighten. "And before my relatives could collect me, a slaver stepped in and took me under his wing."

Shocked, Temis stared at him. "How old were you?"

"I don't know, eight or nine, probably. It doesn't really matter."

She felt the guilt bleeding from him and felt sorry he'd been forced to endure something so ugly at so young an age. "Did they ever, uh, sell you?"

He laughed, a harsh sound. "No. I had other talents better put to use. I didn't really understand my powers then, didn't know what I was. Neither did the slave master. But he saw my calming effect on the slaves and used me instead of expensive drugs to sedate them."

She didn't know what to say. How could he feel responsible for his actions as a young boy when he was clearly as much a victim as the slaves? She knew nothing she said would make a difference to him, not now. He was wallowing in remorse and anger, and she knew how powerful those emotions could be. No, she'd wait for a better time to show him his innocence in the matter.

They traveled together in uncomfortable quiet. Temis dwelled on his tale, on his abilities and the slave auction forthcoming. The questions bouncing inside her head ripped through her mind like a sharp cleaver, the tension causing a roaring headache.

Suddenly her headache ceased, replaced by a surge of masculine warmth. She swiveled in her seat and stared at Gren. "You have healing abilities too?"

He nodded, his expression contained.

She shook her head, amazed at his gifts. She glanced at her timepiece and sighed. Releasing the inner shields she'd built, she tried to relax and open herself to Gren for the sake of the mission. But the more time passed, the more she found herself dreading the approaching deadline. It was time for the auction to begin. Time to adorn the slave's absent, drugged expression and don the silken rags that exposed more than they hid.

Temis and Gren shared an unhappy look of mutual understanding.

"It begins, Temis. Remember, despite what you may think, I do care. And I won't let anything happen to you," he promised. He might be a Thesha, way more than she could understand at the moment, but she *felt* his truth.

"I know. Now let's put this *drun* away before he harms anyone else."

Gren nodded, a familiar gleam in his eyes. The mercenary was back, and for once Temis was happy to see him both arrogant and deadly.

* * * *

When Gren entered the outer walls of Rorn Fenhal's sanctuary into the large slave tent, he looked like a "marble statue of sheer menace," per the woman flirting with the guard at the gate. After Temis had removed her outer cold-weather clothing and boots, he yanked lightly on her chain, pretending she was no more than chattel and not his bonded mate being paraded almost naked among the worst of the system's slavers.

She wore a dark violet top, so sheer her nipples showed through the narrow expanse of silk holding her breasts. The matching bottoms had a low-cut waist, her belly appallingly visible under the see-through silver wrap she wore.

No shoes adorned her feet, a common practice to discourage runaways, and her beautiful face softly bemoaned her supposed drugged pleasure.

Are you alright? he asked for the third time. He had insisted they remain open to one another, and despite her worries about his background, she agreed. At least she trusted him that much, he thought sourly, deliberately shielding his discouragement. He was upset, but he didn't want to distract her from their main purpose.

He looked behind him and felt his blood heat. He'd never seen her more beautiful, and it bothered the hell out of him everyone else was getting the same eyeful.

The violet and silver of her clothing made her eyes appear to glow, in spite of the dull flatness she tried to project. Her curves spilled over her clothing, a delectable offering that no man would be able to resist.

He knocked another man out of the way as he walked down the traditional "welcome line." This one refused to take the hint so Gren was forced to take action.

Giving his anger an outlet, he grabbed the scum reaching for Temis and broke the man's wrist with a casual snap. The man's screams drew everyone's attention, and Gren dropped him without so much as a backwards glance.

One of Rorn's peacemakers approached to survey the commotion, relaxing into a smile when he noted Gren with Temis behind him. He nodded to several other guards responding to the noise and they dispersed quickly.

"Lead Rorn has been expecting you," the man said, staring boldly over Gren's shoulder. "What beauty you bring to our home." He licked his lips and Gren noted the man's obvious arousal through his skintight leggings.

Disgusted and wishing he could simply skewer the bastard with his sword, Gren nevertheless nodded dismissively and continued into the main tent.

Once past the reviewing line, he noted several naked women bound in a nearby cage. None of them appeared coherent, to their benefit, and he confirmed their drugged state with a subtle probe.

That's ten, he said to Temis. *Keep an eye out for the other five. But remember, if we don't see all of them here, they'll most likely be at the private affair after.*

He felt her agreement.

Gren? I'm just worried if we don't move fast enough, the women sold here will be gone before the private auction ends.

No. He forestalled her worry. *Purchases and transfers may be made, but no one may leave until the auction head gives leave to do so. Typically that occurs only after he or she has bid in private.*

Good, I think.

Her thoughts held a hint of humor, and he sent her an encouraging chuckle. Though clothed, he knew how hard it was for her to appear thus. And when Rorn's man, Nero, a peacemaker Temis knew, had seen her in such dress, she'd wanted to sink through the ground.

At least there's heat, he reminded to take her mind from Nero.

Yeah, it could be worse. He felt her subtly glance at the women in the cage. *At least I'm dressed.*

They continued inside the tent, noting the number of spectators present. At least four dozen men and a few female flesh peddlers mingled, sipping fine Jaron wine. Then Gren spotted Fenhal.

Speaking of worse, Temis murmured as she too saw Rorn. She drew closer to Gren, petting his arm with a docility hiding the tension within.

"Gren, how nice to see you," Rorn said with a wide smile, his attention clearly on Temis. "And how wonderful to see you too, Temis."

"I was pleasantly surprised when I received your invitation," Gren said, gauging the other man's reactions. "I was under the impression you and that bastard Sernal were good friends."

"By Flor's feet, no," Rorn protested. "I was merely playing a role. Sorry my men got a little rough back on *Lady Justice*. They were overeager to appear authentic."

"No worries." He spoke without concern even though he wanted to break Rorn's neck, but Temis' firm grip on his arm held him steady.

Rorn noted her hold and gave Gren a quizzical look.

"We've had some fun together." Gren cupped her breast, his attention focused on Rorn's accelerated breathing. "She's the best I've ever had."

Rorn licked his lips, his eyes glued to her nipples. "I can

imagine."

I bet you can, you bastard, Temis seethed while smiling vapidly, her loving gaze on Gren. *And would you mind not touching me there? I'm getting hot and bothered in front of Rorn Fenhal!*

Gren leaned down and kissed her on the mouth. *I'm sorry, but it's aggravating the hell out of Fenhal to have me touching you. Look at him.*

Temis blinked up into Rorn's sneer and smiled.

"I'm doing things a bit differently this time," Rorn said, making an effort toward pleasantness as he tore his gaze from Temis. He nodded at several guests passing by and watched Gren carefully.

"Oh?"

"I've decided to hold the private sale while the general sale progresses. None of my more important clients have issue with that since the ripest picks will be in private anyway."

Gren nodded, pleased with the outcome. The sooner he could rescue the abducted women and remove Temis from the tents, the better. "That sounds fine. Let me grab a glass of wine and we'll join you shortly. I take it the roped partition is where the private sale will be held?"

"Yes." Rorn looked back down at Temis, as if unable to help himself. "You're about to become a very rich man today, Gren."

"That's why I'm here." He couldn't help the evil grin curling his lips, feeling the lure of violence urging him to take Rorn's last breath at the earliest possibility.

"Of course." Rorn nodded pleasantly but gave him a wide berth as he left.

Nicely done, Temis mentally applauded.

I'm going to seriously hurt him before this is over. Just the way Fenhal had been eyeing Temis demanded he break several of the man's limbs.

He felt her sigh.

Now sura, *I need you to be quiet so I can concentrate,* he explained. She muttered something he couldn't understand, then quieted as he sought out the caged women.

It took valuable energy to clear their minds and plant firm instructions not to rebel. After a few tense moments they settled into a forced calm, ready to act on his or Temis' notice.

Wow. Temis' voice held a wealth of respect. *This might not be as hard as I thought.*

Don't prejudge the mission too soon. He moved with her to the private area adjoined to the main tent. There he removed her sheer silver shift from her shoulders, exposing more of her. *Showtime*, he said, and pulled open the roped curtain.

What she saw made her freeze in her tracks. He gently pushed her inside and wrapped a large hand around her waist, holding her against his side.

Remember, you belong to me and no other, he growled the warning through her mind. *And I always protect what's mine.*

Chapter Fourteen

Rorn stared through narrowed eyes as she entered the smaller tent, unable to resist peacemaker Temis Freya clad in nearly nothing. He had wanted her from the first moment he'd seen her, but nothing could have prepared him for *this*.

Ignoring the hulking barbarian at her side, he stared in awe and lust at her perfect form. She had full breasts, pert and begging to be bitten. Her stomach was tight, unmarred and snow white. And her legs ... so muscular yet so lean. He could clearly imagine them wrapped around his body while he fucked her.

"You want me to put them in your room?" Nero murmured.

"Do it."

Nero strode to the pair and escorted them toward Rorn's private "room," partitioned from the private auction by four walls of Mornian steel, allowing entrance through a doorway made of rich, blue velvet curtain.

Rorn watched as Gren nodded to Nero before disappearing with Temis beyond the velvet curtains. Rorn's exclusive viewing area, held mountains of pillows and soft fresha furs, ideal for creating sexual friction. An assortment of erotic toys and lotions sat in a corner on a small table, and Rorn had an uncomfortable walk to the room, his cock as stiff as a rock as he imagined plying Temis with his favorite toy, a rough, studded, leather whip.

He'd deliberately changed the format of this particular auction because of her. Normally he'd have watched his slaves selling on the block during the general selection, then proceeded unhurried to the private stock, where the most desirable slaves would be sold.

But he couldn't wait. Not today. He wanted to watch Temis being fucked by the monstrous mercenary at her side. He wanted to see her dominated and brutally enslaved. And he wanted her fully aware of everything, so that she would know he watched her, would know how helpless she was to stop the mercenary's cock pummeling her in every way imaginable.

Stopping for a moment, he took a breath, calming his raging erection. If he weren't careful he'd burst just thinking about it. And he wanted Temis' submission to be lengthy, a feast for the senses to be remembered for years to come.

Only after he'd watched her denigrated before him and caught it on vidstream would he take her from Gren. The merc's purpose finished, he could then be killed.

His breathing fairly even, Rorn deliberately slowed his stride and entered the blue room with a smile. He ran his hands through his thick hair, pleased at its shine in the mirrored wall he faced.

Gren stood with Temis and stared around him. Temis, he noted, stood obediently by his side, the collar around her neck stimulating in the extreme.

"I saw several beauties out there," Gren interrupted his thoughts. "Am I to miss their sale as well as that of the general trade?"

"No, no," Rorn hastened to assure him, not liking the man's look. The hard sheen in Gren's eyes made Rorn distinctly uncomfortable, especially since he'd left his guards outside the small room. He mentally shook off his discomfort. Not even a mercenary with Gren's reputation would think to attack a man as powerful as Rorn Fenhal, and if he did, the phaser tucked in Rorn's back would end that.

Glancing around at his own opulence, awash in the grandeur of his reputation, Rorn recalled the many slaves he'd pleasured in here and knew Temis would be the one he'd never forget. He stared at her, his mouth curiously wet, and licked his lips.

"Well, Fenhal? Let's get to it. How do you want to proceed?"

Apparently Gren was familiar with the auction, for he waited on Rorn--the auction master, to begin the trade.

"First you'll show me what I'm getting." Rorn waited for Temis to disrobe. His cock was impossibly sensitive, and he wanted to feel Temis' mouth on him as she cried for mercy.

Gren eyed him dispassionately and rubbed his scarred hand along her abdomen. Temis moaned and closed her eyes, swaying seductively against the larger man. Yet Gren appeared completely unmoved. Was the man made of stone?

"After that, what then?" Gren asked in a flat tone of voice.

Rorn was beginning to grow irritated. He wanted to see passion, rage, the unnatural fierceness for which the mercenary was famous. And he wanted it turned on Temis. "I want you to fuck her," Rorn ordered in precise words. His eyes narrowed at Gren's surprise. "Hard. Take her violently. Be as rough as you like, but don't leave any lasting scars."

He turned to the vidscreen but Gren stopped him.

"I'll do it, but not for an electronic audience." His voice was firm. "A recording of such an event would be disastrous in the wrong hands. Besides, if I'm reading you correctly, you plan on keeping Temis for yourself. Once I'm through with her, you'll have her for as long as you want her. That's got to be worth more than vidscreen memories." Gren paused, his eyes narrowed with displeasure.

Finally, a small sign of emotion. But the man's next words made Rorn long for a sharp blade with which to remove Gren's tongue.

"Or is it me you wished to remember without my clothes?"

Rorn glared but wisely remained silent. Nothing would mar this day. He would skewer Gren, *after* witnessing his ultimate fantasy. "Of course not. It's the woman I lust for." *You imbecile.* "I'll disconnect the vidscreen. Now stop talking and start fucking. And like I said, take her hard. Make her fight you."

* * * *

Are you ready for this? Gren asked, toying with the back of Temis' top. He could feel her disgust for Rorn, knew how much she loathed letting the man see her like this. *It'll just be for a minute before I end his miserable life.*

No. You can't, she answered quickly. *Sernal wants him alive.*

"I'm getting tired of waiting." Rorn stared suspiciously at them, and Gren knew he needed to act. Fine. He'd let Rorn have a taste of his fantasy, just enough to let down his guard.

Already the peacemaker looked on edge, his face flushed and his breath coming in pants. Gren could see Rorn inching his hand toward his cock, as if waiting for just the right moment to touch himself.

"Perhaps you would rather be the one to rape her?" Gren offered. He felt Temis' incredulity but ignored her.

"I said I wanted to watch. I'll get to her soon enough. Why, Gren?" Rorn asked softly, the cold businessman back in charge. "What's really the problem here?"

Rorn looked behind him at the curtained entrance, as if gauging how fast reinforcements might arrive.

Cursing silently, Gren forced a smirk. "My mistake. If you want me to fuck her again, it's really no problem. Though I can't promise rape. She's hot under that icy exterior, and she likes it big." He gave Rorn's crotch a dubious look, pleased when the man's eyes blazed. Satisfied for the moment, he turned to Temis. "Temis, disrobe, slowly."

He studied Rorn watching Temis, knowing the moment she discarded her top because Rorn's mouth gaped and his eyes widened. Gren glanced at Temis and strove to remain distanced from the situation. Her breasts were full and pert, and it was all he could do not to bend down and suckle the ripe fruits until she came.

She flushed, caught in the mental fantasy he sent her, and Rorn began breathing even heavier, his hand now tight over his groin. At Gren's mental urging, Temis ran her hands over her breasts and belly, then toyed with her bottoms, allowing small glimpses of her blonde curls to peek through her garment before sliding it down her long legs.

Rorn stared unblinkingly at Temis, almost where Gren wanted him.

Dance around him, tease him. Keep distracting the hell out of him so I can break his neck, he growled.

No! She gyrated, making him want to love her regardless of Rorn's filthy presence. *Don't worry, Gren, he'll pay for his crimes. Now watch and learn*, she mocked, getting into the spirit of her role.

Like an exotic pleasurer, she danced around Rorn, swaying toward him, then backing away when he would have reached for her. On and on she moved, giving Gren the time and room to maneuver around the bastard.

He watched Fenhal reach into his trousers and begin to stroke himself. Hell, Gren could feel his own arousal growing as Temis teased and wriggled around him. A man would have to be a eunuch not to respond.

"I want you to fuck her," Rorn said on a strangled breath. "Do it now. Make her scream for mercy," he panted, his hand quickening inside his trousers.

"Scream for mercy, I like that," Gren said in a low voice. He lashed out with his boot, making contact with the center of Rorn's neck.

Rorn collapsed without a word, hitting the ground with a soft thump, cushioned by the many pillows surrounding them.

Now start moaning, Gren told her as he tied and gagged the crumpled peacemaker, burying him under several furs.

"Moaning?" Temis frowned and hugged her chest. "I'm supposed to be getting *raped,* not to mention I'm freezing."

He sighed and narrowed his gaze, directing a burst of energy to her core.

She cried out and sagged to the ground, on her knees and arching back, her breasts thrust into the air while he mentally stimulated her.

Had they the time and the right location, he wouldn't have hesitated to join her. But right now he needed to reach out to the others.

He continued her pleasure, adding a few grunts of his own should Rorn's guards be listening. And while he continued the farce of lovemaking, he mentally connected with the women caged in the large tent.

Except for some heavy fondling and probing, humiliating but not physically harmful, the women had yet to be sold. He ignored their distress, a difficult but not impossible job, and decided to make a full circle around the private auction. Nero had guided them into the blue room before he'd had a chance to survey the area.

Temis, listen to me. He paused her bliss to inject the order. *I have to make sure the others are here. Keep up the pretense until I return. Use Rorn's phaser if you need protection.*

Breathing heavily, she glared at him from under a wealth of golden hair, looking incredibly sensual. *I told you I can defend myself. And when this is over, we're going to have a long talk about taking advantage….* She stopped arguing at the next burst of pleasure spiraling through her.

He left her with a quick kiss, absorbing a large amount of sexual energy from her satisfied body. *Stay safe,* sura. *I need to focus on the others now. But call if you need me.*

He hated having to leave her, but he needed to secure the others before their back-up arrived. Using the energy he'd gained from Temis, he contacted Lurin, grateful the Thesha had thought to position his ship near Jaron, making communication easier.

Sounding relieved to hear from him, Lurin immediately answered. *Catam says Sernal has landed, and is within sight of Rorn's estate. How many enemy are there?*

At least fifty slavers, and another half that in security. How long until Sernal's here, exactly?

Lurin paused. *Twenty minutes, give or take.*

Tell them to make it sooner while I distract the guards.

No, Gren. Sernal specifically told us to make sure you waited for his signal.

Thanks, Lurin. Gren cut the communications. He'd be damned if he'd allow any more contact between the helpless women and the slavers. Despite that none had yet been harmed, he could feel their unease, their degradation pulsing like a disease. And every breath he took under these hated tents made him want to choke. The negative energy generated under these tents over the years lingered, making him almost sick.

Taking a deep breath, he pushed aside the curtains and surprised the two guards waiting outside.

Gren held up his hands. "I was ordered out." He heard Temis moan loudly again and grinned. "Apparently Rorn wants her to himself, to test the merchandise."

The guards were uneasy but nodded.

"And he said he was to remain undisturbed until he called for anyone. Otherwise he'll be very displeased."

They looked nervous as they nodded their understanding.

Gren strolled away casually, projecting a pleased image when he really wanted to smash someone, to release the tension building inside him. Not to mention Temis was all alone in that room without a stitch of clothing.

I put the rags back on. I can moan fully clothed you know, she said with disgust.

His heart lightened at her pique. Content Temis was fully aware of the situation even if extremely irritated with him, he made mental contact with the last five women on his list. He didn't note any additions, and breathed easier when he saw the limited amount of "clients" under the smaller tent.

He noted two disreputable leaders of organized crime on Melan, a few Afleran traitors, and a legendary smuggler and cutthroat from Ragga named Abjon. He would definitely be the one to watch. The dozen or so other participants didn't look worthy of Gren's concern.

A crowd was gathering around the center stage of the private auction, where the bidding was to begin. Gren counted six guards stationed around the perimeter of the area, plus the two in front of Rorn's room, and wished he'd brought his sword. But he knew Rorn would have the technology to ferret hidden weapons, and he'd earlier relinquished two decoy throwaway blades to Rorn's men without a qualm.

Gren didn't need a weapon to hinder Rorn's guards. He had two hands aching for the challenge. His blood heated, similarly as it did when around Temis, and he felt her respond, her pleasure still pulsing in him.

The energy she'd given him had yet to dissipate, and the build-up was just what he needed to debilitate Fenhal's men.

He glanced at the center stage and did a double-take at the sight before him. He felt for the women, but couldn't have asked for a better distraction.

Two of the slaves had disrobed and were touching each other at the behest of Nero, another minor obstacle Gren would need to overcome.

Moans and groans of approval from the small crowd grew louder and naturally the guards' attention wandered.

Gren easily knocked unconscious two of the furthest from the stage and quickly took their weapons. He left them slumped against one another and walked quickly to the next nearest pair, who happened to be guarding Rorn's private room. With a well-aimed phaser, Gren zapped them both, then fired upon two more, eliminating them as a threat.

His actions finally noticed, the crowd around the stage shouted angrily for help, drawing the remaining security.

Moving in a blur, Gren rolled to avoid a blast from Nero's laser and cut the man down. Then he aimed several pulses at the remaining guards and came to his feet, knowing it wouldn't be long before the outer guards checked on the commotion.

"What are you doing?" Abjon snarled, surprising Gren with a mighty blow to his abdomen.

Lifted violently from the ground, Gren gasped and landed hard on his back, rolling to avoid Abjon's follow-through stomp to the throat. He'd lost his phasers upon landing, and glanced hurriedly to see where they'd flown.

* * * *

"Like I'm going to moan in here all day while he has all the fun," Temis growled, waiting a few moments after Gren made contact with the women before leaving the tent.

She wore only her slave garments and hoped to use the lack of material to her advantage. Instead of distracting Rorn's guards with her beauty, however, she found them passed out on the ground.

Narrowing her gaze, she found Gren silently creeping around, disabling security while the crowd was distracted by ... she blushed bright red seeing the women so engaged on stage.

"By Narok's breast, is that the senator's daughter on her knees kissing--" she paused the thought, shaking her head. She had better things to do than ogle such a graphic display.

Seeing that all hell was about to break loose, she quickly neared the three remaining women, naked and caged on the side of the stage, obscured by a curtained partition unseen by the spectators.

Gren, I need your help here, she communicated at the same time she felt extreme pain around her stomach. She gasped and the pain vanished.

The crowd quieted as someone grunted, then they began shouting encouragement to someone named Abjon. From her vantage she saw the back of a large man, most likely a Ragga with his height, standing over someone.

With a knot in her belly, she imagined that someone to be Gren.

I've released the women from their drugged haze. Take them through the house to the southernmost window, like we discussed earlier. Sernal should be in place by now.

She saw the Ragga lift Gren and throw him ten feet, and she flinched when he made contact with the unforgiving ground.

Hurry up! He sounded pained. *You're distracting me while I'm supposed to be distracting all of them.*

The crowd roared its approval of the fight, pleased at the added entertainment. She heard Gren growl something insulting at the Ragga, who gave a bloodcurdling war cry before lunging at Gren.

Convincing herself he could take care of himself, Temis deftly opened the unlocked the cage and motioned the women to exit. Whispering to the women on stage to follow suit, she turned to encounter two salivating men who had decided to use the crowd's distraction to their advantage.

"I don't have time for this," she muttered and struck at the nearest fool. With his eyes fixed on her breasts, he wasn't prepared for the kick to his face. His partner cursed in astonishment before suffering the same fate.

"Come on, ladies," she said through clenched teeth. "We don't have much time."

Apparently Gren's compulsion made them follow her orders to the letter, for they moved quickly and without question.

As she entered the house, with a grudging thanks to Cherel's knowledge of Rorn's estate, she heard more shouts and phaser fire exchanged. Please, she prayed, let that be back-up arriving.

She raced to the extraction point bypassing several startled servants. All of Rorn's security had apparently been used for the slave auction, for she encountered no trouble on the bottom floor of his mansion.

When she reached the southernmost window she found it open and shivered at the cold breeze infiltrating the house.

"Temis?" came a tentative call from just outside.

She poked her head out and saw Rafe peering at her from atop a nearby tree. When he saw her, he visibly relaxed and slid to the ground. He motioned to his men and entered through the window with two dozen peacemakers.

Seeing her in next to nothing, he had the gall to softly whistle, then handed her a green jumper that she hastily donned.

"You can stop ogling me now," she said dryly, aware that while she dressed, other guards were similarly clothing the women with her. "We have to go back in for Gren."

"Squad one, secure the women and shuttle them out of here. The rest of you come with us." Rafe handed her a pair of boots and her phaser, then followed her through the now empty hallways.

The floor echoed ominously as they ran back outside into the heated slave tent.

"Where did everyone go?" Rafe asked, puzzled.

The crowd had disappeared, as had the disabled guards. She and the others searched the small tent. Nothing. Feeling hollow in her gut, she raced to Rorn's blue room.

Rorn had also disappeared.

"Damn it."

Gren was nowhere to be seen when she and the others swept through the smaller tent into the main tent. There she spied more women being covered and protected while Sernal and his men arrested the masses trying to escape.

"Peacemakers, fan the perimeter," Rafe yelled.

While they secured the area, Temis searched for Rorn and Gren.

Gren? Where are you? Her question met with silence and she grew more worried.

Sernal motioned for Rafe and her to approach. "Listen to this." He didn't look happy as he held the man whose wrist Gren had broken, shaking him for information.

"Like I was telling you, right before you guys showed up this monster Ragga burst through the tent there." He pointed to the large hole in the fabric separating the general sale from the private sale. "He threw that mercenary piece of shit around like he was a doll." The man cradled his wrist and grinned before his face soured. "Then the merc bastard drew blood. I don't know how, but he really hurt the Ragga."

Temis exhaled a deep breath.

"And what else?" Sernal shook the little man, his eyes a promise of retribution.

"Th-then Lord Fenhal followed looking more angry than I've ever seen him. The three of them disappeared into the house through that doorway." He pointed at a faraway door made of broken glass. "Then you assholes showed up and ruined everything."

Sernal yanked him by the collar and shoved him toward one of his men. "Secure this offal with the rest."

He turned to Temis, his golden eyes blazing. "Why didn't you wait for back-up?"

Gren must have been rubbing off on her. Before meeting him, she would have felt nervous under Sernal's thunderous anger. Instead she shot back, "I would have waited, but the mercenary *you* chose decided to do things his way."

She gave Sernal a mutinous glare, worried and angry that Sernal was admonishing her when they should be looking for Gren.

He stared at her, nonplussed. Rafe, however, chuckled. "I told you, brother. He's gotten to her." She scowled at Rafe who held his hands up in mock surrender.

"Why don't we find Gren and then you can interrogate him yourself?" Rafe suggested, to which both Sernal and Temis answered.

"Agreed."

Chapter Fifteen

"I've heard of you," Abjon said as he swung a meaty fist toward Gren's face.

His ribs throbbing, his face bloodied and his shoulder most likely dislocated, Gren used the pain to enhance his reflexes and narrowly avoided another blow to his cheek. Recoiling from the larger man's lunge, Gren leapt to the side and leaned low, kicking at Abjon's knees.

He made contact and the Ragga hit hard, knocking a priceless vase from a nearby table. A murderous curse rent the air and both Abjon and Gren glanced back to see Rorn standing behind them in the mansion's overlarge reading room with a phaser in each hand.

"You," Abjon roared, regaining his feet with graceful ease, a curious motion from one so large. "You promised security for this ambitious trade. And now the woman that should rightfully be mine is out there with Mardu peacemakers!"

Rorn didn't waver, his expression grim as he stared loathingly at both men. "It's not my fault I stole Seriana before you could. Besides, if you really want to blame someone, blame the *drun* next to you. I didn't invite the peacemakers to my party, but I'd be willing to bet he did."

Abjon stared at Gren in surprise, his orange eyes pulsing with a strange light. "You're telling me a mercenary with more murders and thefts on his plate than most of the criminals out there, *this man*, is a peacemaker?"

"No, not a peacemaker," Rorn spat and closed the distance between himself and the combatants. "I suspect he turned to bail himself out of trouble."

Sensing the rage building in the Ragga, the more dangerous of the two despite Rorn's phasers, Gren quickly improvised. "Actually, Rorn, I don't know how the peacemakers arrived when they did. I admit I knocked you out, for the sole purpose of keeping Temis and your beks." He shrugged, mindful of his ribs and shoulder. "Though I have to say your security really is lacking. I took out nearly all of your interior guards myself. And you call yourself a professional?"

A muscle in Rorn's cheek started twitching. "I've had it with you, Gren. You ruined what should have been perfection. I know you brought the peacemakers to my home, my sanctuary." His voice grew rougher, the man's pristine uniform dirtied and his once perfect hair in disarray. "If I can't have Temis, then neither can you."

A sudden burst of weapon fire tore one of the phasers from Rorn's hands. Gren rolled for cover by one of the overlarge settees and saw out of the corner of his eye Abjon do the same a few feet away.

Phaser blasts exploded while the thunder of booted feet raced through the room, the occupants of said boots firing on anything that moved. Unfortunately, Gren couldn't tell if the fire was friendly or enemy.

"This isn't over," Abjon rasped, a hint of blood pouring between his fingers clutching at his neck. "You're going to pay for this. You and the peacemaker." Then in an astonishing burst of speed and strength, the Ragga sprinted for a nearby glass door leading to the outside. He broke through the thick panes, rolling to his feet and continuing his stride into the frozen forest surroundings.

"Stupid bastard," Rorn muttered from beyond Gren's cover and began firing at Gren, shredding the expensive settee.

Unlike the phaser Gren had set to stun, Rorn's was set to kill, as evidenced by the massive black burns left scorching in the blast's wake. Gren couldn't risk being hit, but he needed to find Temis with an intensity that made it increasingly hard to function.

Needing to keep his pain from affecting her, he'd been forced to shield himself. It was maddening to know she was out there and possibly in harm's way. But he knew Temis could take care of herself, much as he didn't want to admit it. And he had to finish Rorn before the man escaped to do more damage to the innocents of the system. Gren would just have to believe in Temis, both for her sake and his own.

"You couldn't share, could you, Gren?" Rorn's voice was raspy, his control all but shot. "All week you had her on her knees, begging you to let her go. I know you fucked her in every way imaginable. Who wouldn't, in your position? But you just couldn't give her up. I would have paid you thousands, you know."

Rorn fired again, this time coming close to taking the top of Gren's head. Gren glanced under the rubble of settee and saw Rorn's feet nearing. The massive firing that had previously interrupted Rorn had faded into the background, coming now from somewhere outside this room. If Gren didn't move quickly, he wouldn't live to see tomorrow.

Just as he was about to send Rorn to his grave with a series of complicated moves learned on Zephyr, he heard Temis.

"Gren?"

Rorn shifted several feet away, facing the direction of the front entranceway. Damn it!

"Temis, do step closer. No, no, my little slave, drop your weapon or I'll kill you where you stand, and your clumsy oaf of a lover as well." Gren couldn't see Rorn's hands and had no idea if the other man bluffed or had actually regained the second phaser.

Apparently he had for Temis sighed and tossed her phaser to the ground in a clatter.

What are you doing? he fairly shouted, trying desperately to stave the pain while communicating. *Why didn't you shoot the* drun?

He heard her gasp and drew in on himself, making a mental note to hunt down Abjon and return his myriad breaks and bruises to the Ragga's body.

"What's the matter, Temis?" Rorn asked snidely, walking toward her. "Embarrassed to admit you liked feeling his cock inside you? Did you really think I wouldn't eventually discover your feigned submission, the lack of needle marks on your arms and legs? You were never drugged, just a dirty little whore playing the mercenary to make me jealous."

Rorn had lost his mind altogether. Gren took the opportunity to roll quickly away from the settee, in full view of Rorn and Temis, and stood on steady feet, his anger boosting his reserves.

"There you are, Gren." Rorn smiled, his eyes shining with madness. "I wanted so badly to kill you after you lived out my fantasies with Temis. But you wouldn't do it. Now I think I'll live out my fantasies with *you* watching. What do you think?"

He shared his gaze between Gren and Temis while he steadily stalked her. Temis stood frozen, not in fear, but in concentration. Gren could see the lack of trepidation in her gaze. If anything, she looked angry as she glared past Rorn at him, as if *he'd* done something wrong.

Knowing Rorn planned to rape Temis and force him to watch, he moved one step closer to Rorn, one step closer to ending the bastard's miserable life. Did Rorn really think Gren would allow him to rape Temis? Or that he could rape her now, with peacemakers and slavers running amuck on his estate? At any moment Gren expected to see a squad of lawmen running through the door.

Instead, out of the corner of his eye he saw Rafe sliding quietly into the room. Now confident Rafe could take Fenhal down should the need arise, something in him relaxed.

"I'll bet you fifty beks you can't rape her." Gren folded his arms and stood nonchalantly as he challenged Rorn.

Rorn blinked and paused, now standing right behind Temis. "What did you say?"

"Make it a hundred beks. There's no way you can rape that woman."

Rorn shoved one of his phasers into the small of his back and stepped to the side. He opened the fly of his trousers, exposing a raging erection. "I can do all sorts of things with this," he hissed and held the phaser to Temis' temple, rubbing himself against her jumpsuit.

"But you should see what I can do with this," Temis said softly as she butted the back of her head into his face while simultaneously grabbing the phaser aimed at her head.

The phaser went off and Gren's heart leapt into his throat. Luckily Rorn's shot fired into the wall, barely missing Temis. Just as Gren reached her, she threw her elbow back into Rorn's stomach and pushed away, turning to fire as she did so.

Before her phaser tagged him, however, Rafe had his hand around Rorn's throat, choking him unconscious, before securing the criminal's hands at the small of his back. The Mardu moved so quickly Gren had missed his movements altogether.

"Didn't I tell you not to leave my side, partner?" Rafe asked Temis calmly, his eyes glowing with reproach.

Temis had the grace to look shamefaced. "I know, but, well, I meant to stay with you. The confusion, the phaser fire--"

Rafe sighed with disgust. "Forget it. Just help the stupid merc sit before he falls down. I swear, one week with the man and you're useless with orders," he muttered, dragging Rorn from the room.

Temis hurried to Gren's side, staring at the hardened set to his features. The left side of his face had swelled, his lips bloodied and his cheek already sporting a darkening bruise. By the way he breathed, shallowly, she knew he'd injured his ribs. And something else about his posture made her think of broken bones.

"What the hell were you thinking?" she shouted her worry. Shaking with anger, she nevertheless wormed her way under the shoulder that didn't tense when she touched it, and led him to a nearby couch.

He sat gingerly and she couldn't help touching his injured cheek with gentle fingers.

"Why didn't you answer me when I called to you?" The silence had been deafening. After sharing her thoughts with the Thesha, unusual though it was, she'd gotten used to being a part of him. When he'd limited her access and then detached that special part of himself, she thought she'd go crazy with worry.

"I thought I'd lost you when you wouldn't answer."

Gren sighed and kissed her with tender lips. "I'm sorry, *sura*," he said with a groan. "But I didn't want you to feel my pain. I knew it would distract you. You did get the women away safely, didn't you?"

She nodded. "They're all accounted for, the slavers rounded up as we speak. I should warn you Sernal's not very happy with you."

He cursed soundly and she grinned. He had a creative streak on par with hers. "I couldn't let the women continue to suffer," he said stiffly. "Their pain hounded me."

"But they were drugged and ignorant of their surroundings." Temis didn't understand.

"Yes, but their spirits felt the abuse. Their pain gnawed at me, Temis. And the dark energy under that tent, it was like a plague. Harm toward women is something my kind cannot tolerate. Especially when inflicted on the innocent."

She stared at him, aware she once again had to face his alien nature with eyes wide open. Communicating mentally hadn't truly bothered her. Telepaths did it all the time and though not common, she'd run into her fair share. But reminders of Gren's Thesha heritage heightened the tension between them.

She still felt in awe of his gifts, that she sat next to a man thought more legend than real. But as she looked at his marred face and injured body, she couldn't help seeing the man beneath the myth.

"Let's get out of here. You need a medtech and I need a break." She sighed. "I don't ever want to look at another slave auction for as long as I live. And I'm not up for more of Sernal's lectures."

He groaned and stood with her, nodding his agreement. To their consternation, Sernal met them at the doorway with a dark scowl.

"You two come with me. I'll personally escort you back to *Lady Justice*. I've got a few things on my mind."

"Just a few?" Gren gave Sernal an arrogant quirk of his eyebrow that set Sernal's temper aflame. Binding Gren's hands behind his back, and none too gently, Sernal escorted Gren to his ship with Temis trailing behind.

"Good idea," Gren grumbled as he was dragged to Sernal's ship, every hard step agony to his ribs. "Torturing me in front of everyone will cement my cover as a slaver. I truly appreciate your consideration," he added in an all-too-polite voice.

The peacemakers around them gave the trio a wide berth as they strode toward the shuttle. Sernal glared at Gren and Temis, not amused, though his actions did provide Gren with a measure of safety. No one seeing Gren bound would believe him in league with the peacemakers.

Gren's sarcasm did at least cause Sernal to ease his grip on Gren's arm. The lawman guided him into the shuttle instead of throwing him into a seat. As soon as Sernal set the ship on autopilot, he turned to Gren and Temis with a scowl.

It was a long ride to *Lady Justice*.

* * * *

Once Temis had left them with an excuse to begin her operational reports, Sernal took a deep breath and turned to Gren.

"You look like shit," he said bluntly, eyeing the large man's injuries. "What the hell happened? And why didn't you wait?" he asked, his voice increasing in volume.

Gren cringed and cupped his tender jaw. "Take it easy, Mardu. I'll explain as soon as you pour me a drink."

Knowing he wouldn't get any answers out of Gren until the mercenary was ready to talk, Sernal muttered under his breath and brought Gren a cup of sweetened shusha wine.

"This is one fine cabin you've got, captain," Gren said with a grin, then winced as the acidic juice hit his lip. "Look, Sernal, I couldn't wait any longer to help the women or I'd have been useless. Their pain weakened me," he said bluntly.

Sernal's eyes widened as he suddenly understood. "Oh. Well, in that case, I understand why you had to move when you did. But did it occur to you to explain this to me earlier this morning, when you did your initial survey?"

"I thought it might bother me, but it's been so long since I've been to an auction I'd forgotten."

Sernal nodded, familiar with Gren's repulsion for the flesh trade, if not for the exact reason why beyond the obvious. "You're lucky it worked out for the best."

"Lucky? Hell no. Temis made everything work smoothly." He smiled, his pride shining through the clear affection in his eyes.

Sernal blinked, not sure to believe what he saw in the Thesha's eyes. "So, ah, who gave you the bruises?"

The loving glow faded and Gren scowled. "Abjon, the bastard. By the way, he was there for a woman named Seriana. I'd advise you to put some protection out for her." He rubbed at his sore ribs. "The Ragga scum ought to be hanged for being so damned stubborn," he muttered, "and strong."

Sernal shook his head. "From initial reports, of the fifteen women rescued, only fourteen made it back to the ship. Apparently one disappeared."

"Seriana."

He nodded. "I've put out a search but I doubt we'll find anything. Our hands are full as it is with the capture of so

many slavers. This is the biggest arrest we've had in years."
Sernal grinned, absurdly pleased the slave trade had taken a
huge hit. "I hate to say it, but thank you."

Gren nodded, his arrogance in place as surely as the
bruises on his face.

"But on another note," Sernal's voice deepened, authority
at the ready, "what the hell did you think you were doing
enthralling my peacemaker?" He deliberately poked Gren
in the ribs, grateful for the man's low groan. "I trusted you
to be on your best behavior."

"It wasn't my fault." As soon as he said the words, Gren
flushed. "It was, but there's more to it than a simple
enthrallment."

Sernal nodded. He'd seen similar lovesick expressions on
both Lurin and his brothers' faces when they'd fallen in
love with their wives. "You've bonded, I take it. I should
have known. Leave it to you to snag the most beautiful and
talented peacemaker we've ever had."

Gren tried to shrug and groaned again. "Sorry. Some
things are beyond wishes and wills."

"But does Temis understand what and who you are?"

Gren nodded.

Surprised, Sernal stared at him. "So she's fine leaving the
peacemakers to make her life with you wandering the
system?"

Gren grimaced, and Sernal knew it wasn't due to the pain.

"So, you haven't told her what she'll be giving up to
come live with you."

"It's been a long day, Sernal." Gren stood without help,
his face pale. "I need to heal, *without* a medtech, if you
don't mind."

Sernal knew Gren would heal better on his own.

"But I'd appreciate it if you could give Temis some time
off? Say a week to return to Zephyr for a much-needed
homecoming?"

"No problem. Have her give Rafe a statement." He
smirked, glad of the power he held over his annoying
younger brother. The operational report for this assignment
would be extremely detailed and obscenely lengthy. "I'll
have him record it to vid." Then he grew serious, his
concern for Temis at the forefront of his mind. "Be sure,
Gren, be *very sure* that Temis makes her decisions on her

own. If you try to force the issue, you'll only make yourself miserable in the long run."

Gren said nothing but left with a frustrated frown, walking stiffly from the room.

Sernal poured himself a glass of wine and contemplated the operation. With Rorn under arrest, the capture of more than fifty slavers attributed to his people, and Temis once again safely aboard, he officially declared his mission a success.

He sighed and rubbed the tension from his neck. Perhaps once he had the situation dealt with, he'd take a trip to Aflera. Hadn't Gren mentioned Jahnja was the perfect pleasurer?

The door buzzed and he checked the small vidfinder by the doorway. Smiling, he admitted Rafe.

"Why are you looking at me like that?" Rafe asked, suspicious.

"Weren't you just the other day complaining about our rookies and their reports?"

"Yes, but--"

"Do I have a job for you."

Chapter Sixteen

Gren walked stiffly toward Temis' room, not in the mood for any more theatrics. Damn, but that Ragga Abjon had thrown him all over the place. He scowled at the peacemakers he passed, pleased when they shied away from him. Now, if only the blonde peacemaker he'd bonded with would show him some proper respect....

He knocked at her door, irritated he didn't have the keycode to enter. She buzzed him inside and he entered slowly, looking immediately to the large bed in the center of the room.

At this point he wanted nothing more than to make love with Temis, followed by a restful night's sleep. But how best to make her come to him?

He decided to ignore Temis staring at him and sank with a loud groan into her bed. Perhaps sympathy would garner some attention?

He took a breath and lay back, unable to keep from groaning again.

"Wait just a minute," Temis said and stood over him, her arms akimbo. "You haven't seen a medtech, have you?"

"Not now, *sura*. Please, no more lectures. My skull is splitting apart and my ribs are killing me." He spoke the truth with just a hint of exaggeration. "I just need some time to rest." *And a warm women to love.*

"What you need is a medtech." She looked worried. That he thought to sleep here, or for his well-being? She'd erected her mental shields the moment they'd boarded the ship, and he was in no condition to challenge her. With the exception of her stronger emotions, he could read nothing.

"Actually no. What I need is time for my body to heal itself." He paused, hoping she wouldn't be difficult about this. "Would you mind sleeping beside me?"

She stared at him in confusion. "Are you sure you don't need a medtech?"

He sighed. "I'm Thesha, Temis. My body heals itself, more quickly when I have energy at my disposal." He eyed her up and down, giving her no doubt as to what he needed.

She flushed and her eyes narrowed. "You've got to be kidding me. You can't even sit up on your own. How are you going to make love?"

"In the astral state my physical body is not a burden." He waited for her understanding, and seeing it, took a chance. "Never mind. It's too much to ask of you after such a difficult mission."

"What?"

She looked irritated, and he couldn't help wanting to hold her again, to soothe the confusion and longing and desire he felt troubling her.

"Nothing. If you'll help me sit up, I'll move to an empty cabin. And if you could trouble one of the females to come to me, peacemaker Toulsa seemed attractive, I'll take care of my needs. Don't worry, I won't hurt her and she won't remember a thing."

Her eyes widened, their smoky gray color disappearing under the heated purple growing dark. Taking a subtle measure of her emotions, he felt smothered with her anxious jealousy.

He worked hard to stifle a pleased smile, keeping his expression slightly pained and oblivious to her dismay.

Temis, however, had no problem speaking her mind. "Toulsa? That plain-faced, inexperienced rookie?" She paced before the bed, delightfully riled.

"Now, Temis, you need to rest--"

She cursed for nearly half a minute, stunning him to silence. "I'm fine!" She flounced on the bed next to him and immediately closed her eyes. "Toulsa, ha." He felt her energy trembling with anticipation even as her anger swelled. "Go to sleep," she grumbled, reaching out to his bruised hand. She held him tenderly, her fingers running along his scar.

Despite his injuries, his blood raced, and he took a deep and even breath, looking forward to his dreams.

* * * *

Temis pushed through the darkness of sleep and found herself in a dream, and in the last place she and Gren had fought while asleep.

She stared around her in bemusement, curious as to the memory that caused such a vision. The wide, dirt fighting ring was obviously manmade, the forest surrounding her full and lively. The sweet smell of ripe fruit and flower blossoms carried on a cooling yet comfortable breeze.

To her left sat the inviting pool of blue-green water she recalled from her last visit. She bent and trailed a hand through it, and gasped at the thrill that shot through her.

"It's kay'en water newly released from the underground springs," Gren said in a deep voice, coming up behind her. She stared at his handsome reflection in the pool, not sure whether she should feel annoyed or intrigued that she'd brought him here. Obviously he'd tampered with her mind to bring her to this place.

"Explain this." She stood, turning to face him, and waited silently.

He smiled, a wicked grin that caused her heart to flutter and her loins to quicken. "This is a fighting ring common to my native world. None but my people, and you, have ever stepped foot here." He looked up at the sky and sighed. "Our moons never fail to amaze me with their beauty." Three full orbs glowed with pale pink light in a darkening blue-gray sky, a few scattered and thinning clouds lining the horizon.

"It is beautiful," she agreed, thinking this place suited him. Wild and mysterious and filled with magic. "But why have you brought me here?"

He stared at her in surprise, his naked chest gleaming under the moonlight. "I did not bring us here. You did." His voice deepened as he looked over her. "But I have no complaint with this arena, nor the clothes you chose to wear."

Bemused, she glanced down to see her peacemaker uniform gone, replaced by a skimpy two-piece silk set that left little to the imagination. She could feel Gren's gaze like a caress and her nipples hardened.

He took a step toward her, the straining erection in his trousers obvious. Then he stopped and pulled off his clothing, standing before her proud and unashamedly aroused.

His skin glowed, not bruised or beaten, but with a preternatural vitality. And as she stared at him, she swallowed around the desire building in her.

"What is it you want, *sura*?" he asked, his voice thick. His eyes glowed and he took a deep breath, closing his eyes in pleasure. "Your body wants mine, but what of your mind, your heart?" he murmured and opened his eyes, closing the distance between them.

Temis honestly didn't know. She could only feel, her mind lost to the erotic sensation of being near him. Like a magnet he drew her easily, until she brushed her body against him, reveling in his sensuality.

He growled low in his throat, his stare piercing as he looked deeply into her eyes. "You know what you want, Temis. You have only to accept yourself, then you and I will never be apart."

Before she could say anything, he kissed her, stealing her very breath. Colors and lights danced beneath her closed lids, and she felt him all the way to her bones. Desire roared through her blood as his hands caressed her torso, stroking her back and cupping her buttocks closer, so that she felt every nuance of his erection against her naked belly.

He rubbed against her, deepening his kiss. She moaned when his mouth left hers, then sighed as his lips sucked and nipped at her throat, as if sucking her will to keep even the smallest part of herself away from him.

"Gren," she gasped as his hands slid between their bodies to encircle her breasts.

"*Sura*, you are so incredibly loving," he whispered as he bent to lick the slope of her breast. His tongue trailed over the thin material of her top, the sensation of wet heat and soft silk an arousing friction.

She arched into his mouth, bursting with pleasure when his mouth latched onto her nipple. His teeth bit, drawing the taut peak further into his mouth, and when he began sucking on her, she thought she would never escape the torturous pleasure.

Her insides wept for him, her clitoris throbbing with dangerous need.

"Please," she gasped. "I need you, Gren." His mouth shifted to pleasure her other breast and she thought she would die. She could feel his arousal straining against her thigh and wanted him deep within her.

With slow hands he disrobed her, his touch everywhere and nowhere near close enough.

After removing her bottoms he rose to his feet and stared deeply into her eyes. "But what exactly do you need, *sura*?" he asked seductively, his eyes glinting with desire. In a sudden move, he picked her up in his arms and walked into the pool of water behind her.

She gasped as heat infused her body, ribbons of energy mixing with the fevered desire already pulsing through her system.

"Yes," he groaned and stopped once the water hit him mid-chest. He pushed her against the wall of the pool, a surprisingly flat and smooth surface. "Tell me what you want from me. I'll give you anything you desire," he promised, aligning his groin to hers.

She closed her eyes when she felt the head of his shaft pressing against her sensitive folds, prodding gently until he reached her pulsing clit. "I--" She cried out in ecstasy as he thrust deep into her womb and stayed there.

"Tell me," he demanded, remaining full, his thick presence a heady reminder of his strength, of the power that resided within him.

He sent a burst of energy through her, a blast of pure heat that made her come around him, squeezing him with her inner walls.

She heard him groan her name but he didn't move, merely grew bigger as she released.

Her orgasm continued, growing stronger and stronger until she came to another place, a world full of light that glowed around Gren's smiling face.

I am in you, sura, *now and forever. I will never let you go, never let you hurt or want for anything,* he pledged, the tender look of love shining in his eyes.

Words failed her as she saw what she'd been trying to deny to herself. The love radiated from him clearly, so bright and pure she could only bask in its richness.

In this timeless place she saw herself reflected in his thoughts and memories. A strong warrior, a beautiful woman, a caring protector of the innocent who didn't know how to turn against what she knew was right.

She stared in astonishment as her inner turmoil was laid bare before her. In Gren's view, the warrior and woman within her were one, each aspect of her personality making the other stronger, truer. He didn't understand why she fought to subdue her feminine traits, her desires and physical needs.

She blinked, trying to process it all, and suddenly found herself in his arms again, the water lapping around them in soft whispers. Gren felt hard inside her, still needing more from her than she'd given.

"Gren?" she asked in wonder as she brushed his hair back from his face.

"Please, *sura*," he gasped, his control wavering as he shook in her arms. "I need you, all of you." She could feel his need to move inside her, yet he refrained.

"You have all of me," she said, squeezing him tight with her inner walls. He gasped and closed his eyes, his head tilting back in surrender. "Make love to me, Gren. Fill me with your heart, your love."

He immediately began thrusting, long deep thrusts that rekindled the building desire inside her. With each drive she felt closer to him, connected on a level beyond anything she'd ever known.

Energy built, making the pool glow as the powerful force of belonging surrounded them. Deeper and deeper he moved, his feelings slowly bleeding over into her until she felt every touch of her skin on him, every drop of climbing ecstasy growing like a fire inside him.

"I love you, *sura*," he rasped and thrust one final time, exploding inside her.

Temis opened her mouth but was paralyzed with feeling, the incredible rapture of love and lust entwining her and Gren together.

When she could finally move again, she wrapped her arms around Gren, hugging him tight. She had never known a more giving lover, and knew she never would. In Gren she'd found something precious and rare, a man of strength, character and integrity. He had a power that could have made him a rich man, yet instead he worked with the peacemakers to save innocent lives.

"Gren," she said, not surprised at the wobbly thread of sound that escaped her throat. "I just wanted to say--"

"Later, sura." He slurred his words, his hands tightening around her hips. "I'm sorry, but I can't--" He groaned and thrust deep inside her, his shaft iron hard. Instead of sharing his ecstasy, this time she observed from a distance, gently cradling him as he lost control.

She felt him come inside her again, felt him shudder as he continued to strain against the waves of bliss overpowering him. And when his body lit like Eyran crystal, she shared in his light, clearly able to see for the first time.

* * * *

When Gren opened his eyes, he saw Temis staring down at him with a loving expression.

"Your outer wounds have healed," she said softly and sat on the bed next to him. With a callused hand she stroked his shoulder, singeing him with desire. "How do you feel?"

He stared at her, in awe of what they had shared in her dream. "My body has healed, if that's what you're asking." He wanted desperately to know that the dream was real, that she had meant all the things she'd felt and said. But he needed to hear her say it. Never had he felt so vulnerable with another.

She smiled, a small curl of her lips that made him want to pull her to him and never let go. He frowned, irritated at the sentimental nonsense running about in his head. Damn, but the woman had him in knots.

Her grin widened at the sight of his displeasure. "What?" he barked, wanting to make her tell the truth. His Theshan power screamed to be used, and he had to wrestle the energy into place. What he wanted from Temis could not be forced.

"Why don't you just ask me?" she offered and leaned over him, her lips just inches from his. She licked his flesh, her tongue brushing his mouth in invitation.

He closed his eyes, unwilling to give in to her physical needs until he heard the truth.

"Ask you what?" he said hoarsely.

She chuckled, a sensual sound that rent his control to shreds. Without another thought, he lowered his trousers enough to free his cock, then pulled her on top of him. He reached into her trousers and shoved his finger inside her.

She moaned, squirming on top of him as he plunged another finger inside.

"Wait," she breathed and shed her trousers in a flash. Then she straddled him and lowered herself, fitting him perfectly.

They moved in unison to the song only their bodies and

hearts could hear, and as she crested into climax, she cried out her love.

He joined her, shouting at the feeling of oneness, of utter peace, and waited for clarity to reclaim them both.

"You can't take it back," he said, trying to catch his breath.

"I don't want to." She stared down at him, her gaze one he'd never seen before. All woman, Temis watched him with love fresh in her deep violet gaze. "I love you, Gren. I'm not sure what it means, but I know I'm lost without you by my side."

He smiled. Temis would never be anywhere but at his shoulder, equally possessive and stubborn, an infuriating woman that drew him like no other.

"I've got some thoughts on the future, Temis. But being together will demand certain sacrifices, on both our parts."

She frowned but nodded, and he kissed her again.

"I take it you're not going to join the peacemakers?" When he shook his head, she sighed. "I didn't think so."

"But it's not all bad." He watched as she dressed, wanting her again. "I know you only knew of me as a mercenary and opportunist, but hopefully you now understand that all to be a ruse." He sat up as he spoke and redressed.

When she didn't respond, he growled, "Temis?"

She laughed. "I know. You're Thesha, and not a simple mercenary. What you are, exactly, I have no idea."

"I'm a guardian, a protector of an ancient race. And as my mate, you have one of two choices."

Her interest perked as she put on her boots and stared at him, waiting.

"You can either retire to my home world, where I will visit as often as I can between missions, or--"

"Or I can travel with you, assisting you in your 'missions,'" she answered tartly.

He grinned. "Exactly the choice I thought you'd make."

She looked surprised.

"It's true, love. I would have been stunned if you'd agreed to staying put on Ak'rea, my home world. No one but the Thesha know of its existence, and once there, you would not be permitted to leave, not for a very long time.

"I would rather you accompanied me on my journey through this life. And I'm glad to see you'll endeavor to please me in the future."

She rolled her eyes and he grabbed her in a massive hug. "You please me, woman, you truly do." He gave her a kiss that melted her to the core. "From now on we will be as one, a unit functioning together."

She smiled. "That I can agree with. But for the record, I want it known *you* will be the one endeavoring to please *me* in the future."

"It could be no other way." He gently stroked her back. "I would give my life for you, Temis."

Her eyes filled with tears and she frowned. "I'm not crying."

"I know." He wiped a tear from her eye.

"Warriors don't cry." Her eyes, though glassy, crinkled into a smile. "But we do prove the most loyal of wives. And speaking of which, you owe me a wedding ceremony."

"I would be honored." He dragged her to the door. "I'll fetch Sernal."

"No, no, no." She pulled free of his grip. "I'm from Zephyr, and we do things a little differently there. Besides, you have to meet my family." Her eyes twinkled. "If they don't approve of you, I'm afraid we'll never be married."

His eyes narrowed. "We're heading there as soon as you pack. Sernal okayed a week's leave. You can tell him now or after that you're leaving the peacemakers. But I warn you now, I'm not planning on spending my honeymoon in Chula fighting with you."

"We'll see," she murmured as he waited impatiently for her to pack.

Chapter Seventeen

"That was the most interesting wedding ceremony I've ever witnessed," Rafe remarked as he sat beside Sernal looking out at the large, pink ocean. Aflera's most exotic resort hadn't been cheap, but he'd made enough beks while working as an undercover informant to buy both him and his brother some peace of mind.

With the slavers neatly processed and the missing women all returned to their homes, with the exception of one mysterious woman no one could trace, life on Mardu returned to normal.

Sernal had been so pleased with the outcome of the mission that he'd rewarded his peacemakers with two weeks of fully paid leave. And as the new "Head of Peacemaker Central," as Gren liked to call it, he had the authority.

"I didn't know the Zephyrans fought on their wedding day."

Sernal chuckled, his eyes closed as he basked in the warm sun. "I'll never forget Gren's face the moment Temis said the bonding oath. He looked so in love, and then Temis brought him to his knees with her wedding gift."

"I thought most Zephyran brides handed their husbands their family warstaffs."

"Most do."

Rafe laughed, happy for Temis and pleased he'd been able to see Gren finally brought down a peg. He'd been invited to the wedding ceremony and rehearsal, but still had no idea what awaited Gren.

Temis had a hulk of a father and three overbearingly large brothers, all protective and all wickedly outstanding fighters. They'd grilled Gren for a week before conceding to the marriage.

She'd let slip how much fun she'd had making Gren beg for her family's permission. "He knows I love him, and he's always had things a bit too easy when it comes to women. It's good he had to work for me."

Rafe smiled at the memory and watched a gorgeous woman with six arms nearing Sernal. Ah, the infamous Jahnja, and the reason Sernal had insisted on visiting Aflera.

Sernal's eyes fluttered open with a sparkling gleam to the gold depths, so Rafe wasn't surprised when he left with the woman clinging to him.

"Another Ambrosia." Rafe nodded to a nearby server and relaxed back into his lounge chair.

His thoughts returned to Temis. As brief as their partnership had been, he'd miss her. She had a hell of an instinct and the fighting skills of a peacemaker with twice her experience.

Yet he knew he'd see her again. When he'd questioned her about the future, she'd turned a mysterious eye to her new husband.

"Oh, we'll be seeing you around."

So, Gren had finally found a woman who accepted his nature and complemented his tough-as-nails approach to life. It would be interesting to see them again after married life had settled.

His brother Catam was now as tame as a kitten, and his younger brother Gar had been the same before his wife died. Rafe preferred neither existence. Who wanted to be so tied to a woman he forgot his wild nature, or worse yet, who wanted to be so tied to a woman that her death broke you in half?

He shook his head. Love was for other men, but not for him. For now he'd enjoy life and all its entertainments. He'd leave love and 'warm emotion' to his lovesick friends.

He nodded invitingly to the two women eyeing him like a fresh piece of rak meat. They sauntered to his side wearing little more than ragged bottoms, their breasts puckering with desire as he stared at them.

Grateful to his Xema heritage, he winked and stood, then escorted them back to his room. He might not be Thesha, but he had skills in the bedroom no woman wanted to be without.

And when they joined one another on his bed, he proved it to them.

* * * *

Temis sighed with pleasure. "You're not mad at me?"

Gren laughed. "Not after *that*." He slid his hands under his head and stared at the black sky littered with stars. "Where did you learn to use your tongue like that?"

"I'll never tell." She drew her fingers over his chest dreamily, wondering what it would someday feel like to hold his babe in her womb. She'd been having these fluttery maternal thoughts since they'd married a few days ago.

"Are you ever going to tell me how you got that scar?" she asked, still trying to ferret out all his secrets.

He gave her a mysterious wink and changed the subject. "I still can't believe we're married."

You'll eventually tell me.

Perhaps. She sighed at his stubbornness, then laughed. She learned they had more in common every day they spent together. "I can't believe we're married either. Now I'm Lady Gren." She chuckled. "Don't you have a last name?"

"Nope." He rolled her on top of him. "Have I told you how lucky I am to be your husband?"

"Tell me again, and this time fill in the part about how much the elders think of me."

He groaned, and she could tell he was already regretting telling her of his conversation with them. *I should never have said anything. Now your ego is larger than mine.*

Ha, as if that could ever happen. She grinned, pleased with the direction her life was headed. The elders had been grateful Gren's guilt and misdirected life finally had purpose. Though a guardian for his kind, Gren had too often drifted through space without a care for himself. And the elders sensed it.

Feeling the true bond between Temis and Gren, they wholeheartedly approved of the bonding.

And they said we could visit Ak'rea anytime we liked, she reminded him. *Nice lie you told me.*

He winced at the mental pinch she gave him. *Now sura, I had to be sure you wouldn't rather live with them than me. You'd be miserable on Ak'rea without me.*

Yeah, she humored him. *Surrounded by Theshas with nothing more to do than pleasure a woman.*

He growled and rolled her under him, thrusting deep inside her on a breath. "No one will ever pleasure you but me."

He rode her hard, increasing their desire until they exploded on waves of golden *wainu.*

"Ah, Gren?" she asked when she could form a thought.

"*Sura?*"

"I don't quite think your jealous streak is under control." She stroked his back and felt him harden again inside her. Incredible. "Why don't we work on that?"

He chuckled and began to move in her again. "For you, *sura*, anything." He sent her a vision of a pale haired baby with dark green eyes. "Anything at all."

The End

SERIANA FOUND

Chapter One

As if surviving illegal piracy, scientific experiments gone awry, and the slave trade weren't enough, Seriana Blue now had to evade yet another smuggler asking too many questions.

After so much planet hopping, she thought she'd found the perfect spot here on Aflera, a vacationer's paradise at the height of tourist season. An upscale resort, a new disguise, and a new job as an independent cook--what could be more perfect? It had been an ideal spot to hide from trouble, until this past week.

Damn her father, and damn Abjon Afier!

"You look an awful lot like the woman on this vidscreen." The wiry man blinked at her from his good eye, studying the image on his palm-sized vidscreen as he compared it to her clever if fading disguise.

Looking down at the image of herself only a year ago, she felt as if she'd matured well past the age of twenty-six. Her head ached, her eyes swam with tears, and her hands, once smooth and creamy, were now cracked and dry from rinsing too many meal trays.

Yet she wouldn't trade a day of any of it.

Speaking slowly in Afleran, she angled closer to the persistent smuggler and thrust her bosomy chest toward him, hoping the sight of her padded flesh would distract him. She breathed a small sigh of relief when it did.

"Like a touch, would ya?" she asked coyly, leaning closer. Her breasts brushed his chest and she heard him swallow greedily. He drew a dirtied hand across her chest, lingering over the pert, crimson nipples peaking over the ragged neckline of the dress she wore. Grinning broadly and profoundly grateful to Racnar's synthetic prosthetics, she winked. "How can you think to compare this prized flesh," she paused to fondle her left breast, "to that scrawny thing on your vid?"

The man licked his lips and shook his head, no longer looking at his vidscreen. With a ragged laugh, she took his hand from her breasts and put it back at his side.

"I'm not sure why you're looking for this girl, but it can't be good now, can it?" *What new story had Abjon concocted to justify his pursuit?*

"Ah." He shifted, adjusting his trousers with a less than circumspect movement. "All I know is the girl is worth a lot of money, scrawny or no." He smiled, his teeth as black as his boots. "Not that I don't agree she could use more flesh, to look more like you."

Seriana stifled a snort. She currently looked as though she weighed twice her actual bodyweight, and in the old picture he carried she'd sported her share of curves. "Such flattery will get you a fasun pie, sure as I can swim."

He blushed with pleasure, stammered a few more compliments, then left carrying a fasun pie in one hand, his vidscreen in the other. The minute he turned the corner from her small cookery she sagged against the wall.

Hell. This made four seekers in less than a week. She would have to move again. At this rate she'd soon be facing Abjon, and nothing could penetrate his discerning, flame-filled gaze.

Her stomach tightened as she thought of him, and she frowned as she returned to her latest recipe for spiced mraun fish. She pounded the thick fillet as she recalled the mountain of muscle chasing after her for the past year. If she were honest with herself, she'd admit it had been a lot longer than a mere year.

From the first moment she'd met the stubbornly handsome Ragga native, she'd felt something in her heart sigh. A mental click, then an emotional tug of war had followed as she realized she felt something for a man as steeped in illegal activities as her father.

But his face, by Aphra's breast, what beauty. He looked as if an Eyran geneticist had created male perfection and placed it atop a body made for war. Hailing from Ragga, a planet known for its inhumanly strong inhabitants, Abjon possessed above-average strength for even one of his race. Instead of the overly muscular build one would expect, however, he was tall and lean, his body corded with muscle, not an ounce of fat to be seen.

His face should have been as hard, as unforgiving. But his brilliant, red-orange eyes gave him a warmth at odds with his frame. High cheekbones, a square chin and chiseled nose all spoke of pleasurer ancestry. Somewhere within his background, his Ragga forefathers must have dallied with the System's most striking people, the Nebites, for his lips were full, sensual and begging to be kissed.

Framing such masculine beauty, thick, lustrous black hair cut in shaggy sweeps across his shoulders shone under the bright, harsh sun. Longer than a true Ragga warrior's but shorter than the usual pirate's, Abjon's hair lay straight save for the single braid at his temple. She'd always wondered why he wore the braid but never had the courage to ask.

Courage. She huffed and turned the fish over to pound some more. It wasn't courage so much as self-preservation that made her avoid Abjon. He'd made it quite clear that he wanted her. Just thinking about his fiery sensuality caused her to shiver. Years of his casual flirting and intimate comments should have warned her he wouldn't give up until he'd bedded her.

Perhaps I would've been better off spreading my legs in welcome a year ago instead of running. Much as the thought sent a river of heat through her, she quickly dismissed the notion with a sigh. If only it could have been that easy. But she had always known intimacy with Abjon would forever change her. The very characteristics that made him a leader in the criminal underworld also made him a virtually unstoppable threat. He was too strong, too smart, too controlling.

Rover Blue, another strong, smart and controlling man, truly loved her, and for all his faults, tried to do right by her. Though rarely home and usually engaged in one illicit adventure or another, he spent as much time with her as he was able. His love, tainted by guilt, allowed her the latitude to come and go as she pleased, easing her path to escape.

Abjon would never be so lax. She knew him well, had studied him for years. Behind that sensual face, cunning intelligence and corded strength lay a barbaric warrior who protected what he thought his.

Seriana had escaped her father, but she'd never escape Abjon if he decided to keep her. And if they made love, she knew without a doubt she'd never be free again. Even if she found a chance to physically escape, the memories of his sultry possession would haunt her forever, binding her to the notorious pirate more tightly than Mornian steel.

Frowning, she pounded the fish under her hands. Her integrity made her proud to be Seriana Blue, despite her last name. In the face of her father's illegal activities, she had adhered to an honest way of life, working on the few legal ventures her father owned. But it was a constant struggle to remain firm in her convictions surrounded by criminals, men and women she thought of as family.

Were she to make love to Abjon, to be a part of a man so incredibly dominant, bound by his fiery sensuality and overwhelming power, she would never be able to preserve that core of integrity that allowed her to live with quiet dignity.

Sighing with mixed regret, that she would never know the sensual pleasures she guiltily dreamed of, she returned to the reality of her situation. Finishing her dish, she seasoned the fish and rolled it around a layer of crushed coment seed. That done, she stoked the fire of her clay oven and set the heating timer.

"Stop thinking about him," she warned herself. "Worry about your newest client. If he likes this, you've got a cool thousand beks waiting you." Not to mention the possibility of a side job, one that would take her off the main island and away from off-planet traffic. Warming to the idea, she cleaned her counters and set her cookery to rights before preparing the final dish sure to please Lord Picky, as she thought of him.

She readied his meal and would normally have programmed the tray to take it to him, were he like her other clients. Lord Picky, however, had a reputation for being difficult, and he had enough currency to ensure personalized service.

Shrugging, she ventured into the small room at the rear of the cookery that she used as a living space and straightened her appearance in the mirror.

Ah well, the nose would have to go first thing tomorrow. In the gathering dark, Lord Picky wouldn't notice the exaggerated droop of the left nostril, not that he'd venture onto the main veranda for dining. He had yet to leave his exorbitantly priced room in the resort. As such, she'd never actually seen him, only his servant Morey. And when Morey answered the door, he typically gave her no more than a disdainful glance before collecting his master's meal tray.

She grinned into the reflecting screen. She really did look nothing like herself. Her eyes were no longer lavender, but a deep murky brown. Her blue-black hair now looked brittle and sandy brown thanks to a hair falsifier. The artificial flesh coating the visible parts of her body gave her a sallow appearance. The padded bosom, buttocks and stomach ruffs she wore emphasized her bulkiness, as did the stodgy island clothing usually worn during the cooler months. Regrettably, she had to show more skin than she felt comfortable with, but wearing Racnar's false flesh, she had little worry of being discovered.

She hoped.

Finished patting herself into place, she heaved her massive breasts, tucked her pointed nipples back below her plunging neckline and assumed the slow gait that marked her current persona, that of Rabel Minatta--gourmet chef to the Colassa, planet Aflera's most popular resort.

Humming under her breath, she paused when she reached Lord Picky's suite. Of course he had the highest room with the largest bek count. Only the best for Lord Picky. For him, she'd been removed from servicing all other guests to cater to his every food craving. Whatever. So long as he liked her meals, she was happy. Now how to get Morey to nudge the man into giving her a shot on his private island....

She buzzed the door and waited for an interminably long time. Frowning, she buzzed again.

Morey opened the door looking ragged. His shirttails were untucked from wrinkled trousers, his slicked hair ruffled and his usually snotty demeanor was almost--friendly?

"Oh good, it's Rabel, my lord," he called over his shoulder. He turned back to her with a grin, and she was surprised to note Morey was much younger than he'd earlier seemed. In fact, with his hair like that he looked almost familiar.

At her stare his mirth faded, and he resumed the cool, aloof manner she'd been dealing with for the past two weeks.

"The meal tray?" she reminded, pushing the floating cart toward him.

"Follow me."

She gaped as he turned and walked into the suite. Never before had she been invited to enter. She normally left the tray with Morey and picked it up when she delivered the next meal. Uncertain, she followed slowly, starting when the door slammed behind her.

"Morey, what's taking so long?" the voice of an elderly man whined.

Breathing a sigh of relief that all was as it should be, she continued after Morey, pausing when he stopped by a door. He turned the knob and waited by the doorframe regally, his nose in the air and his head held high.

"Boor," she said under her breath as she passed him to enter the dimly lit room. The door closed with a soft *nick* behind her, but she was unconcerned. She noted an old man sitting up in bed, his form hard to see since the windows were all shuttered closed. Too bad he paid such fees for the view when he didn't seem to enjoy it. Shrugging to herself, she lifted lids from the dinner plates, the smell of her creations making her mouth water, and arranged his meal. Her stomach grumbled and she tried to remember when she'd last eaten.

Despite her apparent largeness, she had actually shed weight working under the heavy disguise in Aflera's heat. Too busy to enjoy her own cooking, she'd lost even more weight this past week.

Swallowing past the hunger gnawing her belly, she brought her mind back to the task at hand. When the meal looked perfect upon his serving dish, she glanced up with a smile and politely asked, "Where would you like me to set the tray, my lord?"

"Closer, my dear," he said feebly.

Narrowing her gaze, she thought she saw him waver. There, it happened again. His body shimmered into an almost transparent state. Sudden unease shot through her, and she took a hasty step back, only to find herself caught by a large hand on her arm.

"Bring it closer, dear," a hard voice repeated, this time from behind her, and she shuddered at the menace in his tone.

The old man disappeared as bright light illuminated the opulent room. In his place was a silken bed littered with familiar clothing--clothing from home. She swallowed loudly as hot breath met her ear.

Please no, let it be anyone but him....

"Ah, my favorite meal," Abjon Afier growled. "Seriana Blue."

Chapter Two

Seriana could do no more than blink before she was spun around and pressed against a rock hard chest. She caught a glimpse of blazing eyes and a flat mouth before she was thrown into a whirlwind of desire.

Hard lips descended over hers with enough force to make her gasp. The minute she opened her mouth, his tongue invaded and his touch turned into seduction incarnate. Molding his mouth to hers, he swept the soft petals of her lips with enough heat to make her moan. His arms curled around her frame, bringing her tight against his body.

The padding prevented her from truly feeling him, but the rocking motion of his pelvis told her he more than wanted her.

Seducing her mouth, he began sucking at her tongue, stroking and thrusting until she wanted to melt through the floor. He tasted like ambrosia, heady and addicting and enticing all at once. Knowing it was Abjon but unable to stop herself, she reached for his hair and sighed as she felt the whispery soft strands under her fingertips.

He deepened the kiss and hugged her tighter, making her knees tremble and her loins pool with want. She could feel her undergarments wet with desire, could feel her nipples chafing the padding crushing her sensitivity. She groaned in defeat, that he could make her want him so soon, so easily, when she'd spent the past year running from him, running from *this*.

He broke the kiss, breathing heavily. "I've been waiting a long time to do that." His voice sounded deeper, more enthralling than she remembered, and she had to blink not to fall under his spell.

His arms encircled her firmly but without pressure. The contrast between his deadly potential and his gentle restraint increased her susceptibility where he was concerned. She found his strength and his control unbearably sexy.

Breathing deeply to still her trembling, she managed a

faint if steady voice. "How did you find me?"

He said nothing, merely stared from her hair to her overly large breasts. His smile, when it came, was hard, measuring. "I always find what I'm looking for; didn't you know that, Seriana?" He sounded cool, his anger in check but close to the surface.

"Abjon--"

"Say it again, say my name."

She swallowed against his threatening sensuality. "Abjon. Let me go."

He ignored her, releasing her enough to peruse her costume. "Take it off."

She blinked. "What?"

"I said take it off. Do it, or I will."

Nervously eyeing the bulging arms he crossed over his massive chest, she pondered her options.

"I have no more patience, Seriana," he said in a low voice, all the more menacing for its quiet. "If you don't take it off, all of it, right now, I'll do what I've been fantasizing about since you left." He grabbed her hand and held it to his crotch. His erection was huge and swelling larger. He caught his breath, his eyes glittering with need. "Take it off or I will."

She snatched her hand away as if burned, ripping off the hair falsifier. She peeled Ractor's fake skin from her face, chest and arms, not surprised that Abjon's gaze lingered over her still padded bosom. When she had removed all the fake skin, she moved to the pads under her clothing. His bland nod of encouragement had her gritting her teeth. Much as he loomed over her, she'd never really been afraid of him. Of course, he never used to look at her as if she were a meal he had every intention of devouring whole.

When she had discarded all the padding to the floor, she waited.

"I said all of it."

"But that is all of it." She didn't understand. Did he want her to--?

"To your bare skin. And don't forget the false lenses."

She gasped. "I'm not going to--"

He reached her in the blink of an eye, his speed as deceptive as his calm. "I told you not to play games." He ripped her dress right down the middle, leaving her with nothing more than a pair of sheer panties and a thin camisole he quickly discarded.

Frozen, she pressed her legs together and stood under his large hands, extremely conscious of the calluses roughing his palms. Skimming her body, he ran his hands over her hair and down her frame, lingering over her flushed breasts and quivering mound. The heat from his hands made her wet, so wet she could feel the moisture sliding between her folds.

His nostrils flared and his eyes narrowed. Shoving her legs apart, he cupped her mound, rubbing his fingers through her slick heat, making her blush with embarrassment. He stared deeply into her eyes and frowned. She silently cursed him to deep space, so ready to come she wanted to howl with frustration, and all from his simple touch.

"Take out the eye pieces." He didn't remove his hand but kept it still.

Trying very hard not to move against his fingers, not to climax and show ultimate vulnerability to a man like Abjon, she did as he ordered and removed the small disks masking her eye color. "Good," he murmured and slid his fingers across her nether lips and deeper, working her without mercy.

"What," she started and gasped, unable to stop the moan from escaping her lips. "No, wait, Abjon," she keened as his fingers rubbed her throbbing clit. She clutched his biceps and closed her eyes when he stopped.

"Look at me," he rumbled in a thick voice.

She opened her eyes and stared at him while he threw her into a vortex of need and desire so acute it was painful. He continued to finger her, sliding his thick digits over her clit but slowing before she could reach climax. Then he slipped a finger inside her and her entire body clenched.

"Will you give me what I want?" His finger slid out of her while he waited for her response.

She writhed. She tried to hold out. But he rotated his middle finger over her clit, so softly she thought she imagined it. Then he increased the pressure, sliding ever so slowly, and she wanted to scream.

"Please," she begged, needing to end the unbearable tension spiraling in her body. "Whatever you want."

He thrust a finger inside her and flicked her ripe nub with his thumb. Her body rocked and she clamped down on his forearms to stop herself from falling as an intense orgasm ripped through her.

His eyes swirled with red fire, the orange depths of his irises changing, flickering to burnished gold as he watched her.

Drugged by the complacency of relief, she was his for the asking. And he knew it. With deliberate patience, he unbuttoned the stays of his trousers until all of him was revealed. His turgid cock bobbed with need, moisture coating the tip, making the dusky copper length glisten in the light.

"Take me in your mouth," he ordered, his breathing uneven as he grasped the root of his shaft, readying for her.

Surprised by how much she wanted to taste him, Seriana followed him to the bed and watched him sit and spread his legs wide. Kneeling between his thighs, she lowered her mouth to the head of his penis and noticed more fluid seeping from the tip. His reaction shifted the power between them, showed her how much he wanted her touch. And before she tasted him, she glanced up and smiled.

His brows rose in surprise and he opened his mouth to speak, but ended on a groan as she licked him. The look in his eyes made her want to devour him. Touching him, tasting him, had her desire rushing back.

Without breaking eye contact, she lowered her lips over the crown of his penis, sliding over the velvety tip as if savoring a meal. He was large and thick, and putting her mouth over him took some adjustment. But the look on his face was worth it. Pleasured agony stretched his lips taut, made him close his eyes as he strove for control.

Seriana could feel his thighs tremble, and with soft hands she ran her fingers through the curly black hair surrounding his cock. He moaned and surged through her lips, enough to make her close her mouth to prevent further intrusion. The action heightened his desire, for she felt his sack tighten, could feel his balls firm against the base of his shaft.

Using her hand to rub his long cock, she encircled the area not covered by her lips, feathering her touch while she stroked him with her tongue. She greedily engulfed as much of him as she was able. Her clit pulsed with pleasure as she sucked him, and before long he was gripping her hair to control his short, pulsed thrusts. Just deep enough to entice, but not hard enough to hurt her.

"Aphra, but I need to fuck you," he said on a groan. She sucked harder and cupped his balls, rubbing the velvety skin with light fingers.

His orgasm was gradual but soon built into a fevered rush. He began to come, moaning her name as he spurted in her mouth. Great shots of seed rushed down her throat as she greedily drank every drop.

She continued to milk him, needing to give him pleasure for reasons beyond her understanding. When his climax ended, she released him and tried to regain command of her flaming libido. Once she felt some control, once the desire began to ebb, she glanced up at him.

His face no longer bore any trace of vulnerability. Instead he looked every inch the warrior from Ragga, the infamous pirate bent on plunder, bent on conquest.

He dragged her to her feet and rose, righting his clothing as if she hadn't just given him ecstasy. "Put on the blue dress."

Still trying to regroup, she did so. Once she was dressed, he called for Morey.

"Pack up everything and send it to Fidei. Put her clothes and mine in the master suite. You know about the rest."

Morey nodded, his eyes bright with amusement. "Sure thing, *my lord.*"

Abjon took Seriana by the arm in a grip meant to punish. Stunned at his sudden mood change, she had to run to keep up with him.

"Where are you taking me?" She tried to sound firm. "You have no right--"

"I have every right! You're mine, and it's time I showed you just what that means. What happened in that room is only the beginning." He smiled, his expression not the least encouraging. "I'm going to fuck you until you beg me to stop. Then I'm going to fuck you until you beg me not to."

She fumed. So he meant to manage her with sex? She wanted to curse him, she wanted to rail at him, but she knew the truth as well as he did.

Her running had come to an end, and bemused by her

thoughts, she realized a small part of her was glad. Though she'd resented him for the better part of her growing years, she realized something about him called to her on a deeper, more primal level.

Now she had no choice but to deal with the situation. No more excuses. As she stared into his bronzed face, harsh from the sun and the bitter experience of life, she recognized a driving need to *know* him, inside and out.

The final barrier within her broke as she understood that running away had only heightened her desire and her feelings for the warrior dragging her through paradise.

Chapter Three

Abjon stared at Seriana without blinking, drinking in her presence like the finest of wines as the small watercraft sped over the rose-colored waves of the Phaernean Sea.

For two of the longest weeks of his life, he'd watched and waited, baiting his trap for the woman who still tied him in knots just by breathing. He didn't know what had been worse, not knowing where she was, or knowing and being unable to touch her for fear of spooking her into escape before he was ready.

His cock twitched as the breeze lifted her dress to reveal one long, creamy thigh. Lean yet supple, her legs had always drawn him with their deceptive strength. Lively and smooth, they conjured images of honeyed delight, and he could all too easily imagine those limbs locked around his head as he lapped her sweet cream. It had been all he could do not to take what he wanted in the first place, but he had contented himself with giving her a quick climax. And seeing her passion, he'd been hard pressed not to come when she had.

Abjon breathed deeply, keeping his eyes on his quarry while drawing on the discipline that stood him true these many years. He'd been through hostile revolutions, peacekeeper takedowns, and many a crew coup: enough experience to make him the most powerful pirate in the Vrail System. But by Aphra's heart, steeling himself against Seriana's powerful allure literally hurt. His cock throbbed and his heart beat painfully in anticipation of what was to come.

For two weeks he'd watched, anger and admiration warring within him. He still had trouble believing how incredibly deceptive Rover's "charming if a bit naïve daughter" had been. But seeing her disguise and how cleverly she adapted to her environment made him feel an odd sense of pride.

He'd chosen well in his mate, as he'd known those many years ago. If only he'd been sharper in his pursuit, truer to his instincts, none of this would have happened. He should have cemented their bond years ago, his illegal pirating be damned.

She finally glanced at him with those cool violet eyes, no longer defiant but strangely contemplative. Her gaze lingered on his face, in particular his lips, before traveling down his frame. She said nothing and gave him no clue as to what she was thinking.

He stared at her with a satisfied glint in his eyes, remembrances of her heated cries, of her explosive orgasm softening him. He'd known she'd be perfect, but the experience far surpassed his expectation. And when she'd closed her mouth over his cock, the incredible feeling of being inside her.... He wanted it again, the next time within her sweet pussy.

Her pink, ripe lips pursed as his stare intensified, and she looked away with a frown.

He should have fucked her the first time she flashed those innocent eyes at him and saw him as a man, as more than her father's Second. In time he'd stepped out from Rover's shadow into his own light, but somewhere along the way he'd lost control over Seriana, as had her father.

For eleven long, hard years he'd worked to build his empire and stretch his reach across the System. Only the strongest, the deadliest, held on to what they cherished most. He'd thought himself strong, deadly, nearly invincible. And then a twenty-five year old woman with no warrior skill to speak of had disappeared from right under his nose.

Feeling like a fool all over again for losing his intended, his tolerant mood abruptly vanished.

He turned his attention from her when the craft met Fidei's docks. A private island only the richest could afford, Fidei boasted the most stunning tropics in Aflera. Natural flora dotted every nook and cranny of the island. Soft pink, royal purple, and beckoning blue petals littered the path leading to the main house. Despite the beauty of the scene, the flowers held a far greater value than merely the aesthetic. Muted scents of honeyed flin and sultry rinka permeated the thick air, a heady aphrodisiac to the unwary.

He noted Seriana's flushed face, the way she avoided eye contact. *Good. She definitely felt it.* Much as he wanted to fuck her right now where they stood, he'd do better to prolong the chase. No need to let her see how deeply she affected him. Instead, he'd let her know what she'd been missing all these years. He would seduce her, push beyond her endurance, and force her to accept him and only him as her lover and lifemate.

They reached the home's main entrance, a set of steps leading to a monstrosity of wealth and hidden pleasures. Seriana's hands clenched and her body tensed ever so slightly--a sign he'd come to recognize. She might have avoided all the others seeking Rover's wayward daughter, but no one knew her as well as Abjon did.

He locked his hand around her arm to prevent her sudden flight. No, subtlety with this woman had not worked in the past. The time had come for blatant intention. He would strike at her resistance lick by lick and bite by bite, until he had her begging for mercy.

"You're so predictable," he murmured, pleased when she stiffened and shot him a glare. "There is no escape from me, Seriana. The time has come for a reckoning long overdue."

She paused at the top of the landing in front of the entrance. Cured Afleran blueglass clouded the view into the home, but from what he'd already seen Abjon knew Seriana would be reluctantly impressed.

"Reckoning?" she asked heatedly.

He nodded, unable to resist her sparkling temper. "Yes, but perhaps after some dinner. I've other hungers to sate before the sun sets." He licked his lips, and she stared at him, unaware of her equally ravenous gaze.

She shook her head, apparently susceptible to more than just the exotic scents around them. His cock swelled and he again thought about fucking her here and now to set the precedent for the days and nights to come. But he wanted to lull her into a false sense of complacency. She needed to relax a fraction, then his claiming would be all the more powerful.

Pleased with his strategy thus far, Abjon nodded her toward the entrance and waited while she pulled on the door cord. Morey appeared to welcome them inside. With a nod to Abjon, he closed the doors behind them and left them alone.

"Dinner awaits." Abjon once again grabbed her by the arm, this time rubbing the pads of his fingers over her silken flesh, more than satisfied with her sensual shiver.

They passed antiques from the arneo-classic period worth as much as his first ship and he saw grudging admiration for the home reflected in Seriana's wide, violet gaze.

"By Aphra's vision, you must have stolen from half the System's quadrants to afford this place."

What little she knew of his business pursuits. He ignored her poor opinion of him and guided her into her seat. "I trust I won't have to tie you down to prevent further escape?"

She sat mutinously silent.

"Seriana," he said with a pleased sigh, seating himself next to her at the large dining table. He truly enjoyed having her at his mercy. Just knowing she was here, that she was his, made his blood hum. "Running again wouldn't be the smartest thing to do. And though your father thinks you beyond intelligent, I'd have to disagree with him."

Her eyes flashed. "Don't talk about my father to me. If Rover Blue truly cared about me he wouldn't have thrown me at *you*. How can he be so blind?" she cried.

"Your father loves you, and he's one of the strongest men I know," he said with quiet deliberation. "He has an open mind. He isn't so childish as to run from passion when it presents itself."

"Childish? You think it's childish that I want to live my own life? That I want more than stealing and killing and running from System law, always looking over my shoulder?"

He'd promised himself he'd maintain control. He refused to let her goad him and thus redirect the situation. Taking a deep breath, he forced himself to answer evenly. "I was ever willing to discuss your needs and your wants, Seriana. Yet in all the years we've known each other, this is the first you've shared them with me."

"You wouldn't understand," she muttered and looked away.

"Why? Because I am a man? Or because I am a Ragga?" He couldn't help the frustration lining his words. "Just because I can take by force does not mean I always will."

Her eyes shifted to his so fast he thought she'd give

herself a headache, and he amended, "Unless of course I'm pushed to violence by a very stubborn, willful spitfire."

She frowned. "My life is not your concern."

"Of course it is. I promised your father I would always look out for you."

"Oh, so it's *my father* you're trying to impress by hunting me down like a skipped bounty?"

She wasn't ready to hear the truth, not yet, so he pressed the controller in his pocket and food suddenly appeared on the table before them. Deliberately changing the subject, he said matter-of-factly, "You must be hungry. I know you haven't been eating well on Aflera." He peered at her, seeing the defined cheeks and thinner waist that only emphasized her curves, making her look all the more luscious.

"I don't need food." She pushed her plate aside and gazed at him with a sober look on her face. "I'm sorry you're taking this the wrong way, Abjon. But we're not meant to be together. I wish you would understand that."

He waited, wondering where she thought to go with this new tactic. Anger hadn't worked, so what now, passive persuasion?

"Make me understand," he murmured, envisioning her in a lavender silk shift he'd brought from home.

"You're a man used to taking charge, to getting what he wants. But I'm a simple woman." He wanted to scoff. "I don't need riches and perfection. I don't need a man to make my life complete. I only need myself, to be true to a life of peace and understanding with the System."

Did she really believe the Xen tripe she was spouting? He knew she'd spent time on planet Eyra, but she was quoting their mantra almost verbatim. *"Understanding with the System" my ass.* He watched her carefully, reluctantly impressed at her ability to appear so earnest when he could feel the static of bullshit in the air.

He nodded, feigning sympathy, and decided to alter his grandiose plans for making her see reason. With Seriana, action meant more than words. He chose his words carefully.

"It really is about what *you* need." Her eyes narrowed at his tone, and he could see her weighing the decision to believe his sincerity. "I'm sorry, Seriana. I should have considered this before."

He stood up and helped her to her feet, then cleared a place on the table and gently sat her where her plate had been. Stepping between her thighs, he took her face in his hands. He allowed a show of remorse on his face, a look he'd been practicing to appear authentic, and surprised her into speechlessness.

"I've been selfish, placing my wants above your own." She nodded. "My hungers." He looked to the food around them. She nodded again, as if in a daze. "When all along I should have been considering your needs."

He kissed her softly on the forehead and swore he heard her sigh of relief. "I'm not so big a man I can't change."

"I'm so glad to hear that," she said, gracing him with a smile.

He smiled back, the tightness of his expression alarming her.

"And since it's your needs we're discussing, let's lay it out on the table, so to speak." He glanced at her position on said table and grinned.

"Abjon?"

"What you *need*, Seriana, is a good fuck."

He swallowed her cry of indignation, conscious of the sultry taste and feel of her. Silken limbs pushed at him, her mouth fought to be free, and then she was sighing, leaning into him. Like magic, their sensual magnetism flared to life, capturing them both within its web.

Abjon needed her like he needed breath. He wanted to brand himself on her, to make her realize she should never run again. Hardening his resolve to do it right, he willed himself to be strong. If this didn't cement the foundation for their future, he didn't know what would.

Chapter Four

Seriana couldn't breathe. The sneaky, sexy bastard had seen through her double-talk. She'd wanted to deal with him honestly, to see where their passion might lead, but he was so damned controlling. The entire boat ride to the island she'd argued with herself and had finally realized there could never be a "them" because there was too much of *him*.

Yet now, with Abjon's mouth covering hers, with the scorching passion in the tightly coiled body holding her, she hopelessly surrendered to the desire riding her hard.

Groaning under his onslaught, she was barely aware of his hands removing her clothing. His callused palms slid down her cheeks to her neck while he stroked his tongue inside her mouth. Stars, but he tasted like sex, and she couldn't help remembering how his cum had tasted, salty and surprisingly sweet, like the man himself.

He licked at the roof of her mouth, twining his tongue with hers as his hands covered her breasts, weighing them before pinching her nipples with painful bursts of pleasure.

"Abjon, please," she gasped when she could tear her mouth free.

"Please what?" His voice was husky, his hands constantly roving, stirring her flesh with their heat. "Please more? Please touch me, here?" He plumped her white globes, fondling and caressing her to the point of madness.

She lost all thought when his mouth trailed the path his hands had taken, sweeping her breast into a hot, moist well of delight. The sensation was powerfully erotic, but when coupled with his left, roving hand, she drew perilously close to demanding he finish her. Moving lower, tempting her to mold her body to his, his left hand caressed her stomach, then reached her tight black curls, grazing them ever so softly.

The pull of his lips on her nipple tugged at her womb and made her deliciously wet. When he finally delved into her folds, she groaned and whispered his name like a prayer.

She pressed as close to his hand as she was able, conscious that as he suckled her breast, he lowered her back to the table. Breaking away from her chest, he continued to trail kisses down her body, until his mouth rested a breath from her mound.

Settling his chin in her black curls, he rubbed back and forth, as if waiting for something from her. When she raised her head to look down at him, she saw male satisfaction blazing, along with something she couldn't quite name.

"You see, love, you only needed me."

Before she could respond, he spread her thighs wide and kissed her. The heat of his mouth fairly undid her, making her arch into his touch, unable to be still.

She writhed and moaned, in shock and awe that he had the power to make her feel with such intensity.

He laved her with aggressive strokes, his tongue and teeth nipping and sucking with an expertise that bespoke practice. But just as the niggle of jealousy wormed its way into her thoughts, it quickly disappeared when his tongue shot into her channel.

"Oh, Abjon," she moaned, arching up, needing a release for the building tension shaking her very being. She had never felt so much sensation, and it was almost too much to bear.

"What is it you want, Seriana?" he asked thickly, his mouth shiny with her juices, his eyes a vibrant golden yellow, bright with desire.

"You, I want you," she freely admitted, gratified by his harsh breathing and the mouth he readily returned to her clit.

He sucked on her nub and thrust two fingers inside her, pushing her to the edge. As if he could sense it, he began pumping his fingers in and out, all the while toying with her clit, sucking and biting, until she could feel her arousal pulsing like a living thing in her mind.

"Please, Abjon, please," she cried, needing more, needing ... him.

He thrust his fingers harder, his breathing as heavy as hers. Then he changed the slant of his mouth, his tongue bearing down with sharp licks that made her already hard clit almost overly sensitized. He drew back and blew warm breath over her flesh, and the tremor of climax was upon her. Bringing his mouth back down, he drew hard on her taut clit, rocking her into an explosion of desire that brought the world to its end.

Rapture pulsed through her, shaking her with its force. On and on the pleasure flowed, until finally she sank back on the table, her eyes closed in bliss, her body trembling with the aftershocks.

A warm kiss pressed her mouth, and she tasted herself on his lips, an erotic reminder of who had brought her to such peaks. She opened her eyes.

"You have no idea what you need," he said in a gritty voice.

Glancing down, she saw him raging hard. Though she had little energy, she thought to give him the respite he so richly deserved and reached out to him.

"No." His rejection hurt, especially after the incredible attention he'd just lavished on her body. He'd put so much care into his lovemaking. Or had she only imagined the affection, caught in passion's snare?

"You think too much. And you aren't ready yet, not for what I have to show you."

He hoisted her off the table and over his shoulder like the barbarian she'd always claimed him to be.

* * * *

Four days later she remained tied to the large four-poster bed in his bedroom. She had been stunned when, after he'd brought her such ecstasy he'd tied her arms and legs to the bedposts and left her there, alone.

He showed only to feed her and allow her visits to the lav. He refused to speak with her but always treated her gently, never as rough or harsh as he'd been that first day.

On his visits he was in control, subdued and silent. At first alarmed, she quickly disregarded any notion he might harm her. He might scare the rest of the System, but Abjon Afier had never hurt her physically. And after that first night, she knew he had some twisted sense of wanting to please her.

It seemed, however, that talking sensibly with the man would never work. At least she could respect him for not believing her Eyran line about "oneness." She'd never understood the alien concept of withdrawing into oneself, especially when she wanted so much to be a part of the rest of the world.

He hadn't believed her story, but had he listened to what else she'd said? She wanted more from life than the shady world of thievery to which he and her father belonged. She knew very little about the other side of life, the side where it was okay to trust in another.

She tugged at the silk scarves holding her arms. Funny, but until now she hadn't really questioned her father's bond with Abjon. Talk about trust. The two were thick as thieves, literally. For a man not prone to reliance, her father depended an awful lot on a Ragga more stone warrior than mortal man.

She had always sensed more from Abjon than he'd shown others. He saw with more perception, thought with more tolerance, and acted with more decisiveness than anyone she'd ever met. Incredibly, he'd risen from the ranks as a lowly miner, to her father's Second in Command, to leader in his own right in just over ten years. And in all that time he'd maintained a watchful eye over her.

From the first she'd been drawn to him. True, she'd been impressed by his Ragga strength and flame-colored eyes. But more, she could feel something within him that called out to her.

Uncomfortable with the notion, she yanked at her bonds again, shivering in the cool air that met her skin where the blanket had fallen.

Seriana still had a hard time believing the intense pirate who'd beleaguered her for years was the same man who'd made her beg him to take her. By Aphra's breast, the man could kiss. She could still feel his lips over her clit, could readily see his shiny black hair buried between her thighs, the thin braid at his temple trailing over her skin.

She grew wet thinking about it and wished she could press her legs closed. Tied as they were to the bedposts, she had no way of bringing them together. Sighing, she pondered her options in dealing with this situation.

Would it really be so bad to try to get to know him? But for his obvious heritage and time spent since joining her father, she knew little about him. Learning all she could about Abjon Afier only made sense. Perhaps his history would explain his allure. Conceding her curiosity didn't necessarily mean she had to give up what she wanted out of life. *As long as she didn't become too engrossed in the startlingly sensual man,* she reminded herself.

The doorway opened suddenly, startling her out of her introspection. Abjon entered with a tray of food. She eyed him hungrily, but not for sustenance. Instead, her eyes traveled over the broad width of his chest, partially exposed by his unbuttoned shirt. His coppery skin seemed to glow in the dim light of morning shining through the windows.

She'd always been partial to the smoothness of his skin, the lack of hair on his chest and legs she'd studied when he hadn't been looking. Now, bound as she was with no more excuses to avoid him, she was free to look her fill and she did so.

"Problem?" he asked as he placed her tray near the bed. He stood with his arms akimbo, and her gaze flew to his powerful neck, that on any other man would be a spot of vulnerability, but on Abjon looked like muscle-corded armor.

"No problem," she answered with a rusty tongue.

Sensing her need, he brought a cup of water forward.

"I could drink easier without these." She shook her wrists in their restraints.

"I'm sure you could." He tipped her head back and allowed her to swallow the water in small sips. She pondered the subtle change she sensed in him. She couldn't put her finger on it, but he seemed warmer, more connected to her than he'd been the past four days.

With her thirst assuaged, she glanced up into his face only to see a blazing furnace of heat dwelling in his eyes. Cool air trickled over her breasts and she realized what had caught his gaze. Unable to stop the blush scalding her cheeks, she glared at him.

He chuckled. "Sorry, sweet, but you can't expect a man to look away from such perfect fruits." Leaning down, he kissed each breast with deliberate softness, making her nipples erect and aroused with ease. "I could feast here for days," he murmured.

"Abjon," she gasped. "What are you--" She lost her train of thought when he tugged at one nipple. "When will you let me go?"

His lips quirked.

"You can't keep me like this forever," she said in a breathy voice, unnerved by the idea she might not mind being tied up as long as he was there to tend her.

"Hmm."

"What does that mean?"

"It means you and I have some talking to do." He began feeding her small bites of succulent forba fruit, and she was too hungry to care about her bonds as she ate.

His eyes seemed overly intense as he watched her, his gaze alternating between her mouth and her breasts.

"Aren't you going to eat?" she asked, conscious that since he'd entered he'd lavished his attention on her appetite.

"I already ate." He grinned widely, showing strong white teeth. "Now we're going to play a little game. We're going to ask each other some questions. If I like your answers, I'll set you free." He paused.

"If you don't like the answers?"

"I'll keep you like this--"

"You've got to be kidding."

"--forever," he taunted, or at least she hoped he did.

Chapter Five

After he allowed Seriana a brief respite to the lav, during which she made use of the facilities and cleaned as best she could, Abjon retied her to the bed.

She thought to fight him but by the look in his eyes decided not to. It wasn't as if she had the strength to overpower him. As it was, the only sway she seemed to hold over him was his body's response to her naked frame.

After he'd tied her, he left her naked and open to his perusal. She studied him, wondering just what he hoped to gain from all this. Surprisingly, she felt no fear or even anger. Just arousal and curiosity, both of which threatened to consume her.

"Are you ready to begin?" He stood over her and removed his shirt.

"What do you want from me?" she couldn't help asking.

His eyes gleamed, and he removed his boots and trousers, leaving him clad in a thin pair of shorts, which did nothing to hide his fierce erection. "We'll get to that soon enough." He joined her on the bed, straddling her waist but resting on his knees and thighs so as not to overwhelm her with his weight.

She swallowed loudly. His shorts clung lovingly to his massive cock, and she couldn't help noticing how he seemed to swell under her regard.

"I can't wait," she heard him murmur. She blinked up into his eyes and saw him staring at her mouth. She flushed, unable to help herself, and he chuckled. "Let's begin the game.

"First I'll ask you a question, and I expect you to answer honestly. Even if it's what you think I don't want to hear."

"Okay," she said slowly.

"Then you may ask me a question in return."

"I can ask anything?"

He nodded and she thought this might work out to her advantage after all. In addition to the obvious arousal he stoked in her, he might also assuage her curiosity.

"Does my heritage bother you?" he asked.

Surprised, she shook her head before she even thought about it. "No, why would you ask that?" He seemed to relax a little in relief, and she couldn't help but laugh. "Of all the questions to ask, that seems a little obvious now, doesn't it?"

"Lust can be aroused in anyone, Seriana. Like has little to do with it." He sounded different, and she realized he truly had feared she disliked the Ragga in him.

"Okay, I answered your question. Now answer mine. What exactly are you? You're Ragga, but you're something else as well."

He blinked in surprise. "You're very observant." But he didn't sound happy at the admission. "My father was Ragga, my mother Nebite."

She'd only guessed before that he might have Nebite blood in his background. But hearing him say it, she could only stare in admiration. The Nebites possessed a sexuality and beauty envied by those in the System. She could see the sensuality in his face, in the pleasure-slanted eyes that burned with gold as they watched her.

"Does it bother you to admit it?"

"It's my turn to question." He easily ignored her query. "Do you hate your father?"

The abrupt change in subject startled her. "Hate my father? Of course not."

"Yet you ran not only from me, but from him as well."

She flushed. Hearing him say it made her feel all of two years old. She should never have run. She should have stayed and fought for her independence. "I wasn't thinking clearly."

"I agree." He overlooked her glare. "You don't trust him, though, do you?"

She squirmed, not wanting to answer.

He ran a hand over her breast, squeezing and petting. "If you do not answer, sweet," he said in a soft voice, "I will bring you near to climax but not over. Again and again, you'll teeter on the brink, *begging* me for release."

The word "begging" made her reconsider. To her consternation, she'd done enough begging already. "Okay, okay," she said on a breath as he toyed with her nipple. "I trust my father in that I know he loves me. But he's too unprincipled to trust with other things. Currency? No. The lives of himself and my friends? No, I'm sorry to say."

She felt ashamed to admit what she'd felt all her life.

"Don't worry, love, I know how you feel."

She blinked. "You do?"

"Much as I love and respect your father, I understand him. He hasn't gotten to where he is today by being compassionate and, dare I say, *nice*."

He shifted over her body, sliding his heavy erection over her belly.

"Do you like how I make you feel?" he asked.

"Hey, it's my turn for a question."

"You asked it when you said, 'you do?'"

"That's cheap." She wanted to scowl, but his hands crept over her breasts again, and she sighed instead.

"Yes, love, tell me how you feel. Your body knows, but I want you to admit it to me."

She arched under his touch, frustrated at how much he made her want him. "Yes," she hissed. "I like the way you make me feel. I want you. I always want you," she confessed when he suckled one taut nipple.

"Tell me." He moved back so that he sat between her legs, his hands placed precariously near the juncture of her thighs.

"Since I was, I don't know, sixteen or so, I've felt out of sorts around you."

He began stroking her thighs, his eyes glued to hers, and she continued on a gasp.

"You made me feel hot and cold. You bothered me when you stared at me with that blazing amber look, like the one you've got now." She moaned as he slid a finger between her folds and inserted it into her wet sheath. "You always promised with your eyes, but you never made good on that promise."

He stilled his hands and she could tell she'd surprised him. "You wanted me then?"

"I don't know. I wanted something from you, but I didn't know what. I was young. By the time I realized what I felt, I knew too much about you," she added resentfully.

"Ah," he said, sliding back and leaning down to lick the dew from her clit. She groaned and tried to tighten her thighs around him, to no avail. "So my "illegal pursuits," as you think of them, put you off."

"Yes," she gasped as he sucked hard on her clit.

He licked her again before regaining his position on his knees between her legs. Staring down at his tented shorts, he muttered under his breath and ripped them from his body.

"Do you like what you see?" he asked on a ragged breath when his eyes met hers.

She nodded.

"What would you like me to do to you?"

Seriana bit her lip, wanting him more now that she saw his cock glistening with need. Yet to give voice to her inner desires....

"Seriana," he threatened in a growl and flicked at her clit.

She closed her eyes and took a deep breath. It was easier if she didn't have to look at him. For some reason he made her feel shy while overly sensual. It made no sense.

"I want you to touch me like you before, and to feel you in my mouth again. But I want you inside me when you come. I want to feel you thrusting in and out of me, your body rubbing against mine."

His breath sped at her words, and she knew she'd aroused both of them with her desire. She opened her eyes and saw him staring at her, his mouth flat and his cock even larger.

"I wanted to draw this out," he admitted on a rasp. "But I can't."

He crawled up her body and turned around, putting his face in her lap, his cock level with her mouth. Then he began licking and tasting her, and she was lost. Feeling for his shaft with her lips, she eagerly opened her mouth and accepted his gentle thrust.

Like a lover's perfume, his sultry scent called to her, demanding she give him as much pleasure as he'd given her. She took him in, pushing and pulling at his cock with her lips and tongue while he nipped gently on her clit.

The added sensation of being unable to move, completely under his control, increased her stimulation until she was a short breath from orgasm.

His thrusts increased as well, telling her in no uncertain terms how much he wanted her. She managed to break from his shaft. "Please, Abjon, inside me."

With a muffled curse, he quickly shifted until the head of

his cock met the wet heat of her sex. "Look at me, love," he said in a guttural voice. Waiting until their eyes met, he slowly slid inside her, stretching her to the limit and beyond.

He was large, massive, and he fit with a perfection she could only have dreamed. With a deep groan, he began thrusting, softly at first, as if to determine her acceptance.

"More," she cried, needing all of him. His answer was a violent thrust, making her groan with approval. He stroked and stroked, pummeling with a strength that should have hurt, but only heightened the erotic sensation. A sudden brush of his shaft against her clit and she was coming, hard and deep, her contractions gripping his cock with a violent pull that triggered his own climax.

"Seriana," he shouted as he came, gushing into her with a force that took them both off the bed. He shuddered as he poured into her, caging her within his arms tenderly while his body loved hers.

After a while they both recovered enough to gaze sleepily at one another.

The discomfort of her bonds seeped in, and she read the understanding in his glowing eyes. "You promise you won't run?" he asked in a throaty growl.

"Not until you answer the rest of my questions," she managed.

He grinned, a bright shine of affection that made her heart jolt. "I think I can handle that." After a quick kiss on the mouth, he shot off the bed and undid her restraints.

Feeling the blood rush back into her hands and feet, she shivered until he began rubbing her to relieve the tingling.

Once the blood rushed back into her limbs, she thanked him and watched as he climbed back into bed. "You really are a handsome man."

"I know."

Laughing at his arrogance, she accepted the warm embrace he enfolded her in and thought hard about how to say what she desperately wanted to know.

"Seriana?"

"What do you really want from me, Abjon?"

He stiffened beneath her and she wondered if she should have eased into the heavy questions after they'd both fully recovered from their lovemaking. Now the passion and excitement she'd felt faded under the sudden flatness in his all too expressionless gaze.

Chapter Six

What did he want with her? Was the woman daft? How could she not sense his feelings behind every touch, every teasing caress? But then, perhaps she didn't sense it because she didn't feel it herself.

A foreign sense of self-doubt filled him, one Abjon hadn't felt in a very long time. Even when Seriana had vanished a year ago, he'd known he would find her and bring her back to him. He'd never once considered the possibility she wouldn't care for him.

"Abjon?" she asked hesitantly.

He rolled away, his back to her, and sat at the side of the bed. Frustration and rage built inside him that once again he might fall prey to a woman's manipulations.

Dammit, he hadn't imagined the way she'd looked at him for the last few years, or had he? Yes, there had always been a tinge of wariness in her gaze, but mixed with that was a wealth of admiration, of attraction. He had been equally taken by her beauty, her intelligence, and more, her integrity. Ironically, her basic purity had drawn him like no other thing could.

Surrounded by a world of corruption, Seriana glowed with an innocence all too rare in this life. The daughter of Rover Blue, a cutthroat that made Abjon pale by comparison, she possessed a keen intelligence that should have enabled her to see beyond the superficial layers of his craftily built reputation. He'd stolen, yes, and he'd killed to defend himself, but he'd never murdered, and he'd only stolen from those as or more corrupt than himself.

That she still didn't see the real him, after all their years together and, hell, after this morning, made him want to pound something into the ground. He didn't dare examine the emptiness in the vicinity of his heart.

"What is it you think I want?" he asked coolly.

"I think, ah," she paused, and he glanced back at her.

Unlike him, Seriana was small, feminine, and beauty personified. Her long black hair fell in waves around her face, framing the deep lavender pools of uncertainty swimming in her eyes.

"Tell, me, Seriana. We are, after all, still playing the game."

"The game?" Confusion lined her brow before she recalled what had led to their lovemaking. Her eyes darkened to a deep indigo. "Is that all this is to you? A game?"

"I might ask you the same."

She rose to her knees, gloriously naked but so enraged she missed the answering flame of passion in his greedy stare. "You've stalked me, you've haunted me, for as long as I can remember. The first time in my life I tried to be free of my father's criminality, *you* hunted me, and not just for a few days or weeks, but *for an entire year*. I was almost sold as a slave to filthy Melan degenerates because of you.

"And now, after a year of running, of never-ending pursuit, I turned around and made love to you. I, Seriana Blue, made love to Abjon Afier, the biggest, baddest pirate in the entire Vrail System, in the face of my self-imposed rule to avoid my father's way of life. What the hell does that tell you?"

He could only stare at her, so enraptured by her passionate splendor he wanted to lay her down and join their bodies for eternity. It was with some effort he answered. "That you were swept away by desire, perhaps?"

He wouldn't have thought it possible, but her eyes deepened to black, and then she flew at him. Startled, he caught her and tumbled to the floor, conscious to keep his weight underneath her.

Stars, but the woman had spirit in droves. She slapped, clawed, and even managed to bite him before he flipped her onto her back and straddled her, staring in puzzlement.

In all the time he'd known her, he'd seen Seriana do many things, including lose her temper. But he'd never, ever, seen her explode into violence about anything. Dare he hope this was a good sign?

"Get off me, you oaf!" She struck at his chest, and he easily caught her hands and pinned them to either side of her head. "By Aphra's heart, you're not even breathing hard."

He wanted to smile at her pique. "Are you finished?"

"Are you?" she growled.

"Sweet, I've barely begun."

* * * *

She couldn't put her finger on it, but the odd flatness that had moments ago filled Abjon had vanished. Now, as she lay on her back under a mountain of Ragga, she wondered whether to view that as a good thing.

He stared down at her with a face that enraptured her, as it had from the first moment she'd seen him. For years she'd regarded him from afar, afraid to get too close lest she succumb to his temptation. The last thing she'd wanted was to get involved with one of her father's men.

Yet for all her distance, she had noticed things. She'd never seen him act disrespectfully to a woman or to a person of advanced years. She knew Raggas had a hearty respect for traditions and the elderly, but Abjon had been raised apart from his people.

Though he'd supposedly stolen millions, he lived comfortably but not to excess in the house next to her family's home. She'd never seen him with a woman, but his popularity with the ladies was a thing of legend among her father's crew. Abjon, however, remained circumspect about his love life, almost like ... a gentleman.

A gentleman, however, she thought wryly, her temper fading, *didn't sit atop a lady*. Though he'd kept his weight off her by resting on his knees, she didn't like the submissive posture in which she lay. Almost as if he'd read her thoughts, he cautiously rose and lifted her to her feet as if she weighed no more than a feather.

"Back on the bed, Seriana," he said in a thick voice, making her instantly aware of their lack of clothing.

She felt the blush even while she reached for a sheet to wrap around herself. "I don't think so. I want you to answer my question, Abjon."

"Question?" he asked negligently as he leaned against a bedpost, a smirk on his face. "Which question would that be?"

She opened her mouth to blast his insolence when she realized he was enjoying their banter. He looked relaxed, almost boyish in his amusement, and he lacked the battle tension that always seemed to fill his frame.

Much as she wanted to take him to task for making light

of what she'd been through, she didn't want this new, light-hearted Abjon to disappear.

The fact that he'd pursued her since the day she'd left, that even when he'd captured her he hadn't hurt her, but instead had gifted her with pleasure beyond imagining, had to mean something. He'd made no reference to returning her to her father, and he touched her like a man who cared. At turns possessive yet tender, he stared at her with a strange look in his eyes, one that, in her heart of hearts, she hoped to credit as love.

Narrowing her gaze, she stepped forward and poked him. "Don't get smart with me," she growled. Her finger made no headway against the muscled wall of his chest, so she sought an alternate means to subdue him. She dropped her sheet and saw an answering need in his swollen cock.

With stroking hands, she began to pet him, trailing over muscle and sinew, stealing around the rock-hard bulge of his biceps. His breathing quickened and she grinned, a purely feminine power stealing through her.

"You aren't sending me back to my father anytime soon, are you?" she asked as her hands reached down to encircle his lengthening erection.

He groaned and closed his eyes, yielding to her control. She thrilled when he shook his head and brought his hands over hers.

"More, sweet." He encouraged her to increase the friction on his cock, and when she followed his instruction she was richly rewarded with a soul-stealing kiss. Thought soon faded as feeling and sensation overtook them both.

* * * *

The next week passed all too swiftly to Abjon's way of thinking. He and Seriana spent time together, playing, laughing, and best of all, making love at every available opportunity. With her, he could never quite get enough, and every instance spent inside her only increased his addiction to having the sweet, wild woman.

He tried to overlook the searching glances she sent him when she didn't think he was looking. The time spent with her was too perfect to mar with anything negative, so he simply ignored the need to hash out their differences.

Sooner or later their idyllic vacation would end, so until that time, he planned to make the most of it. He grinned as he watched her splashing about in the relaxation pool behind the house. Her full breasts swayed as she laughed, her pearlescent flesh sparkling against the pale pink water.

Her taut abdomen fairly begged to be nipped, and he grew hard thinking about what he planned to do once he joined her. Unfortunately, Morey interrupted his pleasurable thoughts with a badly timed vidcall.

Answering the screen mounted just inside the rear of the house, Abjon warned, "This had better be damned important."

"It is," Morey quickly answered. "Rover Blue has been spotted circling the Colassa as we speak. Already a few of his scouts have questioned the staff."

"By Aphra's breast, I told him I'd bring her back."

"Apparently, he has as much patience as you do," Morey muttered. "I'll keep him distracted as best I can. But the most you can hope for is a day's reprieve."

"Do it. And keep him in your sights once he lands."

"Will do."

Abjon disconnected, his good mood shot to hell. Damn. He hadn't had nearly enough time to connect with Seriana. They'd shared their bodies and their minds on a number of interesting topics, but had yet to share their hearts.

He knew he'd fallen in love with the woman long ago, but admitting it to her--that was something else altogether. Like it was yesterday, he could still remember the pain of his mother's betrayal. Sold at nine years of age to a mining facility, he had watched through tears as she'd left laughing with her latest lover.

Love had almost killed him then. He could only hope he'd fare better this time around.

Seriana called his name, and he met her drying off by the small pool. Her eyes shimmered with humor but quickly sobered when she saw him.

"What's wrong?" She reached out a hand, cupping his chin to bring his gaze to meet hers.

Unable to stop himself, Abjon took her mouth with possession. She sighed under his touch, enhancing his need to claim her as his own. Plunging his tongue inside her mouth, he began stroking, thrusting in and out of her mouth with a need bordering on obsession.

He fondled her breasts, his touch growing rougher as he

noted the hardened peaks, her shivering, dampened flesh quivering with excitement.

When he found her soft and wet between her thighs, his body demanded release.

He yanked his mouth from hers and took her by the shoulders.

"What--" she asked in a daze before he turned her around and forcibly bent her over the nearest table.

Giving her no audible response, he slapped her on the ass and shoved her thighs apart at the ankle, the domination of their lovemaking waking the savage within him.

"Brace yourself," he growled while he deftly unfastened his trousers. Once he freed his cock, he stepped between her thighs and shoved himself deep inside her.

She moaned his name as he rode her hard. Gripping her hips, he pistoned in and out, her harsh breathing and his physical mastery bringing him very near climax.

He reached around to pinch her clit and felt her walls close around him as she quickly peaked. She squeezed him, every contraction of her vagina a new torment to his already over-stimulated shaft.

Pounding harder and faster, he soon followed her into oblivion. Shuddering as his seed drenched her pussy and slid down her thighs, he couldn't contain the brief thrill that stole through him at thoughts of impregnation.

Though he'd never truly reflected on it, having a child with Seriana was a foregone conclusion. Each time he spilled his seed inside her, he brought them closer to an inseparable future. Satisfaction pooled in his heated blood, and with regret he finally withdrew.

She turned her head and watched him readjust himself in his clothing. "Not that I'm complaining, but what brought that on?" She stood and turned to face him, but he couldn't keep the smile off his face as he noted the seed trickling down her leg.

Blushing, she grabbed a nearby towel and cleaned herself. "I swear, you fill me to overflowing every time."

"Good." *And soon enough there won't be a spot on you that isn't marked by my scent. You're mine.*

She laughed. "Such a smooth talker. So tell me why you looked so grim only moments ago."

His euphoria faded. "Your father has arrived."

"Oh." Her face fell. "I suppose he knows where I am."

"Not yet." Abjon placed both his hands on her cheeks, loving the feel of her silken skin. "Love, it's time we talked."

She sighed and her eyes filled with tears, unmanning him.

"Don't cry," he pleaded, wiping her eyes. "Seriana, I--"

"It's all right, Abjon. I knew it was too good to last."

Chapter Seven

"Too good to last?" His eyes narrowed, making Seriana want to break into loud, embarrassingly awful tears.

This week had been perfect. Absolutely, incredibly perfect. If a lingering sense of unease occasionally hit her during quiet moments, she'd ignored the feeling. It had been too heavenly to have Abjon to herself. All that sensual male devoted to fulfilling her every desire. It was unreal.

He'd been all she'd imagined a man could be: tender, loving, sexual and giving. When not making love, they'd discussed everything from poetry to politics.

However, she made no mention of his livelihood, and he made no mention of the fact that she'd fled from him. Instead they'd wiled away the hours swimming and sunning, basking in Fidei's paradise and in one another.

"Now that my father's here, we'll have to get back to reality." She couldn't help the depression that filled her. "You'll go back to pirating, I'll go back to keeping my father's books, and this interlude will fade into a pleasant memory."

"Only pleasant?" He looked amused and her sorrow swiftly turned to irritation.

"I'm so glad you're not concerned about my father. He's killed men for less than what you and I have done this past week."

One brow rose. "You're kidding, right? Seriana, you yourself told me your father was throwing us together. Of course he'll accept me. He's lucky to have me as it is," he murmured.

"You don't understand. My father wanted us together, *bonded by marriage*." She waited for horror to pass over his face, as the word 'marriage' had that effect on the men she knew.

He shrugged. "I still don't understand the problem here."

"The problem is this--I'm not marrying you," she spaced each word out slowly.

"Why?"

"Why?" she blustered, astounded by his obtuseness. "You're a pirate, that's why."

"And if I weren't a pirate? What then?" He stepped closer, gazing down at her with a disturbing intensity.

She stared back, lost in his flame-filled gaze, wishing beyond all hope that she could have this man in her life forever. But she refused to live with someone who would constantly jeopardize their future, all for want of materialistic possessions.

If Abjon were a peacemaker or soldier for the greater good, she could live with his dangerous profession. But to risk life and limb on a daily basis, for naught but profit? And Aphra knew what ends he employed to gain such profit. No, not even for Abjon could she abandon her hope for a better future. Her eyes misted. Just thinking about the loss and heartache their separation would bring made her want to cry forever.

"But you are a pirate," she said softly, breaking eye contact. "So the point is moot."

He cleared his throat. "What if I told you I love you?"

She froze. "Do you?" How she managed to ask that in a calm voice she'd never know. She felt as if her entire existence hung on that one answer.

"I do." His words were solemn, the loving expression in his gaze open and honest.

Tears began pouring down her cheeks and her heart felt as if it were being ripped in two.

"I'm sorry, Abjon, more than you'll ever know." She sniffed, wiping at her eyes. *How can you say you love me and not know who I am inside? I can't keep living like I did with my father. I'm not a criminal and I never will be.* "I won't live with a man who does what my father does. And we both know you'll never give that up."

He smiled then, completely breaking her heart. "So sure of that, are you?" He grazed her cheek with one finger. "We only have one more day together, Seriana. If you won't say it, then show me how much you love me."

The words locked tight in her throat, she threw herself into him, seeking haven in his arms, in the pleasure only he could give. Mouth to mouth, heart to heart, their bodies spoke of a love not to be denied.

* * * *

Abjon and Seriana met her father the following day in his suite at the Colassa. Rover Blue sighed with relief as he enfolded his daughter in a backbreaking hug.

"Easy," Abjon chided, giving Rover a dark look.

Her father snorted, ignoring the Ragga. "By the goddess, Seriana, you are truly beautiful." He marveled as he turned her in his arms. "Seeing you now, it's as if you're an entirely different person than my sweet little girl." He glanced at Abjon knowingly. "She's beautiful, isn't she?"

Abjon gave her a wolfish grin, despite her strong warnings from yesterday and this morning. "Indeed. She's delectable."

Her father stared from Abjon to her, his smile widening, and she felt as if "doom" were written on her forehead. "I told you she'd see the light. So when is the marriage ceremony to take place?"

"I'm afraid there won't be one," Abjon said in a matter-of-fact voice. Her eyes narrowed, as did her father's.

"What?" Rover asked.

"She won't have me."

"Why won't she?" Her father glared at her, giving her a stare that made lesser men tremble.

"I can't," she blurted, wondering why Abjon hadn't seemed more emotional. If he'd truly meant that he loved her, he should have sounded more heartbroken. Instead he sounded as if he could care less.

"Why can't you?" Rover cursed. "I've worried my head off for a year, only keeping out of the search because your giant here promised he'd return with you. Then I hear from one of my sources that he'd found you." He paused to glare at Abjon. "And he hadn't said a thing to me about it. That was a month ago!

"Don't think I don't know what you two have been doing in all that time. This boy's lusted after you since the day he saw you, and you've avoided him for the same reason, I expect." He rolled his eyes when she gasped in surprise. "Hell, Seriana. You mooned over the lad every chance you saw him. What did you think, that I hadn't noticed how extremely 'uninterested' you always were?"

Abjon, she noted, had an extremely satisfied look on his face.

She blushed, knowing everything her father said was true.

She'd admitted as much to Abjon, but her father made her sound like a love-sick *zafu*. Scowling at her father for making her feel like she was twelve again, she let loose the leash on her emotions.

"Fine. You want to know why I don't want to marry him? It's because he's too much like you."

"What?"

"You heard me. I don't want a man who thieves and murders on a whim. I don't want someone who will always put me last, who thinks he's above the laws that give our system justice and equality. What you do isn't right, Father. And I've been telling you that for years!"

Rover blinked at her. "Yes, well," he blustered, looking to Abjon for support.

But her lover simply shrugged and shook his head. "Don't look at me. You dug the hole, you get out of it."

"And another thing. You took Abjon under your wing years ago, making him just like you. This is the kind of man you want for your daughter? A man who would sooner kill another for gain than lift a finger at decent, honest work?"

Abjon began to scowl. "Now wait a minute, Seriana--"

"This is the man you would have me wed? A killer, a thief and mercenary? Hell, Father, he's almost worse than you!"

"Thank you." Abjon tilted his head and said wryly, "For a minute there I thought you didn't like me."

"I love you, you idiot. That's not the point." She continued to berate her father, who stood dumbstruck under her tirade. "I hate keeping your books. I hate living on Mornio, and I hate knowing there's the possibility you might not return when you go raiding. And another thing," she continued in huff, talking as fast as she was able. "You--"

Overwhelmed by the barrage of emotions she'd been suppressing for so long, she missed Abjon's overjoyed grin until he yanked her violently toward him and kissed the breath out of her.

"Thank Aphra," she heard her father mutter. "Damned if her dead mother hadn't suddenly appeared and possessed my shy, quiet little girl."

Abjon ended the kiss, and she had to lean on his arm her

knees were so weak. "She's not shy, and she's definitely not quiet. She's my woman, and it's about damned time she finally realized that fact."

"Abjon." She struggled in his imprisoning grasp. Apparently he'd missed the part about them not marrying.

"No, love, you're mine," he said firmly and turned to her father. "She's not running the few legal ventures in your dirty organization anymore, Rover. In fact, aside from fatherly visits that have nothing to do with your activities on Mornio, you won't be seeing her or your grandchildren until you clean up your act."

Rover's eyes widened. "Grandchildren?"

"Not yet," she growled, embarrassed Abjon was having this conversation with her father, in her presence no less. "And where do you get off telling my father how to behave around me?"

She tried to scowl, but Abjon's heart-stopping smile conquered her anger.

"Seriana, I love you, but you're too tenderhearted dealing with your father. With Rover Blue, only direct intimidation and straightforward orders work."

"Orders?" Rover blustered.

"Orders," Abjon agreed. "We both know my fleet can take yours, anytime I want to," he added, menace in his tone.

Seriana gasped and wriggled to get free, but Rover merely raised his eyebrows. "You think?"

"I know." Abjon stared at her father, and she prayed the standoff between them wouldn't turn ugly.

"Damn me," Rover grumbled and shook his head. "I believe you mean that. Even with all you gave up."

He and Abjon exchanged a heavy look, one that had her curiosity running rampant. "What are you two talking about?"

Abjon tugged her away from her father and stared down at her with a tender expression on his face. "I asked you once before what you would do if I wasn't a pirate." Her heart sped with hope, with anticipation. "And I told you I loved you."

"But--"

"Seriana, I've worked these many years to be able to make a future for *us*." He waited while she digested his words. "I've loved you forever. The only reason I worked as hard as I have with your father was to make a strong enough presence to keep you safe, and to make a good enough living to finally break free. I've been completely legitimate in all my enterprises for a year now. I'm a free trader, one who owns a fancy little island named Fidei, as a matter of fact." He frowned. "If you hadn't run like you did, we could be celebrating our one year anniversary tomorrow in paradise."

She could only stare in wonder. As Rover Blue's Second, Abjon had commanded most of the System's underworld, a position of authority prized by everyone she knew. "You gave up all that power, all that prestige for me?"

"For us," he corrected and kissed her gently. "I've always known how you felt about my lifestyle. Rover constantly talked about you, and I understood more and more about the woman I loved."

Her eyes welled and she heard her father clear his throat.

"Well, go on, girl. Tell him you love him and you'll be marrying. And maybe I'll give some thought to handing over the reins too. I'm getting older, and I definitely want to see some grandchildren before I go."

"Don't push, Rover." Abjon glared her father into silence before returning a loving gaze to her. "I built that house on Fidei for you, love. And I've seen how much you enjoy working in that cookery at the Colassa. Be with me and you can have anything your heart desires."

She had eyes only for Abjon, for the man who had done so much to be with her, aware of the unfettered joy filling her soul.

"I desire you, Abjon Afier. I love you, and I would be happy, no, honored, to join you in Lifebond."

He blinked, surprised. "Lifebond is a Ragga concept, Seriana."

"I know," she said with a sly grin. "I studied everything I could get my hands on about the Ragga culture the day after I met you."

He grinned, his eyes alight with an inner fire. "You did, eh?"

"I did. And our bonding wouldn't be complete without the Ragga ceremony. After all, I can't birth Ragga children without the Lifebond."

His eyes took on a suspiciously wet sheen and he hugged her close. "I love you so much, Seriana."

"And I love you," she said between tears.

They jolted to feel her father's arms around them. "And I love both of you," he said in a thick voice. "Imagine, my brains, Abjon's brawn, and your looks, Seriana. We'll rule the entire System in no time at all!"

"No son of mine will be involved in anything illegal," she warned with a laugh.

"Of course not," her father agreed, a twinkle in his eyes. "I was talking about your daughter."

The End

Printed in the United States
48115LVS00001B/109-117